Come and Talk To Me

June Kramin

Come and Talk To Me is a work of fiction. Names, characters, places, and incidents are either the product of the author's imagination or are used fictitiously. Any resemblance to actual persons, living or dead, business establishments, events or locales is entirely coincidental.

© Copyright May 2012 by June Kramin
© Cover art by: Ink Slinger Designs

All rights reserved. No part of this book may be used or reproduced in any manner whatsoever without written permission except in the case of brief quotations embodied in critical articles or reviews. Visit and/or contact us through our website at www(dot)WritersAMuseMe(dot)com

ISBN:
ISBN-13: 978-1-927044-21-6
ISBN10: 1927044219

DEDICATION

For the man of my dreams. Of course in my dreams, you do have that sexy accent ;)

We all know the song, Army, Navy, Air Force, Marines.... What many of you may not realize is that the Coast Guard is also part of our Military Forces.

This book is a work of fiction. No ill will is meant towards the VA that serves our wonderful, selfless soldiers. I also dedicate this story to our soldiers and the wives who await their safe return, as well as the doctors that patch them back up.

PROLOGUE

Twice in Reggie's life she had long drives alone during which she reflected on her life with Van. First was the drive to Fargo, where she would be waiting for him to come out of surgery. The second was her drive to Colorado to start a new life, after he didn't.

1

"How bad?" Regina asked Van. "Do I stop to get the pizza or you want me straight there?"

There was a pause before he answered. "Go ahead and get it, but then come straight here."

Reggie arrived home fifteen minutes later. She put the pizza on the table and went to her knees at his side. "It's that bad again?"

"The dammit-alls aren't helping at all," he replied with tear-filled eyes. Dammit-all was what they had named his newest pain pills.

"Dammit, Van. I knew you needed more than just another type of pill for the pain. Something has to be seriously wrong. I know that crap is going to mess with your kidneys or something."

"Baby, not now. Please."

"I'm sorry. You're my tough guy. I hate seeing you like this." Reggie stroked his hair as her memory drifted to the first time they met and she witnessed just how strong he was.

Regina was at a friend's house for a Girl's Day brunch. In Hawaii, people adopted a lot of other country's customs; it was a Japanese custom that March third was Girl's Day. She always made it a point to get together with at least one of her girlfriends to celebrate. She was looking forward to an afternoon of champagne, cheeses, fruits and chocolates with her best friend, Sabrina. When she arrived at Sabrina's house, she found something even yummier on the menu – Donovan.

"Who's that, Bri?" Reggie asked her friend as she looked out the picture window into the backyard.

"Scrumptious isn't he? That's Troy's friend, Donovan. He was stationed here from Minnesota a few weeks ago."

"Farm boy?"

"It does a body good."

The girls continued to observe the demolition from inside, watching through the sliding glass door that faced the backyard. Sabrina's husband, Troy, played supervisor while Donovan slammed a sledgehammer into an existing sidewalk. He was almost as big as Van, but he was busy calculating figures while Van took charge of the muscle work.

"Why are you ripping out a perfectly good sidewalk, Bri?"

"Troy wants to lay down some fancy-schmancy brickwork. He was going to talk to you about getting a good deal for him."

"Of course I can."

"That boy has too much time on his hands on his days off. Stay away from military boys, Reggie. The schedules will make you crazy."

After a couple glasses of champagne, Regina became brave and went outside. She walked to where the activity was, but kept her distance in case some concrete came flying her way. After the sledgehammer came down, she stepped closer. Donovan looked up and let go of the hammer. He moved his sunglasses down his nose, giving her an obvious once over.

~*~

"Hello there," he said, once he got his fill and pushed his sunglasses to the top of his head. He liked what he saw. She was barely over five feet tall and had zero body fat. Her tight tank top and shorts left nothing to the imagination. He imagined her breasts would fill his hands nicely and although he didn't want her to leave yet, he couldn't wait to get a look at that ass. Her thick blonde hair reached her waist. He liked the way it moved with the breeze.

"You know, they make a tool for that. I believe it's called a jackhammer."

"Why would I pay good money and rent a jackhammer when I have a Van?" Troy laughed as he walked over and gave her a kiss on the cheek. "How you doing, Princess? You here to corrupt my wife with another Girl's Day escapade?"

"Of course." She held her glass up as if in a toast. "Van?"

"Donovan," he said as he put his hand out to shake hers. "Van has stuck since grade school. Reggie?"

"Regina." She accepted his hand. "I prefer Reggie."

"Reggie it is." He brought her hand to his lips.

She pulled her hand away and tucked her hair behind her ears.

"Do you want me to get you another pill?" Reggie asked.

"I've already taken twice the dose."

"Twice the dose? And it's not helping?" He shook his head 'no' and buried his face in the carpet. "When did you eat last?"

He replied a muffled, "Breakfast," into the carpet.

She stood up, grabbed a piece of pizza and brought it to him. Holding it at his mouth, she ordered him to take a bite "All that medication will rip apart your stomach."

"I'm not hungry."

"I don't give a shit. Take a bite."

Reluctantly he bit into it then once again buried his face.

"I'm going to take you to the ER." When he didn't reply she asked, "Okay?" He nodded. She mumbled, "Shit." Van was sick of doctors and normally didn't want anything to do with them if he could avoid it. If he agreed to go, he was in bad shape.

Reggie picked up the phone and called their friend that lived closest. He was also Van's boss. "Alex?"

"Hey, Reg. What's up?"

"I need you and someone bigger than you to come help me take Van to the hospital."

"His back?"

"It's bad. Is there someone you can call? He's going to need help getting in the car."

"There is. We'll be there in five minutes. Hang tight, girlfriend."

"Thanks." Alex was a great friend but he was barely taller than her. His wife had him beat by a couple inches. What he lacked in height, he made up for in heart. The couple had been great friends to them since they had moved to Minnesota. In a community where not everyone was the most welcoming, Alex and Kirsten had open arms for them. The couples often spent weekends playing Whist well past midnight while downing Linenkugels 'tackle boxes' that offered a type of beer to please everyone. It was Alex who got Van interested in computers and later hired him at his store.

Alex brought a neighbor of theirs who was, by chance, a male nurse. He was built like Van, but a little on the heavyset side. The two looked like quite the pair bounding through the door. Alex had stopped knocking long ago. Even if they still practiced that formality, the situation demanded hurrying in.

"How ya doing, big guy?" Alex asked as he knelt down by Van.

"Been better, ugly. You?"

Alex softly chuckled and gave him a firm pat on the shoulder. "You remember my neighbor, Gary?"

"Yes. Please forgive me for not standing up," he said with a moan.

"No worries, friend. Alex said this is a kind of reoccurring thing with you."

"Yup."

"Did you do something today that you know would have brought this on?"

"I dunno. Breathe?"

Van wasn't normally short with anyone. He had a pleasant disposition and was usually first to offer a smile and a helping hand. He had to be in pain. Gary turned to Regina. "Gather up everything he's on to bring along to the hospital. They're going to want to know what he's taken." She ran to the bathroom with a plastic grocery bag to bring the various bottles of acetaminophen, ibuprofen, and codeine combinations as well as the 'dammit-all'. "We're going to pick you up now. Brace yourself," Gary said to Van.

The two men stood on each side and quickly brought him to his feet, which in turn brought a cry of pain from Van that made Reggie run out of the bathroom. She rushed over to Van and put her hand on his cheek.

"Holy Shit. You are hurting," she said, staring deep into his eyes.

He could no longer hold back the tears that had been building up; they finally rolled down his cheeks. "Just get me to the damn ER," he said softly as if in defeat.

Reggie stared into Van's light blue eyes as she took another sip of champagne. She liked the way the sun showed off the many shades of blond in his hair. Even the small beads of sweat forming on his forehead were sexy. *Yup. Must have had one too many glasses of champagne.*

"You have any beer in there?" Van asked her.

Reggie put a hand to her hip. "I suppose you've put your club down so it's now the woman's job to fetch your drink?"

"Don't let the blonde locks fool you for a second, Van. That woman is pure redhead. Watch out for the horns and fangs, too."

"I resemble that remark," Reggie said as she turned around with a grin. "I'll be back with two beers anyway."

~*~

"Thank you," Van said under his breath, not for the offer of the beer, but for the view.

"Do the words balls and vice mean anything to you, buddy?" Troy asked.

"She can't be all that bad."

"Wanna bet? I haven't seen her date a guy in the two years I've known her. She has a real hellcat of an attitude towards anything with a penis. I've seen her chew them up and spit them back out faster than you can say 'blue balls'. She came here from Oahu, swearing off men and seems to be holding up to her word."

"Then she's overdue, isn't she?"

"You some kind of glutton for punishment?"

"Let's say I'm up to the challenge."

Reggie came out with two beers as promised. "To think," she said as she handed them each a beer, "I was worried the skills I learned cocktail waitressing all those years would have gone to waste."

Van stepped closer to her. "Since that's the case, be sure to come back later for a tip."

She moved her sunglasses down her nose, as he had done earlier, and looked down so it was obvious where she was staring. Looking back up into Van's eyes, she said, "I don't accept small change."

Troy was holding his side laughing. "What I tell ya, buddy? Ball buster."

"Laugh away, my friend. That girl is mine."

2

At the hospital, Regina thanked Alex and Gary then sent them home. "There's nothing you can do. I'll call you as soon as I hear anything." She filled out the necessary paperwork then settled in the waiting room playing *Bejeweled* on her cell phone, trying to pass the time. After about forty minutes, a male nurse came out to see her.

"Are you Mrs. Kimball?"

She looked up from her game. "Yes. Can I come in now?"

"Unless you'd rather stay and beat your high score." He smiled as he looked at her phone. "I'm addicted to that one myself."

"What did people do to amuse themselves before cell phone games?"

"I believe they were called magazines." He laughed. His friendly manner and casual reply eased some of Regina's concerns. "Follow me."

"How is he?"

"Still in a lot of pain."

"Can't you give him anything?"

"We have – a lot."

"Why is he still so bad?"

"Something is really off in his back. We're waiting to take him down for an MRI, but he's been asking for you. No harm in you being there while we wait. Any normal person would be in la-la land right now after all that morphine."

"Morphine," Reggie grumbled to herself. "I'm really beginning to hate that shit."

When she walked into the room and saw the condition her husband was in, Reggie's heart shattered. He was lying on his stomach again; apparently that was the more comfortable position. Van was moving his legs back and forth trying to get comfortable. Straightening up, trying to appear a lot stronger than she felt, Reggie hurried to his side, giving him a lingering kiss on the cheek.

"No better yet? They said they've given you a lot of morphine."

"It's been about as helpful as a lesbian."

"How's that?"

"It ain't doin' dick."

The male nurse laughed then cleared his throat. "Sorry."

"That's okay." Reggie stroked Van's hair. "We get snippy when we're not feeling well." She leaned down and kissed him again. He reached for her hand and squeezed it as an orderly walked in.

"I'm here to take him for his MRI." His eyes met Regina's. "You can wait here if you want or we can come get you from the waiting room. We'll be about a forty minutes."

Since Troy and Sabrina lived right off the beach in Maalaea, after their fill of champagne and snacks, Reggie and Bri went across the street for a swim. They came back to Bri's yard to lie out on the lawn chairs. Reggie was glad the men weren't in sight at the moment or making a racket. A nap was called for.

Having grown up on Oahu, Regina enjoyed the much slower pace of Maui. She met Sabrina at her current job as a salesperson at one of the lumberyards. Troy was always doing something to the house and sent his wife on errands for materials. Bri had commented more than once about how much she liked having a female help her. She'd only had bad experiences with male salesmen; they usually treated her like she didn't know what she was talking about when it came to lumber and such. She didn't, but that was beside the point. Sabrina figured Regina filled the female quota for the contractor division so they couldn't claim any kind of favoritism. Besides a woman at the cash register, Regina was the only female around. She invited Reggie for a barbeque on a Saturday afternoon to show off the progress they had made with her help and they had been inseparable ever since.

Almost lulled asleep by the soft island music playing from the stereo in the house and the champagne wearing off, the two were jostled awake by the two men.

Van kissed Sabrina hello. "Hiya, Beautiful." He then sat next to Reggie, placing his feet on her chair by her stomach.

Troy walked over and lay flat on top of his wife. Sabrina giggled and gave him the lingering kiss he was after before she finally said, "Get off, you nut ball."

Reggie tried to show no reaction whatsoever to Van's intrusion. He finally cleared his throat and wiggled his feet, shaking her chair. "What is it?" she asked, not even opening her eyes. He was quiet and wiggled his feet again. "What?" Frustrated with him, she pushed her sunglasses up. "Is it time for me to fetch you food now?"

"Size thirteen, Sweetheart. Small change my ass." Van stood back up.

"It took you all afternoon to come up with a comeback?" Reggie placed her sunglasses back on.

"We're lighting the barbeque. I need to know if you want chicken or steak."

"I missed the part where I said I was staying for dinner."

"Steak it is."

"It's mostly the L5 again. There's not too much change with the L4," the doctor explained as he showed her the MRI results. "I've had his records e-mailed here. The herniation is worse than his last surgery. We won't know for sure until we're in there, but we'll either remove what we can or have to do some fusing."

"When is this going to stop?" Reggie had to turn her back to the doctor while she composed herself. She was so tired of hospitals and doctors but most of all; she hated seeing her husband in pain.

"Procedures improve. If he takes it easy, he can live normally with minimal pain control."

"Minimal? Do you know what he takes to get by in a day? I'd be dead. There has to be something better than this."

"This will help greatly. Trust me."

They walked back to the room as they talked. She went straight over to Van, kissed his forehead, and gently stroked his hair. He was no longer moving his legs back and forth. She was grateful he was finally getting relief from the pain. He looked pale as well as sleepy. "Hey there, Size Thirteen," she whispered into his ears and gave his earlobe a gentle bite.

"Sorry, Babe. I'm sure it ain't gonna work after all the drugs."

"Can I get a rain check then?"

"Sure." After a brief silence he said, "I'm sorry."

"For what? Like this is your fault, you goof." She gave him another kiss to his forehead. "So what now?" she asked, turning to the doctor.

"If he were my patient, I'd get him on an ambulance to Fargo right now."

"Isn't he your patient?"

"Technically he's a patient of the VA. I have to wait for word from them."

"Why?"

"They pick up the tab on the service-related injuries. Your husband has Champus; that's military insurance."

"I'm aware of his insurance coverage, Doctor Miller. I've been down this bullshit road already several times. He's had a procedure done in Miami. That wasn't a military hospital. They billed Champus."

"Well, I'm afraid we can't do that type of procedure on him here. We're not authorized to so much as move him until we get their okay. It's not life-threatening and he can be stabilized. We can keep the pain under control until we get word."

"More friggen drugs," she huffed. "When will you be able move him?"

"As soon as we get the okay. I'm sorry, but all we can do is keep him comfortable until we hear something. It shouldn't be long."

"Fair is fair," Van said as he delivered two Long Island iced teas. "Now we're even for the beer. I'll still take a rain check on that tip, though." He gave her a wink and walked away.

"He makes a good drink but he's a little full of himself," Reggie said to Bri.

"Come on, Girl. It's been two years. You need to start dating again."

"I don't feel like dating any man right now, Bri. I wouldn't care if Matthew McConaughey knocked my door down."

"You batting for the other team on me?"

Reggie laughed. "I'd become a lesbian if I didn't hate women more than I hated men."

"He's cute and he's sweet. I like him, Reg. Give him a chance."

"I love you, but knock it off, Bri."

"So he knows he's good looking. So what? That smile would melt a blind nun."

"You are too much. Besides, didn't you tell me to stay away from military men?"

"Since when do you listen to me? Please promise to at least be civil over dinner."

"No claws, Bri. I promise."

As promised, Regina behaved through dinner. Van minded himself as well, staying away from obvious sexual innuendos to keep peace over the meal. Troy suggested a walk back to the beach for sunset when they finished, and everyone was game. Unknowingly making their friends uncomfortable, Troy and Sabrina shared several long kisses over the sunset. Everything was a romantic moment for those two.

Idle minutes let Regina feel how much the Long Island iced teas were hitting her. She wanted to get back to lie down.

"Can we go, Lovebirds?" she asked once the sun had completely disappeared.

"Sure, Reg." Sabrina threw an arm around her. Apparently she was beginning to feel the alcohol, too.

After a few paces, Reggie let out a yell and hit the ground hard with her knees.

"What happened?" Van asked as he dropped to her side.

She rolled to her butt and held her ankle. A Kiawe thorn was stuck deep in her foot with good part of the branch exposed, answering Van's question.

"Aw, shit," Reggie said softly as she looked at it. The small wound had a bead of blood at it.

"Shit, Reg. I've had my share of those bastards. We shouldn't be out here without shoes." Van held her ankle as Sabrina sat behind her. "You want me to pull it out?" Reggie's eyes remained fixed on the bleeding wound. "Reggie?"

She held onto her ankle, but stared at the branch as if in a daze. "Hmmm," was all she could reply.

"You want me to pull it out for you?" he asked again. Her eyes fluttered. "I think she's going to pass out," he said calmly to Sabrina.

"Over a thorn?" Troy said with an 'I don't believe it' tone to his voice.

"There's two and they're damn huge." Van raised his voice and turned around glaring, scolding them for making light of the situation. "Reggie?" He held her chin in his hand.

"Hmmm," she moaned again, trying to open her eyes wide.

"She drunk?" asked Troy with a laugh.

"This isn't funny, Troy." Sabrina scolded her husband. "I've never seen her go loopy like this."

Van gave the branch a swift yank, pulling the thorns out of her foot. She let a scream out again. "Ouch, you bastard!" Reggie flopped backwards into Sabrina.

"Well, that's more par for the course," Troy said.

"Reg?" Van picked her chin up.

"Ouch," is all she would reply with her eyes still closed.

He looked at her heel; it had begun to bleed. He squeezed it a little wanting it to flow a little more freely to clean it out. That earned him a prompt slap on the arm. "Stop it! That hurts!" Tears had begun to fall down her cheeks, but her eyes were still closed.

He put an arm around her back, one under her legs and picked her up. She wrapped her arm around his neck and buried her face into his chest instead of fighting him. He walked them back to the house.

"She diabetic or anything?" he asked Sabrina.

"No."

"You've never seen her pass out before?"

"Stop talking about me like I'm not here," Reggie mumbled.

"Well, have you?"

"Hmmmm?"

"Has she?" he asked Sabrina again.

"No, but wait… she doesn't do the sight of blood well. That much I know for sure. The neighbor girl roller-skated by one day and fell. We went rushing out to make sure she was okay. Her knee was scraped up bad. Reggie threw up and about passed out. I forgot about that; it was over a year ago."

"All that fuss over blood?" Troy laughed again. That earned him a prompt smack in the arm by his wife. "Oh goody. Now we're a matching set," he said to Van. "Men and the women who abuse them: Story at six."

Sabrina glared at him and he became quiet.

"You going to toss your cookies?" Van asked Reggie.

"No cookies." She buried her head deeper into his chest. "I feel like I'm gonna throw up."

3

Reggie stormed into Van's room. It had been two weeks since he had been admitted. The sight of her made him smile, even though he could tell she was about to blow.

"Cookie?" He lifted up a small bag of white Oreos that had been brought to him as an afternoon snack.

"No, thank you. You're outta here in half an hour. There's an ambulance arriving shortly to take you to St. Cloud."

"You heard from the VA? Why didn't they get a hold of me?"

"Because I didn't hear from the VA. You're going on my insurance."

"We can't do that, Baby."

"Yes, we can and are. I spent the last four days making the arrangements. I'm not having you sit here another day in pain while they get their thumbs out of their asses!"

"Shhh, calm down."

"Like hell. Those bureaucratic assholes know exactly what they're doing. You were their 'property'," she said, using finger quotes, "but now they don't give a damn about you."

He knew when it was best to keep quiet and let her rant.

"They could have had you out of here long ago only they don't want to foot the bill. They are banking on the fact we'll do exactly what I'm doing. I don't care what the co-pay is, you're going today."

"It's not so bad." He picked up the button that dispensed the pain meds into his IV and wiggled it in front of her. "Yesterday I said I didn't want to get hooked on the morphine and asked if I could have one of my dammit-alls. They said no, so… ding." He pretended to push the button.

"See!"

"See what?"

"They're not doing dick about it. 'Here's more pain meds, Mr. Kimball'." She went over and sat on the bed. "They're going to kill you, my love. You're having the surgery and you're having it now."

"This coming from a girl who faints when she gets a thorn in her foot."

"You afraid of the surgery?" she asked him, reaching for his hand.

"No. They've been over the details enough. I'm okay with it. I was just hoping the VA would pull through."

"You're a flag-loving sap and I love you, but you've always given the military more credit than they deserve. They broke you, dammit, and they should fess up to it, but they aren't so I'm stepping up to the plate."

"You're so damn cute when you're pissed. I especially love when it's not at me."

"Well, no sex for two weeks will do that to a girl."

"Ah ha, the thick plotens."

"The thick plotens? You are high."

He laughed. "I did that on purpose."

She put her hands on his cheeks and looked into his eyes. "Maybe, but you do look stoned and I don't like it. Enough is enough. I'm going to run home for a few things then I'll meet you there."

"Kiss me goodbye first." She leaned down and gave him a quick peck on the lips. "No. Kiss me right."

She gave him another quick kiss. He reached up and held her face in place. He tilted her head slightly and covered her mouth with his, using his tongue in a way that usually meant they were going to end up naked. She moaned softly and leaned into him, wanting more as well. After a few minutes she finally sat up. Her eyes opened up slowly and she smiled at him as her hand moved to his crotch. She chuckled.

"That's hardly the reaction a man wants when a woman places her hand there."

"After a kiss like that, there is no way you would not be aroused. You are high."

"Give me another chance after surgery."

"You ready for your trip, Mr. Kimball?" an orderly asked as he wheeled in a gurney.

"You're early," Reggie said, grateful for the arrival of someone finally.

"I'm late by a day, actually. Sorry about that, but there was an emergency that took precedence over a recurring back injury."

"Yesterday? I had him set to leave for St. Cloud later today."

"St. Cloud? No ma'am. He's scheduled for surgery tomorrow morning in Fargo."

"Fargo? No. He's not going to the VA hospital; he's going to St. Cloud."

He picked up the chart. "Kimball, Donovan. Last four—"

"No!" Reggie hollered. "Don't start that bullshit." She looked at Van with pleading in her eyes.

He reached for her hand and pulled her towards him. "This was the plan, Baby. They came through after all. I'd feel better without us having to foot the bill for this."

"It's too late. I already made the plans."

"Un-make them. What's the big deal? Switch your hotel to Fargo. Come on. This is a good thing." She sighed heavily. "They're good doctors, Reggie. Let the service pay for it."

She climbed onto the bed and buried her head in his neck. "Just wait a little while longer, Van. I've already taken care of this. I want to do it with my insurance."

"I hate to pull rank, Baby. Let the man take me, okay? I don't want to fight. Let's get this over with." He pulled her close and kissed the top of her head.

After sliding off the bed, she stood out the way, helpless, as the orderly transferred Van to the gurney. Before he wheeled

Van out of the room, Reggie called out for him to stop. She walked over, bent down and gave him one final kiss goodbye. "See you in a few hours."

The four friends arrived back at the house in less than five minutes. Van placed Reggie on the couch. "Get me a cold washcloth," he said to Sabrina, "and one with soap for her foot, too."

When she returned, she went to place the washcloth on Reggie's forehead, but Van took it from her to do it himself. Sabrina smiled at Troy. He shook his head and went to the refrigerator for another beer.

"You want one?" he asked Van.

"In a minute." His attention stayed on Reggie. "You feeling better?"

"I feel like an ass."

"But what a great ass it is," he said with a grin.

She opened her eyes just enough to shoot him a nasty look, then closed them again.

He laughed. "You're kinda cute when you're pissed."

"Then you're going to think I'm downright striking with my knee in your crotch."

"Ouch. Is that any way to treat your knight in shining armor?"

"I didn't ask to be carried."

"You didn't seem to mind."

"I was almost comatose. Is that how you prefer your sex, too?"

"I accept."

Sabrina laughed. "I'm going to go heat up the pie for dessert. You two duke it out."

"You are certifiable," Reggie said under her breath after Bri walked away.

"I'm also crazy about you."

"You don't even know me."

"So let me get to know you."

"Trust me: Run for the hills, Farm Boy."

"Farm Boy? Oh, I get it. I'm from Minnesota so I grew up on a farm."

"Did you?"

"Yes, but that's hardly a fair assumption."

"I'd say it was a perfect—" He cut off her protest with a kiss. She swallowed hard. "I have half a mind to slap you right now," she said when their lips parted.

"And the other half?" he asked as he slowly went in for another kiss. She closed her eyes, but their lips never met. Suddenly there was pressure on her heel.

"Ouch!"

"I need to get this cleaned out. I don't want you to get an infection."

"Kiss my ass!" she said as she stood then hobbled away.

"Where and when, Doll-face? Where and when?"

~*~

"You can't stay away forever, Reg. I miss you," Sabrina said into the phone that lazy Saturday as she pulled weeds in her garden.

"We just went to lunch on Wednesday."

"But you haven't been here in two weeks."

"Got that damn sidewalk ripped up yet?"

"They hauled the last of it away yesterday. Troy said they weren't starting on the brickwork till next week. Come over for a barbeque tonight. I'll tell Troy to make an excuse to Van if that's what's keeping you away, but quit it already. Come over."

"You make sure he's not there and I'll be there."

"Done. See you at six."

"Want me to bring anything?"

"Why do you even ask? I tell you no and you bring what you want anyway."

Reggie laughed. "Formality. See you at six."

Sabrina grinned, hit 'end', and plopped on a lawn chair next to her husband. She tossed the phone to him. "Call Van and tell him six-thirty. You can stall the fire."

"You are a devil, Woman. You know that, right?"

"And you love me." He walked over and lay on top of her in the lawn chair again. It creaked as she screamed playfully. "You're going to break it if you keep doing that."

"You ovulating yet?"

"Tomorrow."

"I can't wait."

"You're supposed to wait and save your little guys up."

"I don't want to wait. I'll make more. I promise." He untied her bikini top.

"Go call Van," she said, unsuccessfully trying to push his face away from her neck.

"I already told him."

"You didn't tell him she would be here, did you?"

"Men don't connive like that. I told him to show up for food and beer. He figures I left out the part where I'm going to make him work on something. He's not sitting there obsessing over a pretty face. You know I love her but she's a handful, Baby. I hope you know what you're doing."

"You know why she's the way she is."

"I know. You know how I feel about that too. Seems to me, she has to be ready on her own time."

"She needs a good man to snap her out of it."

"I hope she doesn't end up snapping my good man."

"He's a big boy. He can take care of himself."

"How about you take care of your big boy?"

"I don't want to waste another month, Troy."

"And I don't want to waste a perfectly good hard-on."

"When don't you have a hard-on?"

"Come on, Baby." He nuzzled into her neck.

"All right, but you're having sex with me tomorrow, too."

"If I must."

4

Regina showed up at five forty-five with a dessert, a salad and a six-pack of Smirnoff Ice. She didn't believe in showing up on Hawaiian time. Being on time was important; early was actually better. She smiled wide when she discovered there were no other cars in the driveway. Sabrina told her Van wouldn't be there, but she didn't ask if anyone else was invited. She wanted some alone time with her friends and hated that Van kept her away.

"Hey, Princess," Troy said with a kiss.

"Hey yourself, Boyfriend." She held his hug just a little longer than usual. "Can I help with anything?"

"No thanks. I'm going to start the fire in a bit. You can go work on getting my wife drunk, though."

"Going to try to take advantage of her later?"

"I already did that this afternoon," he said with a wink.

She laughed, pulled two bottles from the six-pack and went outside to join Sabrina. The giggles and the drinks went down far too easily. Reggie didn't realize how lonely she had been the last couple weeks. She was stupid to let Van keep her from coming over.

Going into the kitchen for another round about a half hour later, she stopped short of walking right into him. "Hey, Doll-face."

"What are you doing here? I thought the sidewalk was done?"

"Last time I checked, Troy and Bri don't make everyone work when they show up, present company included." He walked past her with a beer in each hand, sat down in one of the recliners and reached over to give Troy a beer. There was a football game on.

Reggie went back to the refrigerator and seized the bottle of chilled root beer schnapps as well. She stopped by the TV. "Do you need me to check the fire, Troy?"

"I got it, Reggie. Just go relax."

She huffed away and sat by Sabrina. "You're a real pal," she said, taking a swig of the schnapps.

"Sorry. He just showed up. I guess Troy couldn't get a hold of him. Chill, girl. He doesn't bite."

"Says you."

"Yeah, says me. So," she said, trying to change the subject, "did you think any more on the road sales position?"

"I don't want it."

"Why not? It sounds like more money."

"Maybe. It's more work for sure. Volume is higher but the margins are lower. I'll work twice as hard, but still end up, money-wise, about where I am now. I've run the figures."

"Working hard has never bothered you before. You love a challenge."

She sighed and rubbed her eyes with the heel of her hand. "It's not so much the job as how it is that Becker offered it to me."

"How's that?"

"You got it, Cupcake. Use it."

"He did not call you Cupcake!"

"No, but he might as well have. He wants me to show up at jobsites in short skirts and schmooze sales with tits and ass. He's a pig."

"So turn him in for sexual harassment."

"It's hardly worthy of that, but I'm telling him no. I don't need to explain myself. If he pushes, I'll quit and go work somewhere else. I've started a résumé in case it comes to that."

"That doesn't sound right."

"I work at a lumberyard, Bri. It's a man's world. I wouldn't take the shit if the money weren't so damn good. The way I'm ogled every day is barely better than my previous job."

"Hang in there, Hon." She held up her bottle and they clinked them together.

Van walked over to Bri and gave her a kiss. "Hiya, Beautiful."

Reggie smiled. That's what he called Bri last time. She at least liked the way he treated her friends.

"Long time no see," Bri said. "Thanks for coming to play with Troy so I can have some girl time."

"I'd rather sit over here and look at you two rather than stare at his ugly mug."

"Isn't there a game on?" Reggie asked.

"It's half-time and Troy's throwing the food on."

"I'll go get the sides ready," Reggie said as she stood up.

~*~

"That girl can't stand me as far as she can throw me, can she?" Van said to Sabrina when Reggie was in the house.

"It's not you, Van. Trust me."

"Just hates men in general?"

"Something like that. Why don't you go help her in the kitchen?"

"You want me near her when there are sharp objects around?"

She laughed. "Go help her, Van." He stood and walked to the house.

As Van opened the sliding glass door, Reggie called out. "Bri? Can I borrow a pair of shorts? I spilled the dressing all down my front and gotta get out of these…" Van turned the corner as she finished her sentence, "pants."

"Do you need some help with that?"

"Funny. Out of my way, please." She tried to get past him, but he put his arm out, stopping her.

"If I said you had a fabulous body, would you hold it against me?"

"My, you are a witty one. Please move."

"Why the ice storm, Reggie? Can't we be civil to each other, for Bri's sake? She went through a lot of trouble to pretend we both weren't going to be here today."

"She wouldn't do that to me."

"She did. Are you really that naïve?" He stepped closer to her. "'Cause if you are, I think it's kinda cute." He held her face in one hand, leaned down and gave her a gentle kiss.

Her eyes closed for a second then sprang open. "Stop doing that!"

"Afraid you'll like it?"

"Hardly." Again, she tried to get past him.

His arm didn't budge. "Give me a chance."

She ducked under his arm and walked towards the screen door. She hollered to Sabrina that she was grabbing a pair of shorts. "And no thanks on the help," she said as she walked to the bedroom.

~*~

When she was that pissy, Reggie always drank too much, too fast. The dinner didn't help absorb any of the alcohol. It never took her tiny frame much to feel the effects and she'd had enough to keep up with Van, who had over a hundred pounds on her. As she drank, she didn't get mean. Rather, she started to soften. Finally looking at Van really good for the first time, she saw the handsome face, the strong shoulders, the gorgeous eyes, and, above all, his kind heart. She didn't want to want any man, but she was beginning to like him. Her guard had been dropped and she was actually being friendly.

~*~

"Pity she passed out," Troy said as Sabrina tucked Reggie in on the couch where she fell asleep. "She was getting kind of fun."

"I'm going to bed, too. You two behave." She kissed them both goodnight.

The men stayed up and had a few more beers. Van had made plans to sleep over before he decided to have a few too many himself and claimed a spare room for his own, but he didn't stay put for long. Whether or not it was the thunder rolling in across the ocean or the thought of Reggie so close, he couldn't sleep. At two a.m. he went out and sat on the couch to gaze at Reggie's sleeping face. His weight on the couch woke her. She looked up at him with a smile then stretched. She suddenly jerked awake as if she finally realized where she was. Lighting cracked close, causing her to jump again.

"Don't like storms?" Van asked.

"Not particularly. Is it going to be bad?"

"I didn't hear anything. I don't check when I'm not on duty, though."

"You like that? Being out on the water all day? Rescuing people that don't have the smarts to know when to stay on shore?"

"I do, a lot. It's the most satisfying thing I could think of. I couldn't think of anything else I'd rather be doing. Well, there is one thing." He grinned.

She only got out, "What—" before she caught herself and didn't finish the question. Instead, she blushed.

~*~

Lighting cracked again. She pulled the covers close to her chest. Reggie had been through her share of hurricanes and storms. Although nothing more dramatic than losing power for a few hours had ever happened, she never could stand the booming of thunder. Her parents never allowed her to crawl in bed with them when she was scared. Thank God for an older brother who was more understanding and often tried to fill in on love where their parents had lacked.

Van stood up and extended his hand to her.

"I'm fine here, thanks."

He waved it in front of her. "Come on. I'm not going to bite."

"I'm not sleeping with you, Van."

"I don't recall offering to service you. The bed is more comfortable. I'll take the couch."

"I'm smaller. It's fine." He waved his hand again. She let out a huff and stood up. He held her hand and led her to the room. "This really isn't necessary. I'll be much more comfortable on the couch than you will."

"Good point. Maybe we should share the bed," he said as he closed the door.

"I'm tired, Van. I don't want to play games."

"So lie down and go to sleep. Come on." He patted the space next to him. "You afraid of me?"

"Yeah, right." She wasn't about to let him get the best of her. She stomped over to the bed and lay down. She pulled the sheets up and said a gruff, "Goodnight."

"Sleep tight, Doll-face."

5

Regina was tired but she couldn't fall asleep. She lay awake listening to Van breathing. She smelled his cologne on the pillow, nuzzled in and inhaled deeply. Her back was facing him when she first climbed in, but she had slowly turned around so she could look at him while he slept. How could he just fall asleep? Why hadn't he tried anything? Wasn't that the whole point? She wasn't sure if she should be glad he was so nice or wounded that she obviously didn't do anything for him, despite how he acted. What were all those kisses about? She finally fell asleep, pouting but not without having moved a little closer, just to get a better whiff of his cologne of course.

~*~

Van wanted her. He wanted her bad, so bad he hoped she didn't brush past his midsection and discover how bad. He couldn't believe he had gotten her in the bed in the first place; he wasn't about to push it. Something had happened to her; she didn't trust men. He didn't want to give her a reason to not trust him. Maybe he shouldn't have been so forceful with the kisses before, but he knew she had wanted it... needed it. She longed for someone to love her; only it made her afraid. He wanted to be that someone and would try anything. If he hadn't had so many beers, he would never have been able to fall asleep with her next to him. If someone could have died from arousal, it would have been him that night. The rain that fell outside had quickly lulled him to sleep.

~*~

They woke up in the morning with barely room for a quarter between them. Reggie had snuggled up to him for warmth with the cool breeze coming in. He had unconsciously wrapped his arms around her and pulled her tight to him in his sleep.

"Good morning," he said, without hesitation.

Her reply was a little softer. She was embarrassed. "Good morning." She tried to scoot out of bed but he tried to hold her there.

"Don't go, Reg."

"I have to pee." She flew off the bed and out of the room, grateful to find no one else awake.

Instead of returning to the bedroom, she went to the kitchen and started a pot of coffee. While she waited for it to brew, she sat outside on the picnic table. In a few minutes, Van joined her.

"There's nothing to be embarrassed about. It's not like anything happened," he said after a minute of uncomfortable silence.

"I'm not embarrassed. We're two adults." She rubbed her arms as if she were trying to warm up. She wasn't cold, just fidgety.

He rubbed her arms, trying to help. "Go on a date with me, Reggie."

"A date?"

"You know; the customary ritual between a man and woman where they usually go for food or a movie that may or may not result in a good time or even better…sex."

She glared at him. He should have stopped while he was ahead. "Since you put it that way, no."

"Come on. I was teasing about the sex part. Dinner?"

"Man, you're a pain in the ass."

"I won't quit until you say yes. Just a harmless dinner. I'll even let you buy if you're some kind of feminist."

"You'll buy and I want lobster," she said as she crossed her arms.

"Deal."

"Coffee should be ready. I'll go get some."

"I'm going to take off actually."

"Really?" It came out sounding like she was a lot more disappointed than she wanted it to.

"I have to get a few things taken care of. You want to go tonight? Starting tomorrow I'll be on duty for a week and we're getting underway."

A week? I have to go without seeing him for a week? She pulled herself together. "I suppose tonight would be all right if you're going to make me do this."

"Write down your address for me. I'll pick you up at five."

"Four. Take me to Lahaina for dinner. I'd like to wander around Front Street for a while first... if you don't mind."

"All right. Four it is."

~*~

Reggie wanted to look casual for their date, not desperate, so she chose a colorful, floral sundress. It had spaghetti straps and left little to the imagination as far as cleavage went. It had built-in support so she could go braless. It was a hot day; she welcomed the chance for a breeze blowing up her dress rather than heat sticking pants to her legs. She all but refused to wear dresses or skirts to work since her boss had suggested taking the road sales position. This date was a nice change of pace for her wardrobe.

Van's jaw dropped when he saw her. He could have tripped over it if he wasn't careful. "I feel underdressed," he finally said.

"You look fine. I wanted to be comfortable."

"I like the way you get comfortable."

"Are you going to behave? You said a date as friends. I don't want to be batting away innuendos all night."

"I'll behave, Sweetness."

"That, too." Again she crossed her arms.

"What now?"

"What is it with you and the names? Why is it always 'Dollface' or something else? Just call me Reggie."

"Troy calls you Princess. I thought you didn't mind."

"I don't mind when he does it. He doesn't want in my pants."

He moved closer. "What makes you think I want in your pants?"

"You…" She huffed passed him without finishing her sentence. "Can we go? I really have an errand on Front Street."

"I didn't know I was your errand boy. I thought we had a dinner date."

"It's just a stop since we're out there. I really want to go to Longhi's for dinner, too. Okay? Truce? Can we try not to kill each other tonight?"

"You retract the claws and I'll stop with the names."

"Fine."

"I'll try to have you home before midnight so you don't turn into a pumpkin, Princess."

She slammed the truck door and he laughed.

~*~

Van parked by the famous banyan tree, in a spot right off the Lahaina harbor. Having already done the tourist thing and learning the history of the enormous tree, Van casually walked around the car and helped Reggie out. Their destination, Longhi's, was all the way at the other end of Front Street, but Reggie had said she wanted to walk the store fronts before they went to eat and she was sure to want to walk after eating and drinking as much of his money as she could.

Van wanted to go for a quick walk through the harbor. It was clear he was searching for something as he studied all the boats, not just looking around.

"You don't look like you're sightseeing, Van."

"There's been a lot of activity here lately. I wanted a quick peek. Sometimes the ones trying too hard to be obvious are the ones that have something to hide."

"Are we on a date or are you on duty?"

He reached down and took her hand. "Let's go." She found an excuse to break his hold after a few paces as they approached the first gift shop. She feigned interest in something and never went back for his hand.

They strolled down the street admiring the different art galleries and specialty jewelry shops. The price tourists would pay for a gold pendant shaped like a whale's tail or for an oyster they had to open themselves to find a pearl then buy an overpriced setting for it always amazed Van.

They came to about the tenth jewelry store when Reggie said, "This is it. I'll be right out." He waited as he was told. She came out in a huff about two minutes later. "That idiot."

"Do I need to go hurt someone?"

"He called me saying they had a ring I was looking for."

"And they didn't?"

"What schmuck doesn't know an alexandrite from an aquamarine?"

"Meet that schmuck."

"Really?"

"Really. What is it?"

"It's my birthstone. It's a pretty green in the sun, not like emerald green, and it's a real pretty purple when you're inside."

"The stone changes color?"

"It does. It's amazing. I saw one years ago and fell in love with it."

"Why didn't you buy it?"

"Because it was a gazillion dollars."

"A gazillion, huh?"

"Close enough. The kid was either new and knew nothing about jewelry or misunderstood the note."

"Did you bite his face off? Should I call 911?"

"No. I was nicer than I should have been, though. I would have been pissed if I drove all this way for just that."

"Happy to be of service."

She looked at her watch. "It's only five-thirty but I'm starved. I skipped lunch. Can we go eat?"

"Of course. Lead me there, Prin… Reg." Again he put his hand out to her. This time, she accepted it.

They stuffed themselves sharing an appetizer and each other's main dishes. Crab stuffed mushrooms, steak and lobster, grilled shrimp and pasta with a heavenly white sauce were washed down with two bottles of wine instead of mixed drinks. They both declined dessert and began a slow stroll back on the other side of the street. Reggie wanted to walk by the ocean. "It never gets old for me. I don't think I could ever live anywhere away from the water."

They stopped to lean over the railing and stare out at the ocean. The sun was already gone, but it was still a wondrous sight.

"That's why I like my job so much," Van said. "I love the ocean. I don't think I'd be as happy if I was in Duluth or somewhere off a lake." He turned and looked at her. Her eyes were closed as she took in the ocean breeze. He leaned down and kissed her.

Her eyes sprang open but she smiled. She pulled on his hand to continue walking back to the car. After a few steps she finally said, "You promised to behave."

"I should have set a dress code when I made that promise. You're killing me, Reggie."

"Ice cream?" She asked when they came across a storefront at the Pioneer Inn that offered soft serve in a waffle cone.

"I thought you were stuffed."

"I was. Now I want ice cream."

He laughed, pulled out his wallet and walked over to the employee. "What kind do you want?"

6

When they reached the truck, Reggie leaned against her door and looked up at Van. He took the hint, leaned down and kissed her. She immediately opened her mouth wanting his tongue; he gave it to her. He pulled her closer and brought her off the ground with his strong embrace. Her arms went around his neck then her legs wrapped around his waist. Needing the truck for support, he leaned her back. For a second, they forgot where they were. A car's horn blast brought them to their senses. He put her down, but lingered over one last kiss before clearing his throat and opening her door.

When Van sat down behind the steering wheel, he leaned over and kissed her again. This time a hand went over her breast on the outside her dress. She let out a slight gasp, but didn't motion for him to remove it.

Van finally stopped the kiss and sat upright. "We need to get going." Reggie nodded in agreement. It was almost an hour back to her house; that would be the longest hour she'd spend in this lifetime. After over two years of avoiding men, she suddenly thought she was going to explode if she didn't have him soon.

They were on the Pali, the curvy road along mountains and cliff sides, when she pointed to a path past the tunnel on the ocean side. "Pull over here." They still had a half an hour to go.

Time was not being her friend. From him stroking her arm and his kisses to her hand, to her caressing his thigh, they were lucky they hadn't cause an accident. He pulled over to the side of the road.

"No, there's a road here," she said, pointing again. He continued around what she called a road. It barely fit the truck with a few feet to spare before it was sheer cliff. She opened the door and hurried out as soon as the truck came to a stop. Rushing out as well, he met her at the front of the truck. In half an instant, she was high on his hips again. They kissed like wild animals that had been starved for food for days. She frantically undid his belt buckle and scooted his shorts down as best as she could with one hand; the other held onto his neck.

~*~

Van groaned as she touched him while he hungrily kissed down her neck and across her breasts. Accepting her actions and the fact that his shorts were halfway down his thighs as an invitation, he slipped a hand under her dress. His hands discovered what he had been picturing under her dress all night; a thong. Delighting in the eagerness of her response to him as he caressed the small patch of material, he no longer entertained thoughts of wanting to move slowly. Bringing his other hand under her dress, he pulled her to his chest. He scooted the thong aside as he lowered her onto himself.

Reggie let out a gasp as he entered her, tightening her arms around his neck as she buried her head deep into them. "You okay?" he asked. "You wanna stop?"

She shook her head 'no'.

"No, you're not okay or no, don't stop?"

"Don't stop." She opened her mouth and gently bit at his neck.

He leaned her against the truck and claimed her deeper. She bit harder and another gasp escaped her.

She felt too good. Van was afraid he wasn't going to last. He only managed slow, gentle strokes while balancing them against the truck. It was as if things were moving in slow motion. He was brought out of his daze by her whimper. She tightened around him, sending him over the edge. He released into her with more than a whimper of his own. It was an animal howl of pure pleasure. He didn't know how he remained standing.

When he finally caught his breath, Van turned around and sat on the bumper with the two of them still as one. She still clung tightly to his neck. "You all right?"

She nodded a 'yes'.

He brought her face in front of his so he could see it. "Did I hurt you?"

She shook her head 'no'. Her silence scared him.

"Reg, you weren't a... you know. Were you?"

"No," she said, softly. "I wasn't a virgin, Van." She rested her head on his shoulder again and kissed at his neck. "It's just been a very long time for me."

He stroked her hair and kissed her head. "How'd you know about this place? You been here before or did we get lucky?"

"I've been here before, not like this though. Will you do something for me?"

"Anything, Babe."

She sat up and looked him in the eyes. "Will you take me home?"

"Dammit." He pulled her close. "I did hurt you."

"No. You didn't. I'd like to try that again without breaking the orgasm speed record."

He laughed. "I think I can handle that."

"You were right, you know."

"About what?"

"That ain't no small change you have there."

He grinned. "There's no faster way to inflate a man's ego than discussing his unit."

Reggie rubbed her hands up and down his back then across his chest. He held her tight, gentle moans escaping at her touch. She could still feel him inside her. She moved her arms round his neck and picked herself up slightly then went back down slowly onto his lap. "Maybe I don't want to wait until we get to my house after all."

"Lord Almighty."

Another car slowly pulled up, but immediately began to back up when Donovan's truck was in view. Reggie hopped down and straightened her dress. Van buckled up. "Looks like someone else had our great idea. Let's get going."

Their fingers were laced as they sat together in the truck. She was riding in the middle of the bench seat. The passenger seat was too far away now. He kissed the back of her hand and she nibbled at his ear until he said, "You'd better stop it or I'll wreck."

They ran up the two flights to her apartment. The elevator would have been too slow. They hurried to the bedroom without a second to waste, hastily undressing each other, to begin round two. Things moved a little slower at first, but not much. The wanting was too great; the desire had built up for too long. Reggie couldn't hide how she felt about him anymore and she didn't want to. He brought her to pure ecstasy again. She was in bliss once more, somewhere around one in the morning, and again when they woke up in each other's arms at six a.m.

"I can't believe you will be gone for a week." She pouted as she laid her head on his chest, still lying flat on top of him after the morning workout.

"Yeah, but I'll still be averaging sex once a day while I'm gone."

"Swine." She playfully bit his chest.

"Ouch!" He rubbed where she bit him. "I think I could use the rest of a hard week at sea. You sure know how to wear a guy out."

"Is your schedule always like this?"

"It depends." He made long strokes down her back. "It depends where you are and what's going on. I've had a schedule of two days on, two days off sometimes. A couple times a year we might be underway for two weeks."

"Two weeks? Troy's never been gone for two weeks."

"You're on a small island. The patrols are different and Troy has rank on his side. I was in dry dock doing ship repairs once. That was pretty much 24/7 for a month. You've never seen so many cranky sailors before."

"I can imagine." She rested her head on him and sighed. "I don't think I'd like you being gone all the time."

He rolled her off his chest and sat up. "Well you'd better think about it because that's my job, Sweetheart." Standing, in a bit of a huff, he pulled his shorts on.

His harshness shocked her; she didn't know what to say. She pulled the sheet up, covering herself while she watched him get dressed.

After glancing over at the clock, he turned back to her. "I need to report in an hour. I have to go." He leaned down to kiss her goodbye, but she turned her head away. Letting out a heavy breath, he walked out of the room and left her apartment.

Reggie walked to the shower, still in a daze. She let the water run a tad hotter than she could stand and stood under it until it ran cold. When she was done, she angrily pulled the sheets from the bed and threw them in the washer. It was remade with a set of clean silken ones. Sitting on the bed, she pulled a pillow to her face and took a deep breath. Dammit. She could still smell his cologne.

She dropped onto the bed still hugging the pillow, refusing to cry. *Epic fail.* The tears flowed freely. She finally let her guard down; what a mistake that was. To find such grand ecstasy then horrific heartbreak all within twelve hours; a*in't life grand.*

The phone rang and she jumped to her feet. The caller ID read *Donovan Kimball.* She wanted to reach for it but pulled her hand back. "Go to hell." Jerking the phone cord from the answering machine, she spoke through gritted teeth. "I don't need your bullshit in my life. I have enough of my own."

7

Regina made it through work that morning on automatic. By the grace of all that is good, the lunch date she had to keep with the lighting representative was with a woman. She couldn't take another "martini lunch" with an ogling, over-aged light bulb salesman.

In surrendering the road sales position, she had agreed to take over the lighting department in addition to her other duties. It was no big deal. The display was small and stock was kept to a minimum. She could maintain the inventory there and still break down a blueprint and quote an entire house in a day. She could stretch it to two if there was any level of difficulty at all. Three was acceptable by the men who were her peers. It was also accepted that she did all the answering of the phones while they bullshitted about last night's game or some other manly chore worth grunting over. That was accepted of course until they were put on commission -- then she was called a phone hog.

"Geez, Reggie. Give us a chance to answer it before you dive on it."

Kiss my what?

When her commissions were the highest from that first month, she was told she had the best seat in the office. It was received as a humiliation rather than the pat on the back her boss intended when he listed everyone's earnings in the break room. There was a never-ending run of excuses for why she made more. They couldn't accept that she worked the hardest. According to them, she had the highest sales because she had tits.

Reggie vowed to take the face off the first person who crossed her that day. Amazingly, everyone was well-behaved. Rumor had it there was a chalkboard hanging in the men's bathroom with 'Women to avoid this week' on it. Reggie hoped she was on it today, but that still wasn't enough. She didn't want to be there. After lunch, claiming to have gotten a bad sandwich, she called the office informing them she was going home sick. She also called in on Tuesday.

By Wednesday, she vowed to pull her head out of her 'asset'. She would put on the proverbial big girl panties and continue on with life. Busting a contractor trying to get away without paying for a wheelbarrow full of items was a great start to her day. If only she had the authority to kick him where it counted she would have felt better.

By noon, Reggie became lightheaded. She hadn't eaten since her lunch with the rep. Reggie had horrible eating habits to begin with, but when she was upset, they hardly existed at all. Exercise was never part of her daily routine, but she never fought to keep her size-three waist; she simply forgot to eat sometimes. Other times she put away an entire large pizza by herself. It all balanced out in her mind. Today was a pizza day. She ordered six pizzas and notified the 'will-call' boys that lunch was on her. There were five guys outside that ran for all the items that she typed up on invoices for the contractors and two that were dedicated to pulling the entire house loads. She was the only one who went out of her way to show appreciation for the ones who did the legwork and heavy lifting. Again, she heard comments from the other salesmen for why the will-call boys really played favorites. It couldn't be the fifty dollars she spent making sure, once a month, they each had their favorite beer for their tailgate party on Friday or for the spontaneous pizzas. It was surely because,

"They're called boobs, Ed." Erin Brokovich rocked. She thought about picking the movie up on the way home.

Sitting with the boys at lunch, she didn't mind the flirting so much today. She needed to be reminded that someone thought she was pretty. She was paged for a long distance phone call, but asked that a message be taken. It had been Van. *Kiss my ass twice.* Instead of her smugness making her feel better, she heard his voice in her head. *Where and when, Doll-face. Where and when?*

On the Pali last Sunday, dick head. She was losing it. Now she was arguing with herself. She needed to get good and drunk.

"I don't want to drink until I'm sure I'm not pregnant, Hon. Sorry," was Sabrina's answer when she called her best friend. "Come over for dinner, though. Troy went this week with the guys. I wanted to call you anyway. Your timing is good. I'm lonely."

"You mind if I drink?"

"Hell no. Plan on sleeping over too so you can really tie one on if you want. It'll be fun."

The girls had a great dinner and Reggie had a few different mixed drinks. Nothing tasted good tonight. *I can't even get drunk right.*

Sabrina clicked the TV off after they finished a rerun of *Friends*. "So tell me."

"Tell you what?"

"Come on, Reg. How did your date with Van go? I've been dying for you to tell me about it. Why so coy?"

"There's nothing to tell, Bri. We get along like oil and water. You knew that. Why the hell did you even try to set us up in the first place?"

"Don't give me that. There's a spark there and I know it."

"You couldn't be more wrong."

"I know there's more to this and there's something you're not telling me."

"Why?"

"Because Troy said Van won't tell him anything either."

"Really?" Reggie was surprised. She was sure he would have bragged about their night together and laughed about getting another notch on his headboard. The only reason she agreed to come over tonight is because Troy was gone. The thought of facing him after her night with Van was unbearable. *What would he think of me now? Princess? Yeah, right.*

"What's happened, Reggie? You don't keep secrets from me."

"Nothing, Bri. Nothing." She stood up. "I'm going home. I only had a few drinks. I'm fine."

"Stay, Reg. Please?"

She walked over and gave Sabrina a hug. "I love you; I just really want to go home."

"Will you come with me to the dock on Saturday when the guys get back?"

"I can't. I have a work-related commitment." She lied.

"Will you come for dinner at least?"

"I'll be busy all day."

Sabrina crossed her arms. "You know you can't lie to me."

"I'm serious, Bri. I'm driving to Hana to quote a job."

"On Saturday?"

"I do Saturdays sometimes. I can't leave the office all day on a weekday. This is a busy time."

"You can stop by when you get back to town."

"It'll be late."

"So come for brunch on Sunday then."

"Stop it, Bri." Reggie faked a laugh. "You don't need to entertain me. I really have to run. See ya." She hurried out the door before her friend could make another protest or try to set another date.

Reggie unplugged her phone when she arrived at home. The caller ID showed two missed calls from Van and Sabrina had tried to call already. She wanted to be left alone.

~*~

When the Coast Guard Cutter docked at noon that Saturday, Sabrina was there to greet Troy. Van wasn't surprised that Reggie didn't show up. She hadn't been taking his calls. *He had screwed up – big time.* He tried to get past Sabrina, but she wouldn't allow it.

"What happened with you two?"

"It just didn't go well, Bri." He tried walking away.

"That's an understatement, because now she's not talking to me."

"What?" He stopped and whipped his head around.

"I haven't been able to get a hold of her since Wednesday. That's not like her at all. Something happened between you two."

"I'll go find her."

"She said she wouldn't be home, but I think she was lying."

"I'll find her. I'll stop by later and fill you in."

"Thanks, Van," she said as she gave him a strong hug.

He showered in record time at the station then headed for her apartment. Her car wasn't parked where it was before. He thought maybe she wasn't home, but then he found it tucked next to the dumpster. She was hiding. When she didn't answer her door, he went downstairs and looked around the pool. He didn't find her there, but he did find her across the street at the beach.

"Bri said you were in Hana today." Sitting up on her straw beach mat at the sound of his voice, she pulled her towel up to cover herself. "I've seen you naked, Reg. That skimpy bikini isn't going to do anything for me."

"The job was postponed," she said as she defiantly threw the towel down.

"Why aren't you talking to Bri?"

"I'm not – not talking to her. I saw her Wednesday."

"And she's been trying to get in touch with you ever since. She's really upset."

"Are you her keeper now?" Reggie stood up and gathered her things.

He removed her bag from her hand. "Stop it, Reggie. I want to talk."

"We have nothing to talk about. You wanted a quick ride. You got it. You happy?"

"You know that's not true."

"Do I? I said I'd miss you and you freaked out."

"I wanted you to know what you're up against. It's no picnic for me either, you know."

"Now why is that, Van? Don't you have a girl in every port?"

"That's Navy, Sweetheart."

"Fine. Joke away." Reclaiming her bag from him, she walked away. He followed her.

"Look. Maybe it came out wrong. Maybe my timing was bad."

"Maybe? I've been through some crap, but I don't ever recall feeling so used!"

He had to grab her by the arm to stop her from walking into a passing car. "Careful, Reggie." He held her other arm as well. "I'm sorry. I wanted you to know that sometimes I'll be gone. There's nothing I can do about it."

"We had sex, Van. Do you really think I was looking for a commitment after one night?"

"We didn't have sex…we made love. There's a difference."

Making sure there were no cars coming this time, she shook herself free and crossed the street. He silently followed her back to her apartment and was a little more than surprised when she let him come in. "I'm hot. You want a beer?" she asked.

"Sure." She offered him a Mickey's and stepped out onto the lanai. She had left the sliding glass door open when she left for the beach. The crime rate was high here, but being a couple floors up, she wasn't worried about it. He followed her out.

"I'll apologize to Sabrina later," she said, turning to him. "If we run into each other there, let's promise now to be civil to each other. Okay?"

"What do you mean?"

"I'm not going to avoid them, worried that you're going to be there, Van. They're my best friends. Promise we'll be civil in front of them if we happen to be there at the same time."

"Didn't you hear what I said at all?" He reached for her beer and put both of them down on the table, then held her face in his hands. "We made love, dammit. We didn't have sex. I like you a lot, Reggie. I want you in my life. I'm sorry that it sounded differently. If I could take back how I said what I did, I would."

He leaned down and kissed her gently then looked into her eyes again. "It made me crazy thinking that maybe you didn't want to be there for me. I don't know what I'd do if you said you couldn't handle my schedule." He kissed her again, possessively. Her arms came up around his neck as she returned the kisses. They walked back a few paces until she was leaning against the wall. He broke the kiss after a few minutes. "I lied." She looked up at him, confused. "That bikini is killing me." Once again, her legs wrapped around his waist after he picked her up. She was instantly dreaming of reliving their first time together in front of the truck. It was only a week ago, but it seemed like years. She didn't have to dream for long. Apparently they shared the same thought. He was already busy with her bikini top.

8

"What do you mean they're shipping you out? I thought you were here for two years?" They had been together for six months and things had been absolute heaven between them. Once Van was able to knock down her wall, Reggie became the lovesick female she vowed she'd never be. With her past, she thought she'd never have her fairy tale life. She thought she was on her way to it when he broke the news. He was at her place, still in his uniform. He rushed over as soon as he had been told.

"Normally yes, but that doesn't mean anything. I'm at their beck and call, Babe."

"When do you leave?" she asked, biting back tears.

"A month and a half."

She walked to the lanai and leaned on the railing. He came up behind her and held her tight. "Marry me."

"Are you serious?" She spun around and faced him.

"As I've ever been in my life about anything. I want you to come with me. If we get married now, they have to ship me as married. We'd be a package deal. They'll ship you and your stuff and we'll get a place for two."

"I don't want you to marry me because it's convenient and they have to buy my ticket, Van."

"Me either. I want you to marry me because I love you and I don't want to leave here without you."

She turned away and faced the ocean again. She never thought about leaving the islands before. "Where are they sending you?"

"Would it matter?"

She turned back around. "Not really."

"It could be Puerto Rico…it could be California. It could be any hellhole. I know I can do it if you're with me, but can you? Will you marry me and everything that comes with me, Reggie?"

He held out his hand. On his pinky was a plastic pink dinosaur ring with a tuff of hair like a troll doll.

She looked down at it and smiled. "That's my engagement ring?"

"I ran straight here from the station. That's the best the ABC store had to offer."

She took it off his pinky and put it on. "Then I accept." He picked her up and swung her around. "We're crazy, you know."

"Not as crazy as you were for saying yes to that ring. Now I don't need to give you this one." He held out a small box and opened it, revealing a half carat round diamond with six smaller diamonds on one side. In another slot was the wedding band that would connect with it with six more stones, completing the circle. He removed the plastic ring from her left hand, placed it on her right hand, then put the diamond on her ring finger and gave her hand a strong kiss. "How fast can you pull together a wedding reception? I want to get married right away."

"Can we just get Troy and Bri and go to the court house then do something at their place? I don't want anything big."

"You don't want your parents here?"

"I'll call them after the fact. I can't imagine bells and whistles for me getting married after six months of dating. They'll think I'm nuts and try to talk me out of it."

"You are nuts for loving me," he said with a kiss. "That's beside the point. Are you sure that's all you want?"

"I'm sure."

"Tomorrow is Saturday so we can't do anything until Monday. Marry me on Monday, my love." He went down on bended knee.

She said, "Yes," before throwing her arms around his neck as she joined him on the floor. They shared a passionate kiss before Reggie's heart skipped a beat at a realization. She let go of Van and stood. Turning away from him, she leaned against the wall. "Crap."

"Changed your mind already?"

"I need a blood test after we apply for a license. It'll take three days to get the results." He never questioned why she knew that.

"So marry me Thursday." He stood up and gave her another kiss. "I gotta get back. Technically I'm AWOL right now." She walked him to the door and they kissed goodbye. "I want a half a dozen kids... all girls... and I want them all to look exactly like their mom."

As soon as Van left, she collapsed against the door in tears. When she gathered herself twenty minutes later, packing a suitcase and getting away were her only objectives. Not being able to face Van to return the rings, Reggie drove to Sabrina's. Troy answered the door.

"Hey, Reg." He gave her a hug that lifted her off the ground. "I hear congratulations are in order."

She could only answer by holding up a small white bag that held the rings. "Would you do me a favor and give this to Van?"

He accepted it with a raised eyebrow. "I was kind of hoping you guys would come over for champagne tonight. That's what Bri went to pick up."

"Sorry. I can't. I'll see you later, okay?" She hurried to her car and drove away before he could ask any more questions.

~*~

Troy noticed the suitcase in the backseat and groaned. "Oh shit." He opened the bag. When he saw the ring box, he ran for his truck, setting a record for driving the two miles to the station.

Knowing Reggie too well, he knew what this meant. Spotting Van talking to a couple of tourists at the front door, he shouted for him to come over.

"What's up, Boss-man?" Van asked, leaning on the passenger window. Troy tossed him the bag. Van chuckled as he caught it, clearly not understanding what it held; he was still high on the news. Troy hated to be the one to burst his bubble. Van's smile instantly faded as he looked in and saw the box. "What the… why? What is this shit, Troy?" He reached in and pulled out the box. His hands trembled as he opened it, as if he couldn't believe what they held. "Fuck!" Van crumpled the bag and slapped the side of the truck.

"Take it easy, man."

"Take it easy? Why the fuck do you have these?" Troy had never seen Van so angry. His nostrils flared as he spoke.

"Don't shoot the messenger. Get in. I'm taking you to her. I have an idea of what she's doing."

After jumping into the truck, Van slammed the door. Troy cringed, waiting for more yelling.

"What the hell, Troy? Why would she change her mind like that so fast?" Again Van opened up the bag in disbelief.

"I have a feeling, but you need to talk with her." Van smacked his hand flat against the dashboard, causing Troy to jump. "Settle down. Stop taking it out on my truck. It'll be okay. You two just need to talk."

"Where are we headed?"

"I'm pretty sure she's going to the airport. I saw a suitcase."

"Shit!" Van ran his fingers through his hair. It was something he did a lot but this time, Troy noticed a lot more force behind it.

"It'll be okay, Buddy. We'll catch her. I'm taking sugar cane roads. Don't split a vein on this. You'll fix it."

"What's going on, Troy?"

"She needs to tell you that, Buddy. It ain't my place."

~*~

They did beat her to the airport. By the time she was pulling into parking and getting a ticket, Van was running over to her car. She cursed then pulled the car into the first open spot and climbed out.

"Where are you going? Why did you give me this back?" Van held up the bag. "What happed in less than an hour that changed your mind, Reg?"

"I just can't marry you, Van. I'm sorry. It was silly to think I could. I...I got carried away."

"I'll carry you away." He picked her up, hurrying towards Troy's truck as she squirmed to be released.

"Put me down!"

"Not until you tell me what the hell happened." He walked her over to the truck and put her down by the driver's side door. "One of you is going to tell me what the hell is going on!"

Troy climbed out of the truck. "I'm going to get a soda. You two can talk in the truck." Stopping in front of her, he whispered. "Tell him, Reggie. He deserves a chance to make up his own mind."

They climbed in the truck and sat sideways facing each other. "What is it?" Van asked. "Why won't you marry me?"

She exhaled. "I've been married before, Van."

He was only slightly taken aback. "So. Are you divorced?"

His reply shocked her. She managed a soft, "Yes."

"So what's the problem?"

She had a hard time forming the words but they finally came pelting out. "I can't have kids, Van. I can't. You want kids and I can't give them to you. Okay? Is that what you wanted to hear? I'm not marrying you. I'm not going to marry you or anyone... ever." She grasped the handle of the door to try to escape, but he removed her hand from it.

"That's it? You're leaving me because you're afraid I want kids more than I want you? You couldn't be more wrong, Reggie."

"But when you left...you said..." She began to cry.

He pulled her tight to his chest. "I know what I said. I was caught up in the whole moment. I wasn't thinking. I said what I thought you wanted to hear. You know? You're gorgeous and you said you'd be mine. I guess I went crazy."

"But you want kids and I can't give them to you."

Van found some napkins in the pocket of the truck's door and offered them to her. "I've never really thought about it, Reg. Honest. I want you. That much I do know. I don't know about feedings and diapers. I do know I'll go insane if I don't have you."

"You say that now."

"No. I mean that now and always." He held out the ring. "Put it back on, Reggie. Please."

She glanced down at it then looked back up at him. "I want the dinosaur one."

"God, I love you," he said as he brought her close. "Where were you going anyway?"

"Wherever the next flight was heading."

"I have next weekend off. Do you think you can wait until we can honeymoon; maybe on Kauai?"

"I think I can wait," she said with a smile.

They drove back to Troy and Sabrina's at a more reasonable pace. Van drove Reggie in her car as they followed Troy. Sabrina was waiting with champagne. She looped her arm through Van's and said she wanted to hear everything about how he proposed. Troy held Reggie back for a minute.

"Did you tell him?"

"I told him enough."

"It'll only make it harder on you later, Reg."

"He knows I can't have kids, Troy. Amazingly, he still wants to marry me. Let's go with that for now, okay? Promise me you won't tell him."

"He'll ask me someday. I won't be able to lie."

"You can and you will. Please? Promise me you won't ever tell him."

"All right," he said, pulling her in a hug. "I promise." They walked outside and he told Van. "Florida Keys."

"Florida Keys what?"

"That's where they're sending you. A station in Marathon."

Van stood and walked over to Reggie. "You'll still be surrounded by ocean, Baby. It'll just be a different one."

"It doesn't matter. I'll be with you."

9

The government paid for the rent on the house they shared in the Keys. That was about the best thing that could be said about it. The closest base was Key West. Everyone stationed in Marathon lived in rented townhouses or homes. Van and Reggie were right off a golf course with a canal off the backyard. It was a great location; the house was in a desperate state of neglect, though. The middle of it was almost a whole foot lower that the edges. They couldn't help but to laugh the first time they laid eyes on the bedroom doorframe; it looked like a funhouse door. Reggie laughed to tears when she placed a deck of cards on the kitchen counter and it spread down to the other end. She thought about buying a slinky just to see what it would do. They didn't care; it was their first home and they were together. Van teased that the crooked walls might help him by adding more traction. They wasted no time testing his theory out.

Van's schedule had him overnight two nights at the station then home the next two. It wasn't too bad of a deal. Sometimes she wished she was allowed to go to the station, but it was probably best that she didn't. They were still very much at the 'can't keep our hands off each other' stage, even several months into the marriage.

Regina accepted a part-time job at the small lumberyard in town. Scotty's was a chain of stores throughout the Keys. She was hired on the spot once the manager learned of her background. It wasn't as demanding as her last job. New homes weren't built with the vengeance that they were on Maui, but it kept her in the same field and she welcomed the familiarity. On occasion, she was asked to help inventory on Islamorada or in Key West; she loved that aspect of the job. Even a trip an hour up or down the small chain of islands was a fun getaway. They had gone to Miami once, but she didn't care for the rushed pace. It was worse than Oahu and that was always too much for her.

Even though Marathon was a very demanding station, Van rarely discussed work when he was home. Drug trafficking was extremely high in the Keys and that kept them constantly busy. Only when Reggie read something about the largest cocaine bust in history in the paper and asked him about it, did he fess up to being a part of it. There was an occasional rescue at sea and, of course, the patrolling to keep the beaches free from rowdy spring breakers at the numerous bikini contests. All he had to say about that was about helping a twelve-year-old girl remove a thorn from her foot. He was afraid she had become smitten with the uniform; the poor girl would probably chase sailors in her teens. He also reminisced on their first thorn, which she thought was silly, but she did love the kitty earrings he brought her as a gift for the 'thorniversary'.

"I saw these and thought how great they'd look on you."

"I love them!" she squealed. Reggie loved the cats she saw all over Key West, nicknamed 'Hemingways'. They had six toes or more on each front paw. "Can we get a cat?"

He dropped his head down. "I was afraid you'd ask that. I should have gone with the Dalmatians. No, we can't."

"Why not? Aren't we allowed one in housing? 'Cause that's stupid. This should be treated as our house."

"No. I just hate 'em. Besides, I'm allergic."

"But I want one." She closed the gap between them and stroked his chest with the open palm of her hand.

"I'd give you the moon if I could, Babe, but we can't get a cat."

"I don't want the moon, I want a kitten." She added her second hand to his chest and looked up with pouty eyes.

"Not gonna work. I'm sorry. We really can't get one."

"This sucks." She swung away from him and was about to storm off.

He took her arm and pulled her back. He held her face and gave her a gentle kiss on the lips. "I'm sorry."

She leaned into his chest. It wasn't worth crying over, especially knowing he felt bad about it. There wasn't anything he wouldn't do for her and she knew it. "I don't feel like cooking tonight. It's too hot."

"I'll cook."

"Take me out?"

"Anywhere, Babe."

"Lobster?"

He laughed. "You bet." He leaned down and gave her another kiss. "Any chance I could get dessert first? That sundress is makin' me hot."

"Funny. I was about to say the same thing about your uniform. You don't usually wear it home."

"I wanted to see if it had the same effect on you as the twelve-year-old."

"Oh, that sounded so wrong."

"It sounded better in my head."

That was usually the pace when Van walked through the door. Uniform or not, sex was almost immediate. Two days to each of them had been an eternity. One morning, Reggie went to fly into his arms and he put his hand up to stop her.

"What's wrong?" she asked with fear in her eyes.

"I'm hurtin', Baby. I need to go lie down."

"What is it?"

"I blew my back out."

"How?"

He held onto the counter and let out a groan. "Can you help me to the bedroom first?"

She positioned herself under his arm and helped him walk into their room. "Shouldn't I get you to the hospital?"

"I'll be fine. I just need to lie down for a bit. It'll go back in place on its own. Could you get me a couple of aspirin though, please?"

"Sure." She ran off to retrieve them and some water while he undressed. He climbed into bed, face down, after taking them. "Do you want me to rub it for you?"

He shook his head no. "I think that'll make it hurt worse." She gently stroked it as she kissed between his shoulder blades. "Let me rest, Baby. Trust me. It ain't gonna work."

"This will be the first time we've missed a day."

"I'll make it up to you. I promise."

"You want to tell me about it?" She was worried.

"Later. Just let me lie here, okay?"

"All right." She kissed the back of his head. "I don't work until noon. I'll check in on you before I go. I love you."

He grunted a painful reply.

At eleven-thirty, she went in with a sandwich and a soda, but he was sound asleep. She left it at his bedside, kissed him, and went to work. Afraid to call throughout the day and wake him, she resisted. She wished he had called her, but he didn't.

Reggie arrived home a little after eight and went straight to the bedroom. She was scared when she found him lying face-down on the floor. "Donovan!" She rushed to his side.

"I'm okay. I needed a harder surface."

The nightstand still had the sandwich on it, untouched. "You haven't eaten at all?"

"Not hungry."

"This isn't good, Van. I'm taking you in." She went to stand up but he caught her hand, stopping her.

"No. I'm all right." He slowly rolled onto his back with minor grunts and groans then reached out and brushed her nipple with the back of his hand. "I think I'm feeling better already."

"How about something to eat?"

"How about some lovin'?"

"I don't want to hurt you."

"Maybe you'll put something back in place."

"You're hopeless," she said as she removed her clothes. He was already naked.

"And you're beautiful. Marry me."

"I already did."

"Oh yeah."

She straddled him slowly, waiting to hear him wince but he didn't. They began to make love and he chuckled.

"What's so funny?"

"I should have laid down the other way. We're going uphill."

10

They shared a hot shower together after they made love. Reggie hoped the hot water would help Van's muscles. He was leaning against the wall, holding himself up while the water ran down his back.

"Sex didn't help, did it?" Reggie asked.

"Didn't hurt." He picked up his head long enough for a quick kiss then he dropped it back down.

"You going to tell me what happened?"

"There was a fishing boat that was taking on water. They had a life raft, but they were trying to save the boat."

"Idiots. Does everyone play dumb, waiting for you guys to show up?"

"Pretty much. Anyway, I guess it was worse than they thought. One guy was below working a hose from the water pump trying to suck up the water. It was an ancient bastard, about three hundred pounds. The pump – not the guy."

"I get it." She smiled as she gently rubbed his back.

"I went over to holler at him to get out. The boat was taking on water too fast; there was no way he was doing any good. We ordered everyone off the boat and onto ours. He was about to come up when the damn cart that they had the pump on collapsed. It was about to fall down the hole."

"It would have gone through the boat?"

"Worse. It would have landed on the guy."

She gasped and covered her mouth. "Did he get hurt?"

"I grabbed the pump midair and held it there till two other guys came over to help put it to the side."

"You held a three hundred pound pump by yourself?"

"It wouldn't have been so bad; it was the angle though. I really thought something popped."

"Don't you think you should get an X-ray?"

"It feels better, really. I don't think I'm up to company though. Will you call off the Avilla's? Do you mind?"

"Of course not. I'll call Virgie now. Stay in as long as you want. The heat should help."

"I'm already pruney. I'm gonna go hold down the floor again."

"My poor baby." She leaned against his back and gave it a kiss.

"Lower."

She kissed down his spine then made her way back up. "Van?"

"Hmmm."

"You saved his life."

"Just doin' my job, Baby."

Of all the other couples at the station, Van and Reggie had hit it off best with a couple who were from the area. Virgie was raised in Marathon and Bobby was from Miami. He joined the Coast Guard to see the world and was stationed in Marathon instead. Turned out it wasn't such a bad deal; he met Virgie and they were as happy as Van and Reggie.

They shared many nights talking away every subject imaginable. The guys tried a different import beer each time and the girls ran through the finer wines. As Virgie and Bobby discussed wanting to put off kids until they had done a few tours and knew where they wanted to settle, Reggie felt less like she was holding Van back from children. Maybe they wouldn't be ready for kids for a long time either. Maybe in a few years they would talk about adopting.

Virgie completely understood about canceling the night, as Regina knew she would. They made plans for the next two days off since their husbands shared the same shift. As soon as she hung up, Van howled from the bathroom. She rushed in, and screamed at the sight of him on the floor. "Van, no!"

"Baby, call Master Chief. I'm hurtin' bad."

"I'm calling an ambulance!"

"No. I have to go with our coverage. I can't go anywhere else."

"You can't ride all the way to the hospital in Key West like this!"

"I'll be okay. Please, just call him. Call the station. They'll get a hold of him."

She ran to the kitchen to call the station and was relieved when their friend, Derrick, answered. She'd shared a few nights with him in Key West and considered him a good friend. The wives never thought twice about an invitation to go to Key West with any of the crew. No one messed with a crewmembers wife. You were as safe as if you were with your own husband. They were almost more protective, as a matter of fact. She was actually afraid of being looked at in the wrong way by someone, causing a fight to break out.

Reggie explained the situation hurriedly to him and he jumped into high gear. "I'll get a hold of Master Chief, but I'm sending a driver right over. He has to go to Key West; there's no choice."

"But he's in a lot of pain, Derrick. That's an hour away."

"I'll send the truck with the emergency lights. He'll get there quicker. He can't go local unless it's life threatening. Sorry, Reg. I'll send the strongest meds I can find here for him. You can ride along, too."

"He has to lay flat. He's having a hell of a time."

"There's a topper on the truck. I'll throw a mattress in for him. See you in a few, sweet cheeks. Sit tight."

Ten minutes passed before they showed up. The boat wasn't out on patrol so six of the crew showed up. They brought a wooden body board to load him up on the truck. Reggie breathed a sigh of relief at the arrival of the cavalry.

Although they all knew how serious it was, they tried to keep things light. "Hey, Moron," Derrick said when he walked in. "Can I stay with your hot wife while I make the noob here drive your sorry ass in?"

"Keep your black ass away from my wife," Van said into the bathroom rug.

"But I brought her a hot new teddy." He winked at Reggie, who managed a smile.

Derrick knelt down, leaning closer to Van. "You should have let the sonofabitch fall, you jackass."

"You'd have done the same thing in my shoes."

"Yeah, you're right. What a bunch of schmucks. Jones is here. He'll give you a shot in your hairy ass 'cause lord knows I don't wanna see it."

"Up yours. Ah shit, don't make me laugh, man. Get me the hell outta here."

The station's paramedic joined them in the bathroom to give Van a shot of morphine. Reggie hadn't met him yet, but it didn't matter. The thought of that drug made her cringe, no matter who was administering it. He acknowledged her with a nod, but now really wasn't the time for introductions.

Carefully laying him on the board, each man took a corner and carried him out. Once he was loaded into the truck, Reggie climbed in the back with him. Derrick drove, all the others returned to the station in a second vehicle. The truck bounced more than she cared for. With each bump, Reggie looked down to see the pain on Van's face. His eyes squinted together too often and one made him bite his lip so hard, she was afraid he'd draw blood. It took everything she had not to yell at Derrick to be more careful. She knew he was doing everything he could. Relief set in when she realized the morphine must have finally done the trick. About half way into the drive, he drifted off.

Watching him resting now caused her mind to wander and place a heavy load of guilt on herself. She was feeling horrible about having just had sex with him. Hell, she practically demanded sex from him so soon after he was in so much pain. Instead of pleasing herself, she should have insisted they not continue. He swore he was better afterwards, though. Maybe it was endorphins acting like a runner's high and he did feel better, if only for a moment, or maybe he was just being himself; always wanting to please her. When he was better, they really needed to have a talk.

Derrick had opened the sliding window, continually asking for updates along the way. Reggie couldn't respond with much. "The same" was usually her response. Small talk and any other conversation didn't come easy. This was not the place for their normal banter. Even as cool as Derrick tried to be, he seemed to be nervous, too. His replies of, "He'll be okay," only made her worry more. Having had enough of awkward silence, Reggie positioned herself next to Van, noses touching, with the tire well at her back as she stroked his short hair.

Van woke up when they were transferring him to a gurney. Reggie kissed him goodbye and went to get him registered.

"Member's last four?" the nurse asked.

"Excuse me?"

"Member's last four. His social security number, Honey."

"His name is Donovan. Donovan Kimball."

"Don't do me no good. I need his last four. Do you have your military ID?"

"Yes."

"Give me that. It'll be on there."

Reggie handed her the card and waited while the receptionist keyed in the four numbers. Within seconds she had his entire history. That was frightening. She quickly verified his address, phone numbers and rank. Reggie waited to hear verification on his preference on boxers or briefs.

"You can sit in the waiting room. Doctor will be out to see you as soon as they are done looking at your husband."

"Thanks." She sat closest to the swinging door that he had been taken through.

Derrick joined her. She rested her head on his shoulder. "Your hubby is the toughest bastard we have. He'll be fine." He tried to give her a reassuring hug. "I hate to leave you, but I have to head back." Reggie sat upright. "I'm not abandoning you here. Someone called Bobby; he's off tonight. He and Virgie are on their way. They're probably going to keep Van overnight. I already checked. There's housing available out back if you want to stay here."

"I'm staying with him."

"I figured that. So did Virg. She's bringing you a change of clothes. Sorry I can't stay, Reg." He gave her a kiss on the forehead. "You know I would if I could."

"I know. Thanks for coming to my rescue, Derrick, and don't tell me it's your job."

He gave her hand a reassuring squeeze. "Give me an update in the morning."

"I will. Thanks again, Derrick." Reggie wandered to the picture window, allowing Derrick his escape. She'd linger over the goodbye forever if he let her. She didn't want to sit here alone, but she didn't want to get him in any trouble. As she watched the truck drive away, her sadness turned into anger. Why did it have to get so bad before Van got it looked at? Why did her husband have to sit in pain through a horrible drive when they could have gone for help much closer? *He's a person not a goddamn number! Last four? Kiss my ass!* While stewing over her husband's pain, Reggie paced the waiting room. She went to the vending machine for coffee but realized she didn't have any cash on her. They both emptied their change nightly into a jar marked "Maui Fund" so not even a stray quarter was to be found. A swift kick to it brought her brief satisfaction, but no coffee. The nurse had disappeared long ago. There was no one to vent her frustrations to, which was probably a good thing. Complaining about the military to the nurse would get her nowhere. Without a doubt she'd defend the life she chose and boast how great it was.

Finally settling down into one of the chairs, she pulled her legs up, wrapping her arms around them, feeling completely alone for the first time in months.

The doctor came out after an hour, assuring her that Van just had a horribly pulled back muscle and would be fine with some rest. "His CO won't be happy, but I'm giving orders for him to stay home for a week to be sure." He gave her two bottles of pills. "One's an anti-inflammatory and one is for pain. Directions are on them."

"He can go?"

"I see no reason to keep him."

"He can't even sit up."

"He's doing better already. We've given him shots of the meds I've given you and they're helping."

"When he grabbed the pump, he said he heard something pop. Did you do an X-ray?"

"You have a medical background?"

"No... but—"

"Then leave the diagnosis to me. I felt his spine; he's fine. It's a pulled muscle." He pointed at the bottles again. "Follow the directions. He should stay on top of the pain meds or it'll sneak up on him. Don't let him slack off. He can go back to work in a week, but he should take it easy for maybe two."

"It's hard to take it easy at his job."

"I can only offer the advice; I can't make the CO's follow."

"But—"

"I have to get going now. If you need a refill on the meds, come back down and we'll get you taken care of." With that, the doctor walked away.

Virgie and Bobby came scrambling in the room as the doctor left. Reggie turned to them with tears in her eyes. "What's wrong, Reg? Is he bad?"

"They're sending him home."

"That's good, right?"

"You didn't see him, Bobby. I don't think he should be leaving."

"He looks fine to me," he said as he pointed towards the doors. A nurse was bringing Van out in a wheelchair.

Reggie rushed over. "Are you sure you're okay to leave?"

"I'm fhhine, Baby. Don't be such a whhory wart." He was slurring, but not horribly.

Bobby laughed. "Must be some good stuff."

"It's not funny, Bobby," Reggie said. "Can you stand, Van?"

"Suure." He slowly pried himself from the chair, cringing a little, but stood up almost straight. Reggie rushed over to his side to help steady him.

"Can we just go?" she said to Bobby. "I'm sorry you came all this way. Had I known, Derrick could have waited."

"No biggie, Reg. Come on. We're right out front."

Van had a little trouble getting in the car. As soon as they were settled, he leaned into Reggie, snuggled between her breasts, and fell back asleep. She stroked his hair and kissed the top of his head the whole way. She didn't like this at all.

11

Van was still very groggy when they reached their house. Bobby helped him in. "He does seem awfully loopy, doesn't he?"

"He's overmedicated, that's for sure," Reggie said, angrily. "They should have kept him there for at least a night."

"I'm fhhine."

"Bed or floor?" Reggie asked when they reached the bedroom.

"Fhloor."

She threw the comforter down and placed a pillow on it for him. They eased him down. He cuddled the pillow as they exited the room.

"Call me if you need anything, Reg," Bobby said. "Don't call the station. Peckerhead Garner won't do shit to send help. He'll tell him to suck it up."

"You know… I'm getting really sick of hearing how he treats you guys."

"It's military life. What do you do? Some officers are jerks. This ain't Home Ec class."

"It's uncalled for."

"Come on, Reg. You've had bosses that were jerks before."

"This goes beyond a bad boss."

He pulled Reggie towards him and gave her a kiss on the forehead. "Call me."

Virgie had been quiet, but Reggie knew she agreed with her a hundred percent. They couldn't stand the CO, but had already learned that complaining about it didn't get you anywhere.

"I'll stop over tomorrow and check on you," Virgie said as she hugged Reggie goodbye.

"Thanks again for coming to my rescue."

Reggie returned to the bedroom. Not in the mood for a sexy nightie; she slipped on one of Van's extra-large gray t-shirts with USCG across the front. Even though it was freshly washed, she could smell him in it when she brought it to her nose. She picked up a pillow and tossed it on the floor, but it went unused. He was lying on his back; she snuggled up to him and put her head on his shoulder. Instinctively his arm came down around her with a gentle moan, but he didn't wake up.

The following morning he woke up before she did. He was stroking her cheek, trying to get her to wake up. She stretched and cuddled up to him. "How's your back?"

"Better, but now my arm is numb."

She shifted her head to his chest. "You had me worried last night."

"Sorry. I should have sucked it up and not had you call. It's a lot better today."

"No, Van. You shouldn't have sucked it up. It's better because you went in. Stop acting like such a tough guy."

"Who's acting? I am a tough guy." He pulled her tight to his chest. "How come you can look so damn sexy in one of my ratty t-shirts?"

She bolted up. "Let me get you your pills."

"I don't need them."

"The doctor gave me strict orders for you to take them anyway. He wants you to stay on top of the pain, not wait until you can't stand it."

"I really don't need one."

"Then prove it." She dropped down onto her back.

"Is that a challenge, Mrs. Kimball?" Van propped himself on his side.

"Call it what you want." She whipped off the shirt and lay there flat.

He laughed. "A guy misses servicing his wife one morning…" He leaned down and kissed her breast then stopped. He fell back flat to the floor. "Dammit!"

She sat up. "Shit, Van. I'm sorry. I just knew—"

"Get me the damn pills." He put his arm over his eyes.

She hurried off after putting the t-shirt back on.

~*~

Van was a slight bear over the next few days. He hated being helpless, but behaved and took it easy as per the doctor's orders. He didn't know what was worse; being bored senseless while Reggie was at work or wanting to have sex with her every minute when she was home and her saying no. They'd only done a seven-day stretch when he was underway. It was easy to go without sex, as long as she wasn't around. He was going crazy now.

"You have to know it's no picnic for me either, Van. I just don't want to hurt you."

"I'd rather hurt."

"You big baby." She sat next to him on the couch. He dropped his head back in a childish pout. She let out a heavy sigh and reached in the fly of his boxers. "You do have a situation going on here, don't you?"

"It happens the second you walk in the room, Baby."

She left her hand where it was, leaned in and gave him a kiss on the chin. She worked her way down his neck then continued down his chest. "I gotcha covered," she said, lowering his boxers.

"Is this a back injury or heaven?"

Van went back to work the next Monday. He moved a little stiffly, but eventually things returned to normal. Oddly, his CO heeded the doctor's wishes and had him on easy duty for the next week. Van had stopped taking the pills days before he admitted it to Reggie. He hurt, but he didn't want to take them.

"I don't need them anymore, Baby," he said as they lay together on bed. They were both happy to be back in their routine.

"Well, I'm glad, but please promise me you won't play tough guy next time."

"There won't be a next time. It's done. A pulled muscle doesn't last forever."

"Can you prove that?" She teased as she snuggled up to him.

"I thought I just did."

"Prove it again. We have some catching up to do."

12

A few weeks later Van snuck in the bedroom and woke Reggie up with kisses. She yawned and wrapped her arms around his neck. "What are you doing home today?"

"Master Chief allowed me and one of the guys to switch shifts. He needs to get to an appointment in Miami tomorrow. You're off today so what do you say to a day filled with sex then a drive to Key West? I never get to go out with the other shift."

"Okay on the sex, but I already had plans to go to Key West with Virgie tonight. You go with the guys and have fun."

"Can't we go together? You're always there with her when I'm working."

"I guess if you want, but we want to dance. You guys will want to sit at a watering hole."

"Or better."

"Oh no you're not, Kimball. You set one foot in a titty bar and I swear…!"

"You'll what?" He grinned as he ran his hands down her sides and gave her neck a kiss.

"Don't you even think about it! I mean it."

"Promise. Scouts honor." He held up his hand in a Boy Scout salute.

"I always knew you were a boy scout." She pulled him down by his neck for a kiss. "I mean it. No titty bars."

He laughed. "All right. Seriously though, the guys wanted me to go with them. If you have set plans with Virgie, I won't feel so bad. I never get to party with the dysfunctional crew like you do."

The station was evenly divided into two crews. The married men were on one shift and the single guys were on the other. Whether it was done on purpose or not, that's how it panned out. The unmarried crew was affectionately dubbed 'the dysfunctionals'.

That night, the two of them drove separate cars, but followed each other. Van drove the guys and Reggie drove Virgie. Once they parked, they went their separate ways.

"You sure you don't want to hang with us?" Van asked one last time.

"You going to dance with me?"

"No."

"Then, no. You have fun…but not too much fun," she added.

"I think I've got it, Reg. You want to meet here later and drive back together?"

"I don't think so. We won't be staying too late. I have a shift tomorrow afternoon."

"Okay. See you at home then. Keep dessert warm for me," he said with a kiss.

"Yanno," Derrick said. "You two really make me wanna puke."

"Jealous?"

"Hell yeah." He slapped Van on the back. "Sloppy Joe's?"

"Sounds good to me."

"Do we get a vote?" Alan asked.

"You're on your own, my friend, if you want to hit a topless bar. I have already been lectured."

"Pussy whipped."

"Call it what you may, but I prefer to keep the Major attached."

"The Major?" Alan laughed. "More like a Private."

"Ah hell, he ain't been private since I was nineteen."

"Late bloomer. We'll hook up later then. I didn't come here to watch Jimmy Buffet wannabes sing tacky songs for the tourists."

"We'll call you later then. Adios." His friends saluted before they walked away.

~*~

At midnight, well past when they thought they would call it a night, the girls were walking down an alley to get to the car. They walked in the street to go around a group of men who were gathered outside the door to a well-known topless bar. It was one of the skankier ones by reputation. "Hey, Virg! Reg!" One of the guys they knew from the Islamorada station came over to them. They could tell he was a little too tanked. He lit a cigarette. "Why aren't you inside with your old man, Reg?"

"What?" she asked as she froze in place.

"Oh, shit." Virgie held her arm. "Let's just go, Reggie. I don't want a scene. Deal with it later. Okay? Please?"

She shook Virgie's arm free and stormed towards the door. Although the bouncer held back the men from entering, claiming an occupancy issue, he smiled and held the door wide open for Reggie.

She walked through without a thank you for the gesture and scanned the room. The friends Van drove down with were front row to the stage, hooting, hollering, and waving one-dollar bills. She found Van sitting at a table talking to one of the waitresses. At least she had a bikini top on. Well, one that would fit a Barbie doll anyway. Reggie was too pissed to think. She picked up a saltshaker from the table in front of her and whipped it at him. It hit him dead square on the head. Van shot to his feet, sending his chair flying back. Reggie was pretty sure there were flames shooting out his nose. No doubt he expected a fight with a Navy man about to start. When he spotted her, his face dropped and he hurried after her.

"Reg, wait!"

She bolted out the door before he even made it a couple steps.

"What did you do?" Virgie asked as she hurried to keep up with her friend.

"Let's go. Fast." The two quickened their pace to the car.

~*~

By the time Van reached where their cars were parked, Reggie's was nowhere to be seen.

"Shit," he screamed as he kicked the ground. He went back to the bar to tell the guys it was time to split or he'd leave them to fend for themselves and take a cab home. With the trouble he was in, he would even give them the fifty-dollar fare.

Van arrived home a little after one a.m. The front door was locked, but the spare was still under the flowerpot. Point taken; he was in the doghouse. The bedroom door was locked as well. There was no key for that. He gently knocked on the door. "Come on, Reg, open up." When there was no reply he knocked a little harder. "Come on. I'm sorry. I didn't really have a choice. Open the door."

"Didn't have a choice, my ass!" she screamed. "I didn't see you tied up in there!"

"Open the door so we can talk."

"Go to hell."

The door flew open, startling her. He would have broken it down if he needed to, but a credit card did the trick. Using more force than necessary, he had leaned hard into it for effect; getting pissed this was going so far. He knew he was in trouble, but he'd never heard her swear so much before – not at him, anyway.

"Just calm down, would you?"

"You got home quicker than I expected. Didn't take the skank long to get you off?"

"Knock it off already, Reggie. Dammit, you know better than that."

"You swore you wouldn't go in there!" she yelled, standing up on the bed. He pulled her back down. She landed hard on her butt. "Stop it! You're hurting me."

"You'll sit there and listen," he said with a raised voice. It wasn't as loud as hers, but he put some force behind it. "I didn't go in there for what you think. We went in to drag Alan out. I wanted to come home to you."

"Right. That's why you were so snuggly with Skanko the Wonder Whore."

He ran his fingers through his hair in frustration. "Stop it, already. Enough is enough!"

She closed her eyes and turned her head when his hand came up. It was obvious she was bracing herself for a hit. He was taken aback.

"You think I'm going to hit you?" He pulled her close and wrapped his arms around her. "Jesus, Reg. Someone's hit you before?" He rocked with her and she began to gently shake as if she was fighting tears. He held her face in both hands and stared into her eyes. "I'd never lay a hand on you, Baby."

She had begun to cry. "No, but you'll fall for the first set of double D's you set your eyes on." Shaking herself free, she stormed out of the room. He knew he should let her go to cool off, but when he was still lying awake at three a.m., he went out to the couch.

"I want a name and a social security number."

She rolled over to face him. "What are you talking about?"

"I'm going to have the bastard killed that hit you."

"Nobody hit me, Van. Go back to bed." She rolled back over.

He sat down on the couch instead. "Bullshit. You braced yourself for a hit. That was a reflex if I ever saw one."

"You were yelling at me."

"You were yelling first. I wanted to be heard."

"Point taken, Neanderthal, now go back to bed." She rolled back over.

He grasped her shoulder gently and turned her to face him. "Who hit you?"

"No one. Drop it."

He sighed heavily. *One argument at a time, Van.* "The owner of the bar sent a round of drinks over. The guys promised they'd leave after that last drink."

"So that explains you being so cozy with titsy?"

"I sat in the corner out of the way of the show. She sat down by me."

"Ever hear of the words 'go away'?"

"Well, I was about to say that to her."

"But what?"

"A salt shaker hit me in the head."

"Oh." She bit her bottom lip.

"You want to know what I was doing before I had to go find the other guys in that bar?"

"Do I?"

He held out his hand and wiggled his pinky. "Alexandrite. I remembered. You've been looking for one for years."

"You found one?" She sat up and removed the ring from his finger. It was almost a carat in size and heart shaped.

"Every shape to choose from. I don't know why you couldn't find one in Hawaii."

"I found them, they were six grand for a shaving, though."

"It's called chathum. It's a real stone, just lab grown. Always flawless and a lot cheaper."

"You really did your homework."

"The sales girl had nice tits."

She smacked his arm then dropped her head slightly. "I throw a salt shaker at you and you buy me a ring."

"I bought the ring first." He picked up her chin. She looked up with tear-filled eyes. "I'm sorry I made you think I purposely defied you by going in there. I don't need to look at anyone else to satisfy me. It just happened. Okay? Truce already." She had nothing to respond to his apology. "You sorry you threw the salt shaker at me?"

"Not particularly," she said as she put the ring back in his hand.

"What?"

"It would have been one thing if you went in because they were there, but we talked about it in great detail beforehand."

Again he ran his fingers through his hair, but this time his hand came down with a loud grunt. "You're unbelievable. You never can say you're sorry."

"When I'm sorry, you'll know it."

"I'm being punished for being a disobedient dog here. You really believe I should have stood outside and waited for them to come out? This is nuts, Reg. I'm done fighting with you about this." As he stood up, so did she. She stood in front of him and poked at his chest.

"Do you even want to know why I hate those clubs so much?"

"Do tell, Doll-face." That pissed her off and he knew it.

"I know why men go in there and it makes me sick! Anyone with an ounce of dignity wouldn't step foot in a dive like that."

"I told you why I went in."

"But you didn't have to stay!"

"Reg…"

"What do you think I did on Oahu for a job, Van? What do you think a girl like me could do at eighteen to earn a living and support herself in a town like that? Do you think anyone looks at me and thinks 'My, what a nice brain you have'?" His eyes softened. "That's right." She stormed out the screen door.

He joined her, sitting on the rocks at the edge of the canal. He waited for her to be ready to talk.

"When my parents left to go be with my brother and his family, I was eighteen. Eighteen!" She repeated it for effect. "How was I going to stay in the only place I ever knew as home by myself at eighteen? Let alone the most expensive place to live in the whole United States. They think they did me a favor by at least waiting until I graduated, but it didn't help much. You have any idea what a one-bedroom apartment costs? I wasn't anywhere near a beach and it was still ridiculous.

"I leaned that on Maui."

"Yeah, but the military paid your rent. I had no choice." She wiped away a tear. "I hated every second of it; dealing with drooling men constantly trying to cop a free feel, throwing dollar bills at me. Fifty's sometimes. God-awful skimpy outfits that were sequined and ugly as sin, dancing like a half-naked whore for a living; what a wife you have."

"I don't know. I kinda liked that little red, white, and blue number you had."

Her head whipped around. "What?"

"I've been to the White Horse, Reg."

"You…what?" she said, barely above a whisper.

"I was stationed on Oahu for a few months a couple years back to help while their boat was dry-docked. Remember the one I talked about that was in the movie *Overboard* with Kurt Russell and Goldie Hawn?"

"The Point Evans."

"You do pay attention when I talk." He brushed her cheek with his hand. "Yes, that one. We went there to blow off some steam, not get touchy feely with the help. At least I didn't. I saw you, Reg. I thought you were the most beautiful thing I'd ever seen in my life. I thought so then and I think so now. I couldn't believe when I met you at Troy's. I was sure I had died and gone to heaven."

"You knew? All this time…you knew?"

"I knew," he said, taking her hand and giving it a kiss. "I even remember the song that was playing. It was Jodeci's *Come and Talk to Me*. I never wanted anything more in my life than for you to come over and talk to me, but I stayed away."

"Why?"

"I was afraid to go near you. You were outta my league, Baby."

"A stripper outta your league? Yeah right."

"You have no idea how gorgeous you are, do you? I don't care what you used to do, Babe. I knew that's why you were so dead set against men when we met. We were all pigs in your eyes. I'm sorry. We are a bunch of swine as a whole, but there are a few good ones out there, too. Well one, anyway, and you married him."

"I don't know whether to kiss you or hit you."

"How about you kiss where you hit me with the salt shaker?"

"I'm still not sorry."

He sighed heavily again and shook his head. "I'll live with that, but I want sex. Thinking about you in that outfit has me all hot and bothered." He pulled her close.

"I'm not dancing like that ever again, Van."

"I'd never ask. Take me to bed. Now."

She leaned back and looked to the other end of the waterfront. "The hammock is closer."

"That's why I love you. You're always thinkin', Kimball." He held her hand and put the ring on her finger next to her wedding ring. "Perfect fit."

"Promise me no more titty bars."

"No more titty bars. Does that mean you and Virgie won't go to any more all-male reviews?"

"Were you a male stripper to make a living and hate your past?"

"I'll take that as a no." He sighed. "That's double standards you know."

"Hardly." She crossed her arms. "They don't…"

He stopped her talking by putting his fingers over her mouth. "Shut up and kiss me."

13

A few days later, Reggie woke up to the sound of the shower running. It was unusual for Van not to at least kiss her good morning if he wasn't going to stay in bed, which almost never happened, especially after the morning kiss.

She walked into the bathroom, got naked and climbed in the shower with him.

"You didn't come kiss me," she said as she reached her arms around him and rested her head on his back.

"We just docked. I was salty and needed a shower. I'd rather do it here than there, I only brought one set of clothes." He winced as her hands ran up his chest.

"What's wrong? Your back?"

"No. Don't freak out."

Reggie dropped her hands. "Don't freak out about what?" He turned around, revealing a large green bruise high on his chest. "What happened there?" She gave it a kiss, but even that made him wince.

"I got shot," he said, softly, hoping she didn't hear it. No such luck with the wife's selective hearing.

"You got shot?"

"It's not a big deal, Reg. I told you not to freak out."

"Not a big deal? How can you say it's not a big deal? You were shot?" she said again, somehow hoping he would change his answer.

"That's why we wear the bulletproof vests when we're out on patrol. They're not for beauty or comfort."

"I've never seen you in a bulletproof vest."

"I don't ever wear it home." He didn't like the look on her face. "I'm safe when I'm at work, Reg."

"You don't have a vest on your head, Van." She stomped out of the shower.

Van joined her in a few minutes on the four-season screened porch, where she sat staring out at the water. He had a cup of coffee for each of them.

"Aren't you going to bed?"

"In a little bit. I want to talk to you."

"Well, I wanted sex and I didn't get that." He laughed and that made her angry. "You know, I had no idea I was marrying a cop."

"You didn't marry a cop. I have more jurisdiction."

"How so?"

"For starters, if I see fit, I don't need a search warrant in some cases. We also don't stop for doughnuts first."

"Fine, make jokes." She walked outside in a huff then sat on the hammock. It was cool out, but at least there were no mosquitoes. Within a few minutes he was standing next to her. He picked her up and sat down with her in his lap.

"Why do we always have to have these fights on my days off?"

"'Cause I can't fight with you when you're working."

"Touché. What do you want, Reg? I don't want to leave this job."

"Isn't there something else you can do besides being out with the drug runners and illegals trying to slip in?"

"I didn't work this hard to be a pencil pusher like that weenie Garner. It's what I do, Babe. You had to have known what it was like. How long did you know Troy before you met me?"

"Over two years. I never heard about shootings and dead bodies before. I guess there's a little less drug trafficking on Maui."

He laughed hard. "Hardly."

"How so?"

"Are you that blind on purpose or are you really that naïve?"

"Pot doesn't make killers out of people."

"The hell it doesn't. And if you think pot is the worst of the island's problems, you have another thing coming."

She did know a little something about drugs and what they did to people, but that conversation was for later, if ever.

"Troy never talked shop when I was there. I guess I didn't think anything of it. I didn't even know the Coast Guard was military until I met him. The commercials were always, Army, Navy, Air Force, Marines…"

"What a great place…" He continued the song, but stopped when Reggie slapped him on his arm. "It's who I am, Babe."

"Can you be who you are a little safer?"

"I'll hide behind weenie Garner then next time. Okay?"

"He's the one with small man's syndrome though, right?"

He laughed hard. "That's him."

"Pick someone taller."

"It's a deal."

"Can I have sex now?"

"That's affirmative."

"Is it your turn to be on top or mine?"

"I dunno. I was kind of eyeing up the wall."

She hesitated only for a second. "Okay." She let out a squeal, hopping off the hammock and running to the house.

14

Six months passed without much more than a flinch from Van's back. On occasion when it was tight, he popped a pain pill, but they weren't much more than the equivalent of four Advils. It was no big deal. Reggie downed that many for headaches a couple days a month. Her uterus was out of commission, but she still ovulated and became uncomfortable once a month. She preferred Van used that term rather than the word bitchy.

Van came home that morning and was surprised to find her not in bed. He usually woke her up when he got home from work. After a quick search, he found her in the all-season porch, standing there, looking out at the canal.

"Hey, Babe," he said, coming up behind her and wrapping his arms around her waist. "You don't want me this morning, huh? I see how you are." He playfully growled and bit at her neck. When she didn't respond he turned her around. "What's wrong?"

"I'm not sure."

"What do you mean you're not sure? Do I need to take you to Key West?"

"You're not taking me anywhere near that place, Van. I don't care if I'm bleeding to death."

"What is it then? You're scaring me, Baby."

"I'm bleeding."

"You're bleeding?" He leaned her back and looked her over. "Where?"

"I'm spotting, Van."

"Spotting? Ohhh." He hugged her in relief then pulled her back again. "Really?" She nodded, looking a little scared. "That's good, right?"

"I don't know." She bit her bottom lip. "I haven't…you know…for years."

"You mean you used to?"

"I started out normal you know!"

"No, I don't know." He stroked her face. "You've never wanted to talk about it. Calm down, okay? Let's get you to a doctor and get you checked out."

"I'm not going to one of your base butchers!"

"We'll go somewhere else and pay. Whatever you want." He didn't like the sad expression in her eyes. "You're really upset about this."

"It's not really a bad upset," she said, wiping away a tear. "What if…what if this means I can get pregnant now?"

"Reg…don't get all excited one way or another. Please try not to. We haven't thought or talked about this since the day we became engaged. One way or the other is not going to change how I feel about you."

"I know, but what if—"

He put his finger to her lips. "No 'what ifs'. Let me shower and I'll drive you to the clinic." He kissed her. "I love you."

~*~

Reggie insisted on seeing the doctor alone. She was afraid he'd ask questions she didn't want to answer in front of Van. He knew all she wanted him to know.

"I see no cause for alarm," the doctor said. "The bleeding is just a 'sluffing' of sorts. There's no new damage or tears. There's still a tremendous amount of scar tissue. It doesn't look like you can expect much more for spotting."

"Will this happen every month?"

"There's no way to tell for sure. Your body is fighting to heal itself even after all this time. My guess is it simply will continue to try. It is odd to start up after all these years, but don't get too excited. I don't think the lining will ever replace itself enough to support a child. I'm sorry."

Reggie stifled back tears that wanted to flow. She knew she shouldn't have gotten her hopes up, but she wanted so badly so be able to have a baby.

Van rushed over to her when she came out into the waiting room. "So?"

She shrugged. "It's no big deal. We wasted a trip and money." With a smile, he held up a single red rose. "That's more wasted money, Van. Don't waste money on flowers for me. They just die anyway!" She stormed out of the doctor's office and got in the car. Van handed the flower to the receptionist then joined her, started it up and headed for home.

~*~

Van knew better than to dare say a word yet. He knew better, but he couldn't handle her silence.

"If you really want a baby, we can look into adoption, Reg."

"I thought you weren't ready to talk about kids."

"If a baby is what it would take to make you happy, I'll do anything."

"I don't want you to make me happy. I want us to be happy."

"Well, I am happy, dammit. You're the one that isn't all of a sudden. You keep saying it's about me, but it isn't. Having a kid is about you."

"No, it's about us."

He grunted in frustration. "Of course it's about us, but I'm happy the way things are, Reg. You're the one that seems to be dead set on getting upset about it. I've watched Sabrina go crazy every month trying to get pregnant and I don't want that. I don't want you going nuts every month over a spot of blood, hoping and praying you'll get pregnant. If you want a kid so bad, let's look into adoption."

~*~

Reggie was silent the rest of the way home. Van pulled into the driveway, jammed the car into park and walked into the house. She stayed in the car for a while. He was right; she just wasn't done pouting. She finally opened the door to get out, looked down and let out a blood-curdling scream. Van came flying out of the house and down the two steps into the garage. He skidded for a second on a small puddle of water, but clutched onto the car and steadied himself, avoiding a fall.

When he finally caught himself, he asked her, "What happened?" He ran over to her door and opened it.

"There was a snake."

"A snake? I thought you were stabbed with that scream." He looked around. "You scared it off. Come on." He offered her his hand and helped her out of the car.

~*~

Van took a second to straighten up. His back had jerked pretty good sliding to a stop. He walked into the bedroom and tossed his t-shirt towards the hamper. It hit the floor; that was close enough. He was past due to crawl into bed and was tired, but for now he settled on leaning against the wall. He couldn't lie down until they talked this through. She had followed him in and leaned up to his bare chest. He wrapped his arms around her.

"Can we?" she asked.

"Can we what?"

"Look into it." She looked up at him, her chin propped on his chest.

"Adopting? Of course, I meant it. I know you hate everything about the military, but we have lawyers for everything. I can get the ball rolling, if that's really what you want."

"Do you?"

He kissed her forehead. "Yes, Baby." He picked her up and brought her to his chest. She began to wrap her legs around him when he screamed. He dropped her back to her feet and slid down the wall. He immediately lay flat on his back.

"Aw, fuck me!" He pounded the floor with two closed fists. He was wincing, taking deep breaths, trying to pant the pain away. It wasn't working. He let out another shout of pain. "Dammit! Call Derrick. Call him now, Baby. I ain't messin' around. Have him send the truck here."

~*~

"Apparently he gave his spine a little jostle when he slipped on the water," the doctor explained. They were back at the hospital in Key West, with the same doctor.

"A little jostle?" Reggie repeated, upset at the belittling of her husband's injury... again. "Doctor, you didn't hear him scream."

"Even the slightest misalignment can be very painful. Things seem to have readjusted themselves. There was most likely a pinched nerve that cause some discomfort, but it's gone now."

"Some discomfort? I don't know who you're used to dealing with around here, but my husband doesn't shout like that over 'some discomfort'." She took a deep breath and tried to calm down. This wasn't going to help and she knew it. "Did you at least take x-rays this time?"

The doctor sighed. "We have a slap-happy intern here that wanted to rule out everything short of the chicken pox. Yes, he's had x-rays. They show no injuries." Reggie stared at the doctor in disbelief. "It's a pinched nerve, Mrs. Kimball. I've ordered refills of the medications and added something stronger. He did seem a little worse than a few months ago. That could have been because he didn't get the morphine before he was brought to me like last time. In any case, follow the directions again."

"He doesn't like taking the pills."

The doctor had begun to walk away, but stopped at her comment and spun around. "I don't give a goddamn what he likes. This is logged as a military-related injury and if he knows what's good for him, he'll follow my directions."

She wasn't going to let his tone falter her. She stood tall, proud and defiant. "Why is this a military injury if he slipped in our garage?"

"For one, like it or not, missy, he's the property of Uncle Sam. He can't scratch his ass without going through the proper chain of command." She gritted her teeth. "Two, because this is considered a recurring injury. Same location. Same pain. It's like the aftershock of an earthquake."

"This could happen again?"

He ignored her comment and held three fingers up. "And three, because I said so. That test-happy intern is keeping him overnight. You can show up at noon to take him home." He stomped off muttering something about how military men shouldn't be allowed to get married. Reggie kicked a trashcan and let out a stifled scream.

"He's been here for thirty-two hours straight. He really can't be to blame," the nurse said from behind the desk.

"He doesn't give a crap about his patients."

"We've had an influx of crazy wives lately."

"I care about my husband so that makes me crazy?"

"You can love him without ripping him in two, Honey. He chose military life and you chose him. It's best you accept things the way they are."

"I don't have to accept rude and careless doctors."

"You have an ID card that says you do. Sorry." The nurse picked up a folder and walked away.

"Great!" Reggie was red-faced angry and fighting tears at the same time. With no nurse to guard the door, she walked down the hall looking for Van's room. When she found it, she checked behind the other curtain and discovered he had a private room, for the time being anyway. He was sleeping, no doubt heavily sedated. She crawled in bed with him and snuggled up to him like she had on the floor all those months ago. It seemed now like it had only happened yesterday.

With all the anxiety and emotion that had been building up, she fell asleep in his arms. They woke up together with the sun the next morning. It was clear no one had bothered to check on him all night.

~*~

"Settle down, Reggie. I didn't need any checking on, I just needed rest."

She had gotten out of bed and was pacing the room. "The doctor said they were running more tests on you."

"They did everything under the sun. They drew blood twice, I wizzed in a cup, they x-rayed me; what more do you want?"

"I want you better."

"I am better, Baby. You want me to prove it?" He raised his eyebrows up and down.

"This isn't funny, Van. You had me scared bad."

"I'm sorry. I know I swore, too."

"Shit. Who are you apologizing to about swearing?"

"True. You are the one with the potty mouth in the house. Come here." She walked towards the bed and stopped a few feet away, not sure what he was up to. "Closer." She was now standing next to him. "Do me a favor and feel this." He reached out for her hand. His look was serious; she was worried and gave him her hand. He placed it on his crotch; she pulled her hand back and crossed her arms.

"That's not funny."

"If my back was bad, would that be workin'?"

"*That* will be working when you're dead."

"What are you doing here so early?" a nurse asked when she came walking in the room. Reggie jumped at the sound of her voice. Van pulled her close and held onto her.

"She's going to take me home."

"You shouldn't leave until you get the doctor's clearance."

"Is he here?"

"He won't start rounds for another hour."

"Then I'm going to split." He dropped his feet over the side of the bed.

"You can't do that," she said as she flipped through the chart. "I'm supposed to get another urine sample this morning."

"You see my wife here?"

"Yes," the nurse replied. "I already said she should not be in here."

"Isn't she beautiful?" Reggie elbowed him.

"Yes, she's very pretty."

"With her here now, I'm afraid urine is not the kind of sample you'd be gettin'."

Reggie snorted a laugh and brought her hands to her mouth. The nurse stomped out of the room. Van hopped off of the bed. "Take me home, Baby."

~*~

The subject of adopting didn't come up again. Reggie wanted to wait until they were somewhere they could call home. She had gotten emotional between her normal hormones and the excitement of the spotting. She knew Van loved her and that was enough for now.

15

Several months later, Regina slowly woke up to someone shaking her. Van wasn't due home for another day so she was very confused. She read the clock on the nightstand. It was only two in the morning. "Reggie?" The man shook her. The room was only lit by the glow of the clock. It took her another few seconds to realize what was happening. She shot up in bed, suddenly scared.

"It's me. You're okay."

"Derrick?"

"Dang, Girlfriend. I could have had my way with you and you wouldn't have woken up. I've been shaking you for five minutes."

She rubbed her eyes and shook her head. "I'm not feeling so hot. I had a headache and downed a couple of Van's pills." She pointed to the bottle on the stand and laid her head back on her pillow.

Derrick picked up the bottle and turned on the light. "You shouldn't take codeine when you don't need it, Reggie."

"It's not codeine, it's Tylenol."

He held up the bottle and pointed to a word on it. "With codeine."

She sat up and snatched the bottle from him. "Shit. It looks just like the other stuff. I had no idea…why are you here Derrick?" Her mind was finally beginning to clear.

"I need to drive you to see your husband."

"Where is he? Is he okay?"

"Homestead, and he's all right, but you should be there. I'll explain on the way."

She dressed in a hurry then they left in the station's truck. It was a huge custom built six-door Ford F-250. "You can lie down and sleep in the back seat if you want."

"I can't sleep now. You going to tell me what happened?"

"You sure? The details are kinda gory."

"He's hurt that bad?"

"No. Sorry. It's his back again, Reg. We were out on patrol and received a call about a capsized boat, a twenty-five footer. We approached him and it became a game of standoff."

"Why? Didn't he want to be rescued?"

"He was an illegal with a butt-load of cocaine on board. He ended up blowing his brains out rather than getting captured."

"That's horrible."

"Well, Van was on fishin' detail for the body." When she looked at him with her head cocked he said, "Sorry. He was pulling the body up on the ship when his back went out again."

"Dammit all to hell!" She pounded the dashboard.

"You two are sure meant for each other. That's pretty much what he said."

"Why are we going to Homestead and not Key West?"

"We went to the quickest dock we could to get him on land. It was Tavernier Key. There was a civilian EMT there. He had him airlifted before we could say boo."

"Airlifted?"

"He's bad, Reg. Real bad. This ain't no torn muscle or strained nerve."

"I don't give it shit what it costs. I'm glad he'll be at a regular hospital."

"It'll get covered anyway. He's still government property."

"I hate it when I hear that. He's not a fucking jeep."

"He'll be all right."

"Maybe now. Can't you make this tank go any faster?"

"I'm going ten miles over already, Reg."

"I'll pay your damn ticket. Floor it."

"Yes, ma'am."

It was a nice change for Reggie to be able to discuss her husband by name and not four numbers. The nurses offered her coffee and assured her the doctor would be out soon. "He's getting an MRI. It should be about another half hour or so."

"An MRI?"

"Yes. We need a good look-see at what's going on. X-rays wouldn't be good enough in this case."

"Why doesn't that surprise me," Reggie said under her breath. "Is he in a lot of pain?"

"He was given morphine. He's a lot better than when he came in."

Reggie hated that word. *Morphine*. It sounded so final. *The painkiller of last resort*. So addicting. At least Van was better than that. He'd never get hooked on pain meds. Suddenly she remembered her groggy conversation with Derrick earlier. She had no idea he was taking codeine. *Codeine*. She didn't like the sound of that any better. Why hadn't he told her he was taking codeine?

A nurse came over and led her into a room. There was a table and chairs in the middle and the walls were covered with lighted glass boards. Obviously they were for viewing x-rays. "The doctor will be right in." She smiled pleasantly and Reggie thanked her.

The doctor came in after ten minutes and shook her hand. "Mrs. Kimball, I'm Doctor Anthony." She looked at the folder in his other hand. "These are the results from the MRI. I'd like to go over a few things with you."

"Herniated L4 and L5? What now?" Reggie asked after hearing the prognosis from the doctor.

"Surgery to remove the worst of it."

"On his spine? That has to be dangerous."

"It's a common procedure. There's really no choice. He'll feel better immediately. The herniation is putting a terrible amount of stress on the nerve. It's hard to believe he's gone this long from the accident without a procedure."

"Thank Uncle Sam," she said in her best sarcastic tone. "The assholes do nothing but give him pills."

"He's never had an MRI before?"

"Just x-rays and I practically had to throw a tantrum to get that."

"It wouldn't show up too well there unless you were looking specifically for it."

"Goddammit. I hate that place," she complained as she stared at the images.

"Don't be so hard on them. They could be right about the previous times. Maybe there was nothing to see before or it was just a minor injury and this sent him over the edge. There's no way of knowing."

She huffed. "Maybe. Maybe not."

"There's no way of knowing for sure. Anger won't help him. Main thing is we'll get him fixed up."

"When are you going to do the procedure?"

"As soon as you sign the release."

"You'll do it here?"

"It needs to be done right away. I'd hate to move him in this condition. We've been fighting with Champus for an hour. They say no. We'll bill them; eventually we'll get paid."

"I can't thank you enough. I'm so tired of being treated like a number there."

"They're good doctors and it really is great insurance, they have rules to follow like we do."

Reggie held back her comments. She didn't want to carry on; she wanted Van feeling better.

16

They allowed Van to stay for two days after the procedure then orders were sent for him to be transported to Key West for the remainder of the week.

"It'll be closer for you, Baby." Van insisted it was a good thing. "It'll shave an hour of drive time and you can get back to work."

"I liked the idea of you being here for a change."

"I'm just sitting on my ass. It doesn't matter where I am."

Exactly a week after the procedure, he was escorted out the door of the hospital and given leave for only a week of rest at home, much to Reggie's dismay.

"A week? You get to rest a week? You just had back surgery, for crying out loud. Hello…spine…bulging discs…nerve damage. What the hell is the bullshit, Van? You can't be serious. You need to heal longer than a week."

"Baby, I feel brand new. You have no idea how great it feels. I can go back in a week, easy. I wouldn't say that if I didn't mean it."

"Yes, you would." They had an hour to talk about it on the way home. By the time they reached their house, Reggie was still seeing flames. She thought he needed more time to rest and was sure her concerns were more than justified. Before he went to get out of the car, she held his hand and looked him square in the eye. "You never told me you were taking pills with codeine."

"Aw, hell, that's not a big deal. I hardly ever took them. It was hurting one day so I called down there. That's what they sent back with the driver. They said to try that to see if it helped and it did."

"I took some by accident the other night."

"Didn't you look at the label?"

"It looks the same except for a small 'c' in parenthesis on the bottle, Van. The pills are exactly the same size and everything."

"Are you okay? Did something happen?" He reached for her face and held it with concern.

"No, but it really knocked me out. That was the night Derrick came to take me to you. It was a long time before he was able to wake me up."

"I have a lot of weight on you remember. Things don't affect me the way they do you."

"I took two; you're prescribed three – three times a day."

"But I don't take them that often." He sat back in the chair. "Are you worried I'm abusing the pills, Reggie? Because you were the one stuffing them down my face before, if I recall correctly." He angrily climbed out of the car, grabbing the bag of medications that were sent with him -- ones for pain, an anti-inflammatory, an antibiotic, one in case the pain increased, and one pill in case he became constipated from all the pills. How ironic. She hurried out of the car to help him into the house.

"I'm not saying that. I know you take it easy on them."

"Then what?" he barked, defensively.

"You never told me things were bothering you again. You didn't mention having to get stronger pills."

He shoved the bag at her. "Well how 'bout you regulate that from now on like you do when telling me which bars I can go into." He let go of the bag, walked into the bedroom on his own and closed the door.

The phone rang. She almost ignored it to go speak with Van, but she figured it would be best if they both took a few minutes to think about things before getting into a heated argument. It was Troy calling; she was never so happy to hear anyone's voice before.

"That bum of a husband of yours home yet?"

"Oh, Troy." She began to cry.

"He giving you a hard time, Princess? Do I need to come tune him up?"

"I'm sorry for crying. I know it'll pass. I'm sure they sent him out too early and he's hurting and crabby. You know what a peach I am. I'm sure I said something wrong."

"The offer is good you know."

"What offer?"

"To tune him up. We're in Orlando."

"You're not!"

"Yup. Bri's nieces were going to Disneyworld and she wanted to go. Guess who was dragged along?"

"A big strong hunk like you?"

"Bingo. You think that good for nothing will be up for company tomorrow? We'd get there around five."

"He'll be up for you guys and if he's not, I don't care; I need you. Can you stay for a few days?"

"Two if you'll have us."

"We have a spare room. You can stay here."

"I know. You've said that every time we talk. We're glad we can finally take you up on it. I've missed you."

"I've really missed you, too."

"Want to get Van on the phone? Think I should talk to him?"

"I don't think so. We just walked in the door," she lowered her voice, "and it's not very pretty right now."

"Hence the tears. Sorry, Princess."

"It'll be okay. Can I talk to Bri, though?"

"She's been clawing at the phone. I'll see you tomorrow."

The girls talked for twenty minutes before they decided to hang up and finish catching up tomorrow. Reggie went in the bedroom, walking slowly, not wanting to wake Van up if he was sleeping.

"Who was on the phone?"

"Our best friends in the whole world."

"Calling to check on the gimp?"

"Yes." She sighed. She didn't want to play into his mood. "I didn't think you wanted to talk on the phone."

"Good call. I don't."

"They called from Orlando. They're going to stop by tomorrow."

"Really?" She was glad the news perked him up and that he didn't get upset about not wanting company or mad because he couldn't do anything with them.

"I said it was okay if they stayed here for two days. I hope it's all right with you."

"Of course it's all right. I can't do much with Troy, but you can take them down to Key West."

"They're coming to see us, Van. They're not going to worry about going down there. Coming from Hawaii, Key West isn't such a big deal."

"At least we don't have to worry about keeping the sex noise down."

"Stop it, Van. Just stop it. I'm not doing this pity party with you." She turned to walk away but he caught her hand.

"Why is one of us always leaving in the middle of a conversation?"

"'Cause they're called fights. I love you, you damn shithead." She crawled on the bed with him and snuggled into his chest. "You're the one who is always there for me. You're the strong one; the level-headed one. I get to be the bitch." He chuckled, but she continued. "I'm sorry you're hurting. I know I can't imagine what it must feel like, but I can't take you talking yourself down. You'll heal and be good as new."

"No I won't, Baby. I'll have restrictions. This may not be the last surgery I'll have to have."

"So we'll get through it together. You put your damn pride aside and take it a little easy. Let someone else carry the heavy shit for a change. And…you take what pills you need. You follow the directions. I'm not worried about you overdoing it, Van. I was scared that you didn't tell me. I don't want you to hide when you're hurting from me. I don't want you ever thinking you have to play tough guy for me. You *are* my tough guy."

He held her tight. "I'll do my best to take it easy when I can, but I don't want you jumping every time I wince in pain. I'll deal with this my way, okay?"

"Fair enough." She gave him a quick kiss on the lips and hopped off the bed.

"Where you going?"

"I have to check the paper and see if there's an all-male review that Bri and I can get to." She held her serious face for a second before she laughed. She went back to him for another kiss. "I bought you something. I'll be right back."

She lit a couple candles in the bedroom then turned off the lights. "You bought me vanilla bean candles?"

"Nope." She walked into the bathroom and pulled the pocket-door closed. After a minute, she slid it open a few inches and stuck her leg out. She had it bent then pointed it out straight. She put it down and stepped into the doorway, backlit only by a flickering candle, wearing a red, white, and blue very skimpy bikini. Her hair was down, the way Van liked it best. She slinked over to him, slowly moving her arms up and down her sides. He was in a trance. He smiled as the music playing in the background registered with him; Jodeci's *Come and Talk to Me*.

He swallowed hard. "Lord Almighty. Go easy on me, woman."

17

Van and Reggie had a great visit with Troy and Sabrina. Van's spirits were up and it was like old times. The girls did pop away for an afternoon at Key West so the boys could have some time alone. Although Van was okay while they were there, Reggie thought maybe he would open up more to Troy. He never was one for talking on the phone; maybe a couple beers would loosen him up. He wasn't supposed to drink with the medications, but she wasn't about to deny him a few with their friends there.

Duvall Street reminded Sabrina a little of Front Street. They had to get daiquiris from Fat Tuesday and walked around with open drinks, just because they could. One thing that never stopped amazing Reggie was being able to walk from bar to bar with a drink in hand.

"How are you holding up, Hon?" Sabrina asked when they finally stopped to kick their feet up at Jimmy Buffet's *Margaritaville*.

"Me? I'm fine. It's Van I worry about, Bri."

"He has doctors, a whole crew, and you. I'm not worried about him. You look weary. Who's looking out for you?"

"I'm fine. Really. It's hard when he puts himself down, is all. He's always been my strength. When he gets depressed, I don't know what to do with him."

"Have you talked to his doctor about an anti-depressant?"

"That's all I want; him taking *another* pill."

"It's that bad?"

"All they do is feed him pills, Bri."

"But now he's had surgery. It's bound to get better, right?"

"That's the plan anyway. He's going to be on restrictions and he's not going to like it or listen, if I know him."

"Threaten to hold out sex."

"Who's that going to punish?" Reggie laughed. "How are you guys doing? Any luck with your lab work?"

"There's no medical reason why I'm not getting pregnant. We were told to stop stressing about it. It'll happen when it's meant to happen."

"It'll happen, Bri." Reggie gave her hand a comforting squeeze. "Let's get back. We'll stop and get some Force Five wings for dinner. I wanna see Troy's eyes water when he tries them!"

"You know he loves hot food."

"This place gives you a t-shirt if you can make it through the batch."

"Oh, this I gotta see."

~*~

"You look like you've lost a few pounds, but other than that, you're still an ugly bastard." Troy handed Van a beer. "You holding up?"

"When I'm not flat on my back, I'm great."

"I thought you liked being flat on your back." Troy grinned.

"Only when I'm being held down by my wife." Van allowed himself a chuckle.

"There it is."

"There what is?"

"The laugh. I thought you'd lost it."

"Don't give me shit, Man. It hasn't been easy. Reggie's been coddling me to death."

"So let her."

"Are you the one high on pain meds?"

"You'll heal and you'll be the same hero jackass we all know and love. It won't kill you to take it easy for a few weeks."

"What hero work can I do with a limit of picking up no more than twenty pounds?"

"Only twenty pounds? All hell. I guess asking you to help me pee is outta the question then."

Van exploded in another loud laugh. "Shit. Maybe when I re-up we should try to head back to Maui."

"You do that," Troy said as he clinked beer bottles with him. "I'll do what I can from my end."

~*~

"Desk Jockey? What's this bullshit, Garner?" Van threw a letter on his CO's desk. He had been back to work for a few days and had an unwelcome surprise in his work mailbox.

"Just what it says. The range is below acceptable on your back. They don't want you out on the water and putting the other members of the crew at risk."

"At risk? My ass! What is this bullshit really about?" Van slammed his fists to the desk.

His CO stood. Regina had him pegged when she said he had short man's syndrome. He was five-foot four-inches. He was an inch taller than she was but for a man, he was considered short. He had to prove how big he was on a daily basis and, in his mind that equaled to being an asshole. Nothing was up to his standards, nothing was done fast enough, and he didn't know how to speak in any voice other than a yell. He picked up the paper and envelope then shoved them into Van's chest. "Desk Jockey or take an early out."

"Bullshit!"

Garner walked to the front of his desk. "No bullshit. You think you can stay doing what you want just because you like it? What military do you belong to, Kimball? You have to follow rules like everyone else."

"A few degrees of bending? That's what you're calling this? Petty Officer Clark is fifty pounds overweight if he's an ounce. I can run circles around that bastard and out bend him."

"He can lose weight. You, on the other hand, have gotten increasingly worse over the last few months and it shows. You've been out three times with that back. They know it's only going to get worse. You're a liability out on the water."

"Liability?"

"It's a matter of time before you slip up and cost someone their life."

"I acquired this back saving a life, asshole." That would probably cost him. You never spoke back to a commanding officer, let alone swore at one. He knew he had nothing to lose. "This isn't about my back! This is between me and you!"

"The hell it is. Regulations are regulations."

"You'll never let it go that I keep covering your ass, will you?"

"Like hell."

"You are the disaster waiting to happen. You're the one who has the crew in danger constantly with all your miscalculations. You trying to get rid of me because you're afraid I'm going to tell someone about all your fuck-ups!"

"Don't let the door hit you in the ass on the way out, Kimball. Just take that gorgeous wife of yours back where you found her and lead a cushy civilian life in paradise. Drink piña coladas and find a nice waterfall to screw her under."

"You son of a bitch!" Van landed a solid punch on Garner's chin and sent him flying over his desk, backwards. Van stormed out of the office, but not before punching through the glass on the door first. When he reached the gate, the MP's stopped his car.

"We received a call from Garner."

"And?"

"We're not supposed to let you leave."

"You calling in backup to keep me?"

"Nope. I want to shake your hand. I've been waiting years to see someone pop that prick." He motioned to the bandana covering Van's knuckles. "I don't want to know, do I?"

"Nope."

The MP stood at attention and saluted Van instead of shaking his hand. Van smiled and returned a casual salute back.

"Tell him I removed the barrier myself and punched your lights out, too." He waved at the second officer who was removing the sawhorse that served as a roadblock.

"I'll think of something. You're my new hero, Kimball."

Van laughed and drove off base. The smile was short lived. He decked his Commanding Officer and went AWOL. There was going to be hell to pay.

~*~

The phone rang at one in the morning. Reggie's hand landed hard on it as if she was trying to shut off an alarm. After another ring, she picked up the receiver, but was still half asleep. "Hello," she mumbled into the phone.

"Reg?"

"Derrick?"

"You awake?"

She looked over at the clock. "It's one a.m. why would I…" she sat up, suddenly awake. "What's wrong? Where's Van?"

"He's fine. He's here at my place."

"Your place? But he's on duty tonight."

"He kinda…left."

"Left? How? Why?"

"It's a long story. I just wanted to let you know he was okay and he was here in case the MPs show up lookin' for him."

"The MPs? What the hell happened, Derrick?"

"He took a swing at Garner."

She gasped, knowing what that could mean. "Why?"

"He's out."

"Out? Who?" She was confused.

"Van, Reggie. He's out."

18

As Reggie hung up after saying she'd be right over, there was a knock at the door.

"Shit!" After throwing on a robe, she went to answer it. She slowed down her pace and decided it was best if she played stupid. "What are you doing here?" she asked Garner when she opened the door slowly and pretended to be sleepy. "Is Van okay? What's up with the MPs?" she asked, looking behind him.

"Is he here?"

"Why would he be here? He's on duty."

"He went AWOL. Do we have permission to search the place?"

She pushed the door open, leaning against the door jam. "I know goddamn well you don't need my permission, but I appreciate the formality." The MPs walked in while Garner stayed outside the door.

"Has he tried to call you?"

"Would I be worried about him right now if he did?"

"Military wives are a rare breed. There's no telling the lengths you'd go to – to lie for your husband."

"True enough. I'd also put a slug up your ass if he's lying somewhere hurt because of you."

"I always knew you were a real lady there, Reggie."

"Mrs. Kimball, to you," she said, crossing her arms. "What's the matter? Did you forget to put a tracking device on this piece of property of yours? How is it you lose a man?"

"He's in deep shit. I'm not going to even try to sugar-coat it for your pretty face." His eyes began to wander down her front and she was suddenly very uncomfortable. She grasped the front of her robe and held it tight. He smirked, reached over, ran his hand down her face then gently stroked the hand that held her robe together.

"Do you get much on the side, Reggie? You know, when Van's away and on duty?" He leaned into her with his hip. His erection pushing against her made her want to scream, but she was frozen with fear. He slipped his hand inside her robe with his fingertips touching her breast. "…Because I can make things easier for him if you want me to." He leaned into her, pressing himself against her harder and his hand going a little further inside the robe. He brought his face closer, like he was going to kiss her. "If you can fit me in some—"

He stopped talking when he looked in her eyes. They had been full of fear, but they were now open wide and looking over his shoulder. He looked in the direction of her gaze; there was an MP behind him. They had gone out through the back sliding door and came around to the front of the house. Garner quickly dropped his hand and stepped back. "Tell him to be sure he gets back to the station as soon as he shows up, if he knows what's good for him." The MP hesitated, briefly looking over at Reggie before he followed his CO back to the work truck.

She closed and locked the door, leaning against it for strength to remain standing; it wasn't enough. She slid down to the floor and shook violently. She rubbed her hand against the carpet trying to wipe off his touch then clutched her robe tighter. She breathed deeply and clenched her eyes tight to fight her tears. She wanted Van now more than ever, but she knew she could never tell him. He'd kill Garner for sure. Reggie had no idea what made him punch his CO, but she was sure he had it coming. Of course, the military would never see it that way. She had to go to Van, but she wanted to wait a minute. There was no doubt in her mind that they'd try to follow her, thinking she knew where he was. After waiting ten minutes on the floor, gathering herself, she ran to her bedroom to get dressed.

Reggie parked at the grocery store parking lot and waited; she hadn't been followed. She ran the equivalent of two blocks to get to Derrick's townhouse and came bounding up the stairs. He was waiting at the door and gave her a strong hug.

"Is he okay?"

"Just drunk. His hand is cut up a little, but he doesn't need stitches."

"His hand? Why?"

"He punched out a glass panel. Come on." He led her to Van, who was passed out on the couch. She gave his sleeping face a kiss and knelt on the floor. She picked up his hand; Derrick had already cleaned and bandaged it.

"Won't they come here?"

"I don't know. Maybe. I figured he was safer here for a while than at the Monkey."

"You guys aren't supposed to go in the Brass Monkey. The wives don't even go."

"After punching out your CO, I guess a little bar hoppin' on the wrong side of the tracks isn't going to do any more harm."

"What happened, Derrick? Tell me."

"One of the dysfunctionals called me and told me to come get him. Not everyone listens to the 'no Brass Monkey' rule, Reg."

"Not that. Why did he punch Garner? What did you mean when you said he was out? I don't get it."

Derrick let out a heavy sigh and walked over to Reggie, offering her his hand. He helped her to her feet and brought her to the loveseat.

"From what I gather, Garner, that chicken shit, put a letter in Van's mailbox at the station sometime after supper."

"What did it say?"

"He was being taken off regular duty and getting assigned to strictly desk work."

Reggie gasped and put her hands to her mouth. "That would kill him!"

"It isn't right, I know, but he and Garner have always clashed. I'm sure he saw a way to stick it to Van good and seized his opportunity."

"Why doesn't he transfer Van if they don't get along?"

"Why transfer when you can totally screw up someone's life?" She stood up, furious. "That groping bastard!"

"Groping?"

"Whatever," she said, trying to brush off her comment. Derrick couldn't know either. She cursed herself for shouting it. "He's a bastard. How can someone like that be in the position he is and mess with everyone else's lives? Van loves what he does. How can one person do that to him?"

"It's just done, Reg. It ain't right, but it's done. If it could have been reversed before, it sure as hell can't now. They'll throw him out for sure if they don't send him to the brig first."

"They can't do that!"

"He hit an officer. They can."

"You gotta help him, Derrick."

"I don't know what I can do." He turned at a knocking on the door and saw two MPs standing outside. "Aw, shit."

"I was so careful to make sure I wasn't followed."

"They're making rounds. I have to let them in." Derrick went over and opened the door. Reggie stood there nervously waiting to see what would happen. There were two MPs, but their CO was no longer with them. "Where's numb nuts?" Derrick asked.

"He went home. Told us to keep going. He here?"

"He's here. Don't take him, Joe. Just let him sleep it off. I'll bring him in the morning."

Reggie's heart raced. The MP was standing there, but her mind saw Garner.

The MP walked into the living room and addressed Reggie. "Are you okay, Mrs. Kimball?"

She looked at him and took a few small steps back. Her mind was shutting down. She didn't want another man touching her; she was getting agitated. After looking over to Derrick, her eyes went back to the MP Derrick called Joe. She made short shakes with her head and kept repeating softly, "No."

Derrick's head titled at the expression on Reggie's face. "What the hell is going on? Why do you want to know if she's okay, Joe?"

Reggie continued to shake her head 'no' and reflexively clutched at the opening of her jacket. She had backed into the TV before she realized she had been backing up at all, and lost her balance.

The MP reached for her trying to steady her and she let out a scream at his touch.

~*~

The scream registered over everything else that had been going on. Van sat upright and flew off the couch. In the half of a second of thought that he gave the situation, he wanted to remove the cause of the problem. Act first; sort out the details later.

He tackled the MP and sent him to the floor. He was too drunk to put up much of a fight so the MP had him on his back in one quick twist. He sat on Van's chest and held his arms above his head.

"No!" Reggie screamed. She was going to jump on the MP, but Derrick caught her by the waist. "Watch out for his back!"

"Quit it, Van! Sit still!" Joe yelled. When Van stopped struggling, Joe released his hands and got off of his chest. The other MP came over and the two men helped Van to his feet then walked him backwards to the couch. Derrick let Reggie go and she flew into Van's lap, straddling him. Her arms went tight around his neck and she buried her face in them.

He held her tight. "What the hell is going on?"

19

"Reggie?" Van stroked her back, but she wouldn't budge or speak. She tightened her grip.

"What did you guys do to my wife?"

"We didn't do anything to her, Van. It was Garner," Joe said.

"What?" Derrick stomped towards Joe. Van squeezed her tight and whispered, "Baby?" She only tried to climb higher in his lap. Van rocked with her, suddenly scared.

"What happened, Joe?" Derrick asked.

"I didn't see much. I don't know what he did. All I know is his hands were somewhere they shouldn't have been and he was a little too close for comfort for my taste. I'm sorry, Man," he said to Van. "I would have taken him out, but I thought maybe I was wrong. Your wife just closed the door."

"When?" The second MP asked. "I didn't see any of this."

"You were already back at the truck. I went to tell Garner the house was empty."

"Fuck!" Van held Reggie's face in his hands and leaned her back. "Did he hurt you?" She shook her head 'no'. Her eyes were glazed with fear and her lip trembled. He pulled her close again. "Damn, Baby." He stroked her hair. "What was all the bullshit of her screaming in here?" he addressed back to Joe.

"I dunno. I think I scared her getting close. I was only trying to catch her from falling and knocking the TV over. I wouldn't touch your wife, Van."

"I know. I'm drunk; I'm not an idiot."

"I'm sorry," Reggie whispered.

"No, Baby. No!" Van held her close. "You don't get to be sorry here. You didn't do anything wrong. Derrick?"

"I don't know anything, Man. I just picked up your drunk ass."

Van was at a loss. Things still weren't registering properly. It was too much, too fast.

Joe had been staring out the window at the canal, deep in thought. "Van?" Van looked up at him. "I know what happened is stressful for her and all but…something doesn't seem right."

"What do you mean?"

"I wanted to let you stay here. You know, sleep it off. But she's acting a little beyond that."

"What are you saying?" Van's mind was racing. He hadn't really understood what they had been saying at all about what happened. He was worried the guys showed up too late to his house and…he didn't even want to think about what else could have happened.

"She acts like she's been hit."

"What? That's insane," Derrick yelled.

"Don't give me that," Joe said back. "We've all been through the same courses. Something isn't right. She's scared ten ways from Sunday and it doesn't fit."

"You think Garner hit her?" Van asked.

"No. You. Unless you put me at ease about this, I'll take you in, Buddy."

"No!" Reggie cried, still holding tightly onto his neck. "He's never laid a hand on me. I swear."

"She was just felt up by a jerk, Joe. Sorry to be so crude, Reg," Derrick said in apology. "You guys know better than that. Van wouldn't hit anybody. He's the one doin' repairs on kids' feet while we're watching the bikini show."

The other MP finally spoke up. "I know him. That's my vote, too. You're off base, Joe."

"I had to ask. She has me worried. What the hell do we do about Garner now?"

~*~

"I wanna go home, Van," Reggie whispered into his ear. She held him tight as if wishing it would magically make it so. She was tired of the yelling, tired of fighting tears. She hated the accusations that flew at Van even if only for a second. She hated the past she dragged into the relationship. Her heart was still racing furiously. Above all, she didn't like the lightheaded feeling she was getting. She was embarrassed about the screaming and about what happened at the house. She wanted to go home.

"Take her home, Van," the second MP said. "We've already been to your house. We don't need to go there again. We'll show up in the morning and bring you in. Joe, I didn't see nothin'. We can get the XO and Garner there together and hash this out tomorrow."

"I wanna go home," Reggie said again a little softer.

He stroked her back, trying to offer her comfort. "One thing doesn't have a damn thing to do with the other. I decked Garner. He'll have it in for me, but he's going to pay for what he did to my wife."

"I know what I saw." Joe said. "That was bullshit. I don't care if he was the President of the United States. That ain't right."

"I wanna go home, Van," Reggie whispered again even softer then her head gently fell limp on his shoulder.

~*~

"Aw, Baby," Van whispered and kissed her cheek.

"She passed out?" Derrick asked as he walked over.

"She's tired and gets stressed easily. You're lucky she didn't see my knuckles earlier. I'm surprised she hasn't puked yet."

Derrick placed his hands on her neck as if checking for a pulse. "She's okay," Van assured him. "She can't take this shit."

"She shouldn't have to, Van."

"So now what? I'm drunk, AWOL, and my wife is passed out."

"We'll take you home," Joe said. "We'll deal with it in the morning."

"Not before I drive over and kill that sonofabitch."

"You're not doing anything tonight, Van. If I have to sit on you all night myself, I will. You're drunk and beyond irrational. Before you do something you can't take back, get a good night's rest. Take care of your wife, Man."

"I'll carry her down." Derrick reached for her.

"I'll carry my own wife." Van pushed his hand away.

"I don't give a goddamn about your back, Shithead. You're loaded and you're not taking that pretty package down those stairs. She's been through enough tonight. She doesn't need your sorry ass falling on her, too."

Van looked over at the second MP, not knowing what to make of his silence. He was the newest of the team. Their paths hadn't crossed often, but they had always been friendly. He finally spoke up.

"My wife is due with our second kid in a month. If that sonofabitch touched her, I'd want to kill him, too. I know I didn't see anything, but I'll say what it takes tomorrow to set things right. I'm staying at your place tonight if I have to take a floor and I'm not taking no for an answer, Brother."

.

20

The second MP, Petty Officer Owen, drove Van and Reggie back to their house. He went through the house first, making sure it was truly empty, then came back and carried in Reggie. Once she was settled in bed, the men walked out to the living room.

"You don't need to stay. I'm not leaving her alone."

"I'm staying. If he shows up, I want a witness to whatever goes on."

"Then thanks," Van said as they shared a quick man-hug. "I'm about to fall over. The guest room is made up. You don't need take the floor."

Van was only in bed for a few minutes when Reggie's head began to go side-to-side and she softly repeated, "No."

"Baby?" Van tried to gently shake her awake.

"No!" she said a little louder. She was still asleep, apparently having a nightmare. He'd already had to prove himself once tonight. He didn't want her giving their houseguest any more reason for doubt that he wasn't abusing her, but he didn't want to scare her any worse either. Van didn't see that he had much choice. Placing his hand over her mouth, he gently shook her awake. He held her close, hoping it would be a comfort and not put another fear in her. "Baby?"

She flailed once as she woke with a start and let out a cry that was muffled by his hand. Realizing where she was, she relaxed instantly. "Oh, Van. I'm sorry."

"You know…why do you only say sorry when you shouldn't?" He laughed softly, trying to make light of things for her. "What is it, Reg? What's happening? Is there more that I need to know?"

"No. That's all that's happened tonight."

"What about before tonight?"

"There's nothing to tell."

"Someone has done something to you, dammit. Tell me the truth already." Van was still trying to keep things to a whisper. He was wishing they had the house to themselves.

She swallowed hard. "You know what I did before. Every now and then some guys were rough. Nothing really bad happened. Bouncers were usually never far away. You get so you can send those things deep in your mind. You know? Usually I can. Tonight…it…it came back."

He pulled her close to him. "He's going to pay, Baby. If I have to kill him myself…he's going to pay."

"No you're not. It wasn't that bad."

"The hell it wasn't. You don't have nightmares for nothing. What if you keep having them now? I don't want you reliving this shit."

"I won't. Really, I won't. Killing him won't help matters for me and it will only make things worse for you. I've been through…worse. Just a little. He didn't get much, I swear, Van."

"You trying to convince me or you?"

"I'm trying to tell you the truth. Please. I don't want you in any more trouble over me. This will go nowhere, like everything important always does where the military is concerned. You make a big deal out of it and the only thing it will accomplish is I won't be able to face anyone."

"Oh no, you don't. You don't get to feel guilty over this. You did nothing but be beautiful and breathe."

"How's your back?"

"Don't try to change the subject."

"You took a bad spill."

"Savorski broke my fall."

She giggled. "I love you. Can you just hold me?"

"Come here." He lay flat on his back and held his arms up to her. She snuggled into his chest; which was her favorite way to sleep. They were both out in minutes.

21

Even though it was after three when they went to bed, everyone was up at seven, waiting for the bomb to drop. They were drinking coffee in the screened porch when Joe and Derrick showed up. They were in their dress blues. This couldn't be good.

Van held his arms in front of him as if waiting for handcuffs. "You hauling me away?"

"How about a cup of coffee?" Joe asked.

"I'll get it." Reggie jumped up. Her heart was racing again. She needed to be moving around or she was worried she'd pass out again.

The men waited for her to come back before they spoke. She handed them their coffees and sat on Van's lap. She knew she couldn't fight them if they were going to take him away, but she needed to be as near as she could be to him.

"So?" Van finally broke the silence.

"We pulled Bert outta bed at five this morning." Derrick said. Bert was the Executive Officer of the station.

"I bet that made him happy."

"We wanted to beat 'pencil dick' there. We did, by about half an hour. Bert had heard enough to get a good base of the truth before Garner started flapping his gums. He's really not sure what to do, Van. He knows there's tension with you and Garner. You think he doesn't know why, but he does. He knows about Garner and all his fuck-ups. Sorry, Reggie, screw-ups. That will be dealt with when this is settled. He still doesn't condone the punching, although I think secretly he wants to pat your back as well."

Joe continued from there. "He didn't know about the paperwork. He swears he never would have pushed it through. Garner is in some shit for jumping the chain of command on that, too, but Bert can't undo it now that it's been done."

"Dammit!"

"He's not doing anything to you as far as the punch, but if you refuse to go desk jockey—"

"I won't."

"They have an honorable discharge waiting for you in his office."

~*~

Van sat in the chair with his lips pinched tight. He couldn't even say a word. The only thing he loved was ripped from him. It took a few minutes, but it finally occurred to him, it wasn't the only thing he loved. The other was right there on his lap. He gave his wife a squeeze.

"What about what he did to Reggie?"

"Unless she wants to bring up charges, there's not a lot that he can do. Even if she does…I hate to say it, but there's probably nothing they can do."

"That's bullshit!"

"It's his word against hers and they'll think she'll say anything for you. I'm not saying I agree with it; it's just the way it is."

"But what about what you saw, Joe?"

Joe looked to Reggie and was about to speak when she leaned closer into her husband. "I won't do it. I'm not saying anything. It's not going to do any good anyway. I won't go through the embarrassment, Van. I won't."

"So Garner walks and I get booted?"

"That sums it up," Joe said.

"It's a shitty deal, but you could have been looking at three years in the pen for decking an officer. I'd say you got the lesser of two evils."

~*~

That night Van and Reggie lay in bed holding each other. They hadn't said much throughout the day. Van needed things to sink in and Reggie had given him space. She was afraid it hadn't completely hit him yet and was waiting for him to blow. He finally spoke after they lay there for almost an hour.

"He's fixed it so I couldn't even be a cop, you know."

"Don't hate me for saying this, but maybe you shouldn't be, Van. I know you love the whole hero thing, but I don't want to be married to a cop. I'd do it if that's what it would take to make you happy, but I wouldn't like it. I'd worry every second you were away." She leaned up and kissed him on the chin. "Can't you find something that would make you happy that didn't put your life on the line? Can you try to find happiness in something that would bring you home to me every night in one piece? No injuries, no bruises from bullets?"

"It's all I've ever wanted to do, Baby."

"I know," she said, taking her spot on his chest and stroking his sides. "But maybe this is a fresh start for us. Let's go somewhere and do something different for both of us. I think I've taken the 'lumber girl salesman' thing as far as I can take it. I'm burned out. Let's make a fresh start."

He let out a heavy sigh. "You want to move back to Maui?"

"You know, honestly? I don't think so."

"Really?"

"Really. I miss Bri and Troy and all, but I like the mainland. I like driving from one state to another. I like the change of seasons and the cheaper prices. I don't want to move back, not now anyway."

"So then, what?"

"How about your home?"

"You want to move to Minnesota?"

"Sure. I can be the Wicked Witch of the Midwest. See how that goes for a while."

He laughed and held her tight. "You were freezing in the winter here when it dropped to forty."

"So?"

"Put a negative sign in front of that. You have no idea what you're getting yourself into."

"I think you can come up with a way to keep me warm." She kissed his chest again. "Really. I think I can take it. I'd rather add a jacket than be hot all the time. These muggy summers here are running me down. Maui was never this humid."

"You want one extreme to the other?"

"I'd be happy anywhere with you. I told you that."

"You don't even get along with my sisters. Why would you want to live near them?"

"That's only because we haven't had the chance to know each other." She leaned up and propped herself on her arm. "Maybe if we spent more time together, they'd get past thinking I'm pure evil just because I don't go to the same kind of church they do."

"That's right. They'll see you are evil in so many other ways."

"They need to loosen up." She cuddled up to him again. "They'll have to love me once they get to know me better. Who could be better for you than me? Don't answer that," she said, playfully smacking his chest.

"You're sure about this? I wouldn't ask you to go there, Baby."

"I want to. Really. As long as that's what you want."

"I was a park ranger in for a bit around Bemidji when I was in college. It's a pretty area. I wouldn't mind living there. There's a ton of lakes so you'll still be surrounded with water."

His tone was almost back to normal. She thought he might be okay. Soon they could put the military life behind them and live like normal people. Maybe he could find a job he liked that wouldn't be so taxing on his back and if he had a boss that was a jerk, he could quit and find something else without being forced to take the abuse. She didn't care what she did next. She was excited to look for something new. Right now, however, she was excited in another way. "My love?"

"Yes?"

"You want a cookie?"

"Oh, I want a cookie."

~*~

One night after dinner a few weeks earlier, Reggie was getting ready for a shower. "Leave the dishes, I'll get them when I get out."

Wanting to help, he had started to do them anyway and dropped a glass in the sink. "Dammit!"

She came running into the kitchen in a towel. "What happened?"

"Don't come any closer!"

Her eyes became wide when she saw the paper towel on his hand. "You're bleeding."

"It ain't bad. I'll take care of it. I don't want you seeing it and getting sick."

"I want to help you."

He snapped at her. "I got it! You won't help me by passing out. Your 'limp dick' husband can't pick you up like he used to, you know!"

She stomped off towards the bedroom and slammed the door. After a few minutes, he came in the room and sat on the bed next to her. He had his finger wrapped with duct tape. She picked it up and gave it a kiss. "Nice bandage."

"We were all out of Bob the Builder."

She laughed then looked up at him with serious eyes. "I wish you'd let me do the dishes. You know you get frustrated about your hand every time."

As much as Van tried to deny when he was experiencing stronger bursts of pain, Reggie always knew when his back was bothering him. She always knew when he had to pop an extra pill. He was also having issues with the feeling in three fingers in his right hand. A nerve was pinching him, worse on some days than others, and he had problems with his grip. She learned not to baby him since he was sensitive about it, but she tried to do things like the dishes so he wouldn't have to mess with them.

"I hate feeling useless. I should be able to help you around here."

"You're not useless, dammit. If I really needed help, I'd ask. And if I ever hear you use the phrase 'limp dick' again, I'll beat you senseless. You hear me?"

"Promise to spank me instead?"

"I mean it Donovan William." She backed away from his kiss.

"Oh, the middle name. I am in trouble." Nothing snapped him out of a bad mood faster than trying to get her out of one that was on a rebound from his.

"Damn straight. Nobody puts my husband down. Especially you."

"All right," he answered like a scolded child. "I can haz cookie now?" he asked as he laid her backwards on the bed.

Reggie's newest hobby had become printing cute pictures off internet sites like LOLCats and Icanhazcheeseburger. Each one sported a funny cat photo and captions with goofy spellings of words. Since they couldn't get a cat, Van tolerated the pictures plastered on the refrigerator and had started referring to wanting her as 'having his cookie'.

"You can haz cookie now," she said with a kiss, quoting one of her favorites.

22

Within two weeks of the punching incident, the movers had packed up their house and their things were on the way to storage in Big Lake, Minnesota. When you left the service, they were responsible for sending you back to where you originated. That would get their things close enough until they made up their minds as to exactly where they wanted to settle. They waved goodbye to the movers and climbed in their truck. Van and Reggie were going to take their time driving up. They wanted to stop at Disneyworld as well as visit Reggie's parents and brother. They were making it a second honeymoon.

Van put his hand on Reggie's leg. "I just have one thing I need to do before we go, Baby."

She smiled. "Of course." He drove a couple miles, stopped at a row of townhouses and parked across the street on the Gulf side. "Who lives here?"

"Just one of the guys. He borrowed my Gerber tool my last shift and I never got it back. Wait here. I'll only be a second."

"Okay, my love." Reggie stood by the water while she waited. In all the time they spent there, she was still always amazed that the water came right up to the roads. She was used to waves and currents from Hawaii and always thought it strange that there was no tide to speak of. She closed her eyes and took in one last deep breath. "Goodbye, Florida." She looked back across the road looking for Van. She didn't see him, but the name on the mailbox almost jumped off and bit her like a snake. *Garner*.

"No!" she cried and ran across the street.

By the clanking going on, she could tell things were being knocked over in the carport. She ran under the stilted town home, finding them in a utility room. Metal racks were knocked over and Van held his former CO by his neck, a good foot off the floor.

"Van, no!" she screamed as she held one of her husband's arms with both of hers.

"This bastard isn't getting off scott-free, Baby."

"Yes, he is! You're out of the military, but you'll still go to jail! Stop it!"

He only pressed Garner further into the wall. Garner's hands held onto Van's as he hung there, flailing.

"Stop it, Van, please! For me!"

His features finally softened and he lowered Garner to the ground. Van raised his finger to say something to him, but he had no words. He turned and began to walk out of the room. Reggie followed.

Garner straightened his shirt. "I knew you liked it," he said at Reggie's back.

Van spun around but Reggie was closer. She brought her leg up hard and fast. The fluidness and grace of the move would have made her ballet instructor proud. She made contact. Garner hit the ground.

Van looked at her and smiled.

"Say I look cute when I'm pissed and you'll get one, too, Kimball." She stormed past him and out the door.

They turned onto US1 and rode in silence for a long time. Reggie had been angry enough that she shook for a while, but refused to let herself get lightheaded. She hated how she reacted to stress and cursed under her breath for miles. After steaming all the way to Key Largo, she finally blew. She leaned over and punched Van in the arm. Of course, it did nothing to him. He laughed at her efforts. That made her even angrier. He pulled the vehicle off the road at a small unofficial rest area.

"I'm sorry. I wasn't going to let that asshole get away with no ramifications for what he did to you."

"So, you'll what? Kill him yourself and let me spend the next twenty years alone while you rot in jail?"

"I wouldn't have killed him, killed him, Baby."

That was another running joke between them. They had watched a comedian in Key West who did a whole skit on how saying the same word twice changes its meaning.

"Not funny, Van!"

A fisherman pulled up and honked that he wanted to get down a path Van was blocking. Van drove down the road a little way and parked low on a hill against the bridge. He killed the engine, unbuckled his seat belt and slid closer to her. "Nice shot, Bravo Tango Whiskey." He kissed her neck.

"I'm happy to put the military behind us, Van. A simple BTW or just friggen say 'by the way' from now on, dammit."

"5 by 5, Baby."

"Stop it!" She laughed. She didn't want to, but she did. "Fine, you heard me loud and clear but now stop it. Please. I really want all of this behind us…everything."

"Okay." He continued kissing her neck. "Hey, we haven't done it in Key Largo, have we?"

She pretended to go through a mental checklist, counting off on her fingers, naming the different keys. "Nope."

"Ya wanna?"

~*~

The drive to Minnesota took them a total of nine days to do. They took two days for themselves at Disneyworld and two days with her parents, which was two days too many. Thankfully her brother and his wife and kids were there for one of the days. Reggie enjoyed her aunt time. It was a good reminder for her of how much work kids were, but she also knew she still wanted them very much.

They took their time driving and stayed at hotels so they weren't completely worn out each night. When they hit Minnesota, they visited the Mall of America where they played like kids at the theme park. They stayed across the street at a water park where they swam until it closed. They drove into Bemidji the following day and spent time investigating the town. Van suggested they spend a few days driving around before they committed to buying a house.

Reggie instantly loved the town. There was a small mall with a JCPenney and Kmart, but also a downtown that was still very active. There was a huge lake right off the main road and two others that were even more stunning fifteen minutes in each direction.

They found an eager real estate agent that had a list of properties to show them, but Reggie fell in love at the third showing. Unlike many of the other lots where the neighbor's houses almost touched, this one had a double-wide lot. The house was in desperate need of some fixing so the price was perfect. They signed the purchase agreement and 'christened' the house when the realtor left.

They drove to Big Lake that night to tell his family the great news. His mother planned a welcome home dinner and had his sisters over. Reggie hoped it would go over better than their last visit.

A year ago they had driven up to Big Lake to visit for his father's birthday party. "You two don't go to church?" His younger sister said. You would have thought she had been shot by the way she reacted.

"Not currently, no." Reggie answered. "Van's schedule has always been so crazy, we never got into the routine of it."

"Well, you'll find something," she said with a pat to her leg.

"I suppose we will." Reggie struggled to put on a smile. She knew Van had attended church regularly as a Lutheran growing up. They had never discussed going after they were married. She went to Catholic school, but when she graduated and her parents left, she rarely attended a service again on her own.

She sat, silent, while the family carried on about playing in church, singing in church, helping with Sunday school... It was a large part of their lives and she respected it. She just hoped it wouldn't be something that would form a constant wedge between them. Reggie considered herself a believer in God; she didn't feel like she had to sit in a church on Sunday and prove it to anyone else. She had attended a church a few times on Oahu with a 'significant other' and didn't particularly care for the style. She liked to go for an uplifting sermon or some 'make you feel good' music. She didn't care for the 'you are not welcome to receive communion if you don't belong to this church' attitude. *Uh huh. There's a nice welcome. Oh wait, you did say 'welcome, sinner' when I showed up. I feel all warm and fuzzy inside now. Thanks.*

The man she attended with was colorful, to say the least. How could he do what he did, yet sit there for an hour on Sunday to show everyone how 'good' he was? It was a two-faced act that Reggie always carried in her memory. She began to see things for what they were. Whether or not someone went to church, and to which one, wasn't a concern to her. She had always prided herself on being a bitch, but never a judgmental bitch. Someone's religion or the color of their skin was never an issue for her.

Her friends ranged from every nationality on the planet. Hawaii was diverse if nothing else. The islands consisted mostly of Japanese and Filipino, but she also had classmates from Fiji, Tonga, China and Korea. She never put a label to color and only asked for that in return. Being white, she was the minority. She never wanted to treat someone as she had, on rare occasion, been treated when mistaken for a tourist in a shadier area of Oahu.

Although mixed marriages were commonplace and the island was streaming with gorgeous babies they referred to as 'hapa' from the combination of their parents nationalities, for some reason there was still indifference to the fact that Sabrina was black and Troy was Caucasian. It was one point that especially held them dear to her. Love had no boundaries for them. She wished more people were that way.

"So, did you look into churches near your new house?" Van's sister asked immediately after they said they had put money down on a quaint two bedroom with a nice yard. She had hoped after their last fight, the subject wouldn't be brought up again.

"The realtor told us about a great non-denominational Christian church out of town. We thought about going to check it out once we're settled."

"Why would you do that? You're going to go to a Lutheran church, aren't you? You'll only have to take classes for about a year so you can become a member."

Reggie sighed. "I wasn't that keen on the last Lutheran church I went to. I guess we'll have to see. I really don't get the whole class and the member thing anyway. Why can't someone just go there and everyone be okay with that?"

"It's the way it is. Van's Lutheran; you should go to a Lutheran church."

"Do we have to do this again, Kristi? Really?" Reggie had two glasses of wine and was tired from the drive. She was in no mood to have the church fight again.

"It's the right thing to do," Kristi continued.

"Right thing for who? You don't know me or even like me. How can you presume to know what's best for me?"

"Van went before he met you."

Reggie stood up and walked out of the house. Van followed her. She stood by the car with her arms crossed. "You never stick up for me! You just sit there and let them run me up and down every damn time!"

"I don't let it get to me. We don't usually talk about things like you do. Someone pisses someone off and we don't talk for a couple days, then we act like it never happened."

"Dysfunction at its finest," she said, turning away.

"You know how I feel about it, Reggie. We'll go if you want to go."

"But what about you?"

"I'm fine. There's other ways we can get involved in the community if you rather not do the hellfire and brimstone routine. We can do volunteer stuff for veterans, the food shelf…

you can volunteer at the animal shelter and get all the cat loving you can handle." She lit up when he said that.

"I think I'm going to like it here, Van," she finally said.

"Because we're still three hours away from my family?"

"Yup."

~*~

Despite wanting a change in career, Reggie again found employment with a local lumberyard. It was what she knew and she did it well. She was already calculating their home improvement savings in employee discounts.

Van received a monthly allotment for his injuries and they were still able to keep their military benefits such as their IDs to be able to shop at a commissary, which Reggie wanted nothing to do with. Van still had periodic doctor appointment for follow-ups. Reggie was sure they were a waste of time since they never revealed anything and just offered him more pills. He, of course, had to go where they sent him, never to anyone local. It was usually to a doctor four hours away to the cities; sometimes it was only the three to Fargo. At least he was reimbursed for gas.

Since Van was honorably discharged and couldn't find work in the same kind of field because of his job-related back injury, the service had to offer him training in a new field. Reggie had recently purchased them both laptops with a tax return and he had really taken to trying to learn their ins and outs. The opportunity for computer training class came up and he was excited about it. Reggie was a little less than thrilled.

"In Fargo? Why do you have to do the classes in Fargo?"

"Because that's where they are."

"There's a college right here in town."

"But these classes will be paid for by the VA and so will the housing."

"Goddammit, Van! We're out of the friggen' military and you're still at their beck and call."

"It's a Monday through Thursday class. I'll be home for three-day weekends and I can get up and leave early Monday mornings. You won't even know I'm gone."

"Like hell." She went outside and sat on the swing that was in the yard, left by the previous owner. Sometimes it made her sad, causing her to think about kids, but sometimes it was nice for her to plop in herself, too. Van joined her outside, carrying two beers.

"I really want to do this, Reg," he said, handing her one.

"You're going to do it no matter what I say."

"No, I won't. If you're really going to be upset about this, I won't do it."

"Then that makes me selfish."

"Yes and no, Baby. I ask a lot of you. My schedules have always sucked, not to mention the crap with my back. If you don't want me to go, I won't."

She got off the swing, straddled his lap and wrapped her arms around his neck, holding him tight. "I don't want you to go…" After a long hesitation she said, "but go."

"Really?"

"I don't want to keep you from something you want to do just because I'll be lonely."

"It'll go fast."

"How long is it anyway?"

"Six months to a year."

"I know you; that means a year. Dammit, Van, just say a year. When you say a drive is two or three hours it's always three. When are you going to learn to give me the high end so I'm happy when it's the low end instead? It'll be a freaking year."

"Really. I could finish in six months. It depends how many certifications I take. I commend you on your usage of the 'swear, once removed' technique, by the way. It is a slight improvement."

"Bite me."

"Can I?"

"No. I'm still mad."

"We don't have time for mad. We have to start saving up so I can still average once a day while I'm gone."

"You're underway all over again." She dropped her head to his shoulder.

"It'll only be for six months."

A year later, he brought his bags home for the last time. The course was finally over. The time miraculously flew by. They were online every night together using instant messenger; it was almost as if he were home. A few months into the course, Van discovered an online game they could play together. Reggie had really enjoyed it. She always loved castles and stories about medieval times. The game was *Stronghold*. You built castles and maintained your own kingdom. Eventually a war broke out between your kingdoms and Reggie usually won; whether or not Van let her win was yet to be determined. She always knew he was in trouble when he'd load his trebuchet with dead cows for ammo. That always brought her to tears laughing. He called himself Sir Kimball the Gimp and she was Lady Reggie the Kittenless. That was still a sour subject.

Now that he was home for good, it finally seemed like they were going to have a normal life. He had a great job with a computer company that he really enjoyed and he got along great with his boss and other co-workers. Their weekends were filled with fun with other couples. Reggie thought of this as home and wanted to bring up the subject of adopting again when Van called her at work. "You gotta come home, Baby."

"What is it?"

After a long silence he said, "My back."

"How bad? Do I stop and get the pizza or you want me straight there?"

23

Van and Reggie were in Fargo at the hospital. He was about to be taken into surgery.

"Some man of your dreams I turned out to be, huh."

"Don't be silly. Of course you're the man of my dreams." She lay next to him in the hospital bed and ran her fingers through his hair. "Of course, in my dreams you speak with a Croatian accent and your name is Luca."

He laughed. "You're such a bitch."

"That's why you love me." She leaned in and gently kissed his cheek.

"You sure you'll be here when I wake up?"

"Of course. Why wouldn't I be?"

"Maybe because you said three strikes and I'm out."

"No. I said you didn't get a third one; I was gonna shoot you instead." She stroked his cheek then kissed it again. They had fought so well and so often, their love talk would have sounded like a fight to someone who didn't know them.

Usually in the morning when he picked up his coffee, she'd throw the beer bottles he left by the sink into the recycle bin two feet away so he'd know he was in trouble for leaving them on the counter again. Undaunted, he'd smile and kiss her on the cheek and sang, *"I love the way you poison my coffee just a little each day."* It worked every time. She'd give him a smack on the butt then a kiss. If he was really lucky, they went back to bed for 'second breakfast'.

"Close enough." He let out a heavy sigh. "I'm so sick of this bullshit."

"You'll feel better when it's done."

"That's what they said last time. I don't know, Babe." He started to choke up. "I can't do wheelchair."

"You're not going to end up in a wheelchair. They never said wheelchair to you…did they? Is there something you're not telling me?"

"It's never going to end. I'll be there eventually."

"Stop it. You'll come through with flying colors."

"I've let you down."

"Quit it, Van. No, you haven't. What did I say to you when you asked me to marry you?"

"Refresh my memory. I'm still in shock you said yes."

"You were worried I wouldn't like military life. What did I say?"

"That you'd live in an outhouse with me."

"An outhouse in Timbuktu to be more specific." She leaned in close. "I don't care if that outhouse has a wheelchair ramp. I love you."

"I want to be all the man you deserve."

"You are that and more, Luca… I mean, Van."

He laughed. "Bitch."

"Jackass." She kissed his nose. "I'll see you in three and a half to four hours."

"Not if I see you first." He gave her a forced smile then winked.

~*~

The doctor walked out to the waiting room two hours after the surgery had started. Reggie hurried to her feet with a smile. "That was fast. You said it would be closer to four hours. I take it everything went great."

"Not exactly." He tried to pull her to sit down.

She shook his hand away. "What do you mean 'not exactly'?"

"Please sit." He pointed towards the seat.

"I'd rather stand. What have you done?"

"It's nothing we've done. His heart gave out."

"His heart gave out? He's twenty-seven years old! What do you mean his heart gave out? Did you have to stop the procedure?"

"Mrs. Kimball…he's gone."

"Gone?" she screamed. "What do you mean gone?"

He reached for her hands again and managed to pull her down to the sofa with him this time. "He's passed on. His body couldn't take the strain anymore."

"You killed him?"

"We didn't kill him, Mrs. Kimball. If we suspected he'd have this kind of reaction to the anesthetic, we never would have attempted a third surgery."

"What do you mean reaction to the anesthetic? You just said his heart gave out."

"It was a combination of things. He was on so many medications…the strain on his system—"

"You don't have a fucking clue, do you? You don't know him like I do. He'll snap out of it and be fine."

"No. Please sit back down. He's gone."

"You're lying. I want to see him."

"I can't take you in to see him yet. They're closing. I wanted to come tell you right away. I didn't think a nurse should have to—"

Not able to sit any longer, she ran down the hall and pushed through the swinging door that the doctor had come from.

"Donovan!" She shouted as she ran down the hallway looking in the surgery rooms. When she found what had to be him, she swung open the door. "Van!" The nurses were rolling him onto his back. The intubation tube was still in his mouth, but it was disconnected from the tanks. She looked up at a nurse who was standing there with a blank stare.

"You can't be in here ma'am," she said. Someone grabbed her arm, but she shook it free.

"No!" She held Van's arm with one hand and held his face with the other. She leaned in close to him.

"Come on, Soldier. Time to get cracking," she said, gently shaking him. "We have a long night ahead of us. You know how you hate not being able to feel your legs when you wake up." She gave his lips a kiss to the side of the tube. "Come on, my love. There's nothing that gets the best of you. Fight it." She gave him another kiss. The surgery staff stood in shock. "Fight it!" She screamed louder, shook him harder.

The doctor walked in and with a nod, the staff took the cue to leave. "We did everything we could." He placed his hand on her shoulder, but again she shook it away.

"You killed him."

"No, he just gave up."

"Liar!" She turned around and slapped the doctor's face hard. She wilted onto Van's chest and finally cried. "No. No, you're not leaving me."

"Is there someone I can call for you?"

"Leave me alone!"

"I can't let you leave here like this alone. I need to call someone."

"Go to hell." Her head remained flat on Van's chest, but her hands went up to his face. From there, she ran her fingers through his hair then left them there, laced within his locks. Only days ago, she reprimanded him for not keeping the haircut appoint she had made. Now grateful, she ran her fingers through it again, brought her face to his and kissed his cheek. She rested her cheek to his and whispered into his ear. "Come back, damn you. You're not leaving me." She began to sob.

Reggie hadn't remembered much after that. When she opened her eyes in the hospital bed, she was in a pair of dingy green scrubs. She vaguely remembered being dragged down the hall by two orderlies and away from Van. She had no recollection of getting into the scrubs or the bed. After sitting up, she was more than slightly disoriented. There was a glass of water by her bed and a small white pill. She drank the water, but didn't touch the pill. A nurse walked in while she sat there steadying herself.

"Oh good, you're up." The nurse looked to be about her mother's age. She was very heavyset but very pretty.

"Why am I here?"

"Oh, Honey." She sat down and took her hand. "Do you remember what happened?"

"I remember your bastard doctor killed my husband."

The nurse gave her hand a squeeze. "We gave you a mild sedative. You were a little…emotional."

"Are you married?"

"Thirty years this month. Four kids and two grandbabies," she said with pride.

"And how would you have reacted to the news?"

She picked up the pill. "Please take this. I don't want to have to give you another shot."

"A shot?" She remembered now being held by the orderlies while she was jabbed in the arm.

"It's a valium. It'll help calm you down."

"I don't want to be calm. I want my husband."

"Honey, he's gone. You had your visit. He's in the garden room now."

"The garden room?"

"Sounds nicer than morgue," she said with a whisper and another pat to her hand. "I know it's rough, but you have to accept it and begin to make arrangements. You were his only next of kin. I have no one to call. Please take the pill and we can talk and make some phone calls for you."

"Make me." She threw the cup against the wall then walked over to the window. The nurse must have pushed a button because two orderlies walked in within a minute. "Damn you! No!" Reggie screamed and backed into the corner. "What the hell are you people?"

"We want you to relax. We're not trying to hurt you. You need to take the edge off and think clearly. We need to call his family."

"You're not calling his family. I'll call his family after I see him!"

"Your husband is dead, Honey."

"Stop calling me honey! I'm not your fucking honey! I want my husband damn you!"

The two orderlies closed in on her. She flailed violently, landing a square kick to the family jewels on one before the other managed to pick her up and hold her tight to his chest.

"Just settle down, Honey. We want to help you. We need to know who to call for you."

"Leave me alone. I'm not leaving without my husband."

The doctor who operated on Van walked into the room. "Let her down," he said to the orderlies. "Please come to my office so we can make arrangements to move your husband."

"You're not taking him anywhere!"

Reggie ran out of the room in search of the morgue.

24

"Reg?" Regina slowly moved her head from side to side. She opened her eyes, but everything was blurry. "You awake, Reg?" It looked like Van smiling down at her. *It couldn't be.* She blinked a few times, trying to get things into focus. The face smiled. "Hey, Princess. Are you ever a sight for sore eyes."

"Troy?" her voice cracked.

"I'm here, Baby doll. I'm here." She sat up and threw her arms around his neck. He returned the strong embrace. "I'm not letting you go." She cried hard with all the accompanying noise her dry throat could make.

"They killed him, Troy." Sobbing, she repeated, "They killed him."

"Shhh." He stroked her hair while she cried. "I've got you."

When she was finally cried out, Troy leaned back with her on the waiting room couch. "They say you've been giving them quite a hard time."

"They won't let me see him, Troy."

He pulled her forehead to his lips and kissed her firmly. "I know, Princess."

"How'd they find you?"

"His records. The next ICE listing for Van after you, was me."

"ICE?" she asked.

"In case of emergency."

"You didn't have to fly all the way here for me."

"Yes, I did." You can't stay in the waiting room forever, Reg. We need to get you back home and get this all sorted out."

"Sorted out? They killed him. What's to sort out?" Her eyes were filled with tears.

"Come on. I have a hotel room in town. We'll figure it out."

She had forgotten they were still in Fargo. "But..." she was actually out of questions. She wanted to leave the hospital but once she left, she knew she had to let go of Van for good.

Troy stood and offered her his hand. As soon as Reggie was on her feet, she lost her balance.

"Whoa." Troy caught her and sat her back down. "You all right?"

She reached for her head with both hands. "Just light-headed."

"What'd you eat last?"

"Breakfast yesterday, after Van went into surgery. Whatever they gave me must be slow to wear off."

"Reggie...his surgery was Monday."

"I know. Yesterday."

"This is Thursday."

"It can't be."

"You have been refusing to leave and haven't bothered to eat? Reg..." He pulled her to his chest and mumbled. "Dammit."

"I don't remember anything after..." she put her hands to her face and began to cry again.

He pulled her in for another hug. "Let's get you outta here. We'll get everything figured out."

As soon as they were in the car, Troy called the hotel for room service. He ordered a cheeseburger and fries, a steak, a salad and, a chicken and pasta plate. He wanted it ready ASAFP and gave the kitchen staff exactly that for an order.

"Where's Bri?"

"She was at her mom's in Georgia. She'll be here around midnight."

"She didn't have to leave her mother for me."

"Trust me, she was more than happy to cut it short. Besides, you know she'd drop anything or anyone for you." She sniffed again. "It'll be okay, Reg. We'll take care of you." She dropped her head into his lap and cried again.

~*~

When Sabrina showed up, Reggie was sound asleep, curled up on the bed. "Don't wake her, Babe. She's really out of it."

"What the hell happened, Troy? How could he die?"

"I've been on the phone since she's been asleep. Nobody can give me a direct answer."

"What do they say?"

"They run in circles, from too many drugs in his system to an allergic reaction to the anesthetic to his heart just giving up."

"You buying any of it?"

"I dunno. I guess any combination of it could be right. I don't know anything about medicine. You hear horror stories all the time about simple procedures going wrong. We watched that horrible movie two weeks ago with that woman dying when they tried to remove something from her face. Reg is going to blame the VA, but it would have happened in any hospital."

"You're right. You know how she hated military life."

"I know, Babe."

"She always talked about asking them to monitor his kidneys and stuff. She was worried about his system with all the medications. Maybe there was something to all of that."

"I'll see where I can get tomorrow. I couldn't leave her alone today." He looked over to be sure Reggie was asleep. "That's another issue, too."

"What?"

"She was beyond a handful from what they described. She kicked an orderly…you know…" Troy pointed to his crotch. "They tried giving her something to calm her down but she wouldn't take it. They said she refused to call his family. I don't know why they just didn't do it."

"What was she doing all this time?"

"Hanging out in the waiting room. She hasn't even eaten in days, Babe. I caught her from damn near falling over. She thought it was Tuesday."

"Are you shitting me? You know how she gets when she's upset, but that's crazy. What about the nurses? Didn't someone do anything?"

"I'm sure they tried to get her to eat but knowing her, she just shooed them away. I talked to two nurses about her. There was nothing they could do after calling me. I just wish they had done that sooner." He pointed at the room service trays. "She didn't put much of a dent in it, but I got her to eat what I could. I'm glad you're here, Babe. She needs you. I'm not equipped for this."

"I'd say you did a hell of a job."

Troy's eyes welled up with tears. "He was my best friend, too." Bri held him tight. Together they cried, mourning the loss of their friend.

They stayed a few days together in the hotel. No one minded sharing the close quarters; in fact, they preferred it. Regina slept between the two of them that second night, like a scared child who had been awoken by a thunderstorm and crawled into her parent's bed for comfort. Troy and Sabrina both rested an arm on her while she slept.

When Troy came back from the hospital the third day, he was furious.

"They did what?" Regina shouted.

"They said they had no choice. The autopsy revealed all it was going to and they closed the case."

"How dare they ship his body to Big Lake without my permission!"

"That's what was on his record when he joined. It had never been changed. They were responsible for his life insurance."

"Meaning?" Reggie asked.

"It amounts to the funeral and burial paid for. His body goes to the funeral home he chose in his hometown when he joined. They were in touch with Champus about a next of kin list. As soon as you left the hospital with me, they notified his family."

"They had no right to do that."

"The hospital said they had no choice. You were deemed unstable and they had to get him out of there."

"Shit." Reggie sat down. "I just wasn't ready to move him. I couldn't accept…"

"I know, Reggie." Troy sat next to her. "I didn't think they'd do it. They said nothing to me."

She twisted a tissue in her hands. "I can't do a funeral with his family. You know we've never gotten along. I'm sure they're pissed I haven't spoken to them yet." She leaned her head to his shoulder. "It was hard enough to say goodbye to him the first time."

"You don't have to, Reg. You've said your goodbyes. Come home with us," Sabrina said. "His family can take care of the funeral."

"I can't do that. What would they think when I don't show up for my own husband's funeral?"

"Do you care what anyone thinks? Come home for a while. We'll help you take care of your house in a few weeks, a few months… whenever you're ready to face it."

"I have to go." Reggie stood up and stuffed the few clothes Sabrina had bought for her into a plastic bag.

"Reggie," Troy said, stopping her. "Don't go flying outta here crazy. You don't need to do this."

"Yes, I do. He's not going to have a funeral without me there."

"You just said you couldn't do that."

"I don't want to see his family, but I need to be with him. I need to be able to say goodbye, Troy."

He could think of a dozen things to say to her to try to talk her out of it, but all he could say was "Okay. We're taking you though."

~*~

Reggie finally gathered the courage to call Van's mother when they reached their Bemidji home. Cold would not describe the conversation. The doctor's release was the only information they received about what happened; they didn't understand her lack of communication. She lacked the strength to explain it.

"He'll be buried in the family plot and have a good Lutheran service." His mother emphasized Lutheran.

Van had wanted to be cremated. His mother couldn't possibly want to go against his wishes. Reggie shook out of both fear and anger at this woman and her stubborn ways. She tried to put some force behind her voice, desperately wanting her to understand. "That's not what he wanted, Mrs. Kimball. Van had said he…"

"I'm not burning my baby. We've had this plot for generations and that's where he's going. Service starts at noon tomorrow," she said, before hanging up.

Reggie was unsure of her plans now. She wasn't sure she could stay in Minnesota without him; there would be too many memories. Maybe he should be with his family. She couldn't drag his ashes around while she found home. It would be too hard on her.

The conversation went through her head the entire drive to the funeral. It wasn't right, but she justified it for three hours. *It's not him, Reggie; it's just his body. His heart will always be yours.*

25

Although it would mean another three-hour drive after the service, Reggie didn't want to get a room in Big Lake. Troy would have flown her to the moon if she asked; he didn't mind doing the driving between towns. They arrived in Big Lake an hour before Van's service. Reggie asked to be left alone for a while and they understood. She gave them directions to the church as they dropped her off at a small park by a strip mall.

"I need a minute. I promise I'll see you there."

Once the car was out of sight, she walked to the mall and went into a hair salon. "Can I help you?" the receptionist asked.

"Do you guys do *Locks for Love* here?"

"Sure, we can send it off for you. It's another ten dollars though. Are you cutting off all that gorgeous hair? We only need ten inches."

"I want it all off please."

The hairdresser, whose nametag read Lori, complimented Regina's thick mane while she brushed it out. She insisted that she leave it above her shoulders. "It would be a major adjustment to go too short right away. I'd hate to overrule you, but trust me. If you hate it when I'm done, I'll go shorter." The stylist tied a ponytail holder around her hair at her neck to keep it from all falling to the floor in a mess then snipped it off in several swipes and offered it to Reggie.

"Say goodbye to an old friend."

Lori was too excited about her new creation to take notice to the tears forming in Reggie's eyes. Reggie feigned a smile when the stylist proudly proclaimed, "Ta-da" twenty minutes later as she spun her around to face the mirror. It was a cute cut and style. It sat a couple inches above her shoulders and was nicely layered. She asked not to be given bangs; she liked being able to tuck her hair behind her ears. It was nice, but Reggie would have been content if she had done it herself in her best Hollywood fashion, doing an imitation of some crazy lady butchering off her own hair for whatever dramatic purpose. Having paid dearly to get it done must show some kind of sanity and restraint for her actions. *Right?*

Throughout the cut, Reggie twisted her long lock around her hand. How Van loved her hair. She wished she could send it with him instead, but she knew it wouldn't be fair. Two wigs could be made for the children with cancer out of what was cut off. Van would have wanted that. When the stylist reached for it she asked, "Can I take a few strands?"

"Of course." She removed about a quarter inch round chunk of it. "You have more than enough hair here. I'd say you had enough for two, maybe even three wigs; it's so thick and long. You've made some children very happy." Again Reggie had to force a smile in return.

"I need to braid it. You want the honors one last time?"

"No thanks. It's all yours." She paid her bill, tipped the girl another ten dollars and walked towards the church.

~*~

"Where is she?" Sabrina whispered from the pew. The service was half over and she had yet to see Reggie come in.

"She'll be here," Troy whispered back.

They sat quietly, listening to the remainder of the eulogy.

"Donovan is in a far better place now," the Pastor continued. "We should be rejoicing for him. He is…"

"Bullshit." A voice came from the front doors of the church. Everyone turned around.

Sabrina let out a loud gasp. "Oh, dear God!" Her head fell into Troy's shoulder.

~*~

"Bullshit," Reggie said again. "Excuse me if I don't feel like rejoicing right now." No one moved as she walked towards the front of the church. She scanned the faces of the crowd. A lot were relatives she'd met only a time or two. There were some friends from Bemidji and Van's boss. Someone had spread the word; she was glad they would get the chance to say goodbye to him. She couldn't have broken the news to anyone, still finding it impossible to believe herself. Everyone stared at her as she slowly walked to the front of the church.

After climbing the few steps that brought her to the casket, she stared at the handsome face of her husband. They had done a good job, she thought. He looked like he was merely sleeping. She reached in and placed his wedding ring back on his finger. They had given it to her when she left the hospital with Troy. She was upset that they had taken it off. Next she removed the hair that she had carefully weaved around her fingers, placed it into his hands and squeezed it tight.

"I'll love you forever," she whispered as she stroked his cheek and rested her head on his chest. "I'm sorry about the salt shaker." She hadn't even noticed Troy was behind her until he touched her shoulder. Spinning around, she threw her arms around his neck and fell into him. Her body suddenly felt like rubber and her knees went weak. Sabrina had gotten to them when Troy bent down and picked Reggie up. He carried her out of the church and no one looked back.

Reggie curled up in the back seat of the car on the long drive to her house. No one spoke for over an hour.

"I have to get back to work, Bri," Troy finally said.

"We can't leave her like this."

"I'm not saying we should. Pack her a bag and bring her home. She has nothing to keep her here."

"His family is as bad as hers, the poor thing. I swear we're all she has, Babe."

"Van always said his family was a little too conservative, even for his taste. They never left their town. Everyone knew everyone's business and no one missed a Sunday sermon. He was glad he joined the Guard and was able to see more of the real world. Reggie was especially a change of pace for him."

"They really did seem like oil and water in the beginning, didn't they?" Sabrina said with a laugh.

"I never thought he'd break down that wall she had up."

They thought she was sleeping, but Reggie listened quietly to every word.

"I never told you but he called me after some fight they had, wanting to know who hit her."

"Did you tell him?"

"Am I afraid of you two?"

"What did you tell him?"

"I played dumb. That was always her call. If she wanted to leave it buried, I respected that. I always have. I'd still pummel the bastard myself, Bri."

"I know." Bri paused. "I'll book us flights home for tomorrow when we get to her house. You're right. She needs to come home."

"So what's with the hair? She losin' it?"

"I don't think so. I think she's wanted to cut it for a while and only kept it because Van loved it. She put some in his hand."

"Yeah, I saw that."

"I suppose in her eyes it belonged to him. Maybe it's a fresh start for her, too. She's going to be a long time getting over him."

I'm never getting over him. Reggie thought to herself. She finally drifted off to sleep dreaming about him.

~*~

"Ouch! You're pulling my hair, Van."

"Sorry, Baby," he said as he moved his arm.

They had been making love, but a shift of position brought an abrupt halt to things. She pulled her hair free, twisted it, then tossed it up over her head. "I should go get it all cut off."

"Don't you dare," he said, pulling her close and sinking his face into her neck with a playful bite. "You know the only thing that is better than your gorgeous long hair against your naked body?"

"What?"

"Your gorgeous long hair against my naked body."

She laughed. "Some days I do want to chop it off though."

"I'll get you a whole litter of kittens if you don't."

"But you'd die from sneezing."

"So put a lock of your hair in my coffin. Don't cut it, Baby. Please?"

"For you, okay." She nuzzled into his neck. "You going to finish the job?"

"I don't know. Thinking I hurt you kinda killed the mood." He kissed her lips. "Wait. I know." He grinned and kissed down her chest.

"But what about you?"

"It's not about me tonight." He kissed past her naval and kept going south.

They snuggled afterwards; she was still gently moaning and let out an occasional soft giggle. *Damn he was good*. "Promise to do that again sometime and I'll keep the hair for as long as you live."

26

"I'm not going with you, Bri. I need to stay here for a while and get things sorted out." Reggie was sitting at the kitchen table with her arms wrapped around her legs, her chin resting on her knees. She hadn't said anything since they woke up until now. Bri and Troy had been making arrangement to take her home, talking around her like she wasn't there.

"Hon, you can't stay here by yourself. I don't trust you to eat. I know how you get. Come home with us for a while; at least a week or so."

"I don't want to go home, Bri. This is my home."

"This was your home with Van. Now your home is with us again."

Her eyes welled with tears and she sunk her face into her legs. Troy reached from behind and held her tight. "Come with us, Reggie. Please. I have to get back and I don't want to leave you here."

She picked her head up and wiped her eyes. She didn't think she could possibly cry any more. "You're not letting Van down by leaving me alone, Troy. I need to stay here."

"Why? There's nothing here for you anymore, certainly not his family."

"This place is all I have left of him. I'll never have anyone else. I want to stay where he fixed thing up for us. We were supposed to have a life together *here*."

"How can you say you won't have anyone else again, Reggie?" Sabrina said. "You're young and gorgeous. Give it time. You'll heal, Hon."

"No, I won't!" she screamed. "He was my one! *The* one! You only get one, dammit!"

"Are you high? Listen to yourself. Out of all the billions of people on the earth, you're only allowed one? What a crock of shit!" Sabrina wrapped her arms around her. "We don't need to think about that now, but please, Hon, come home with us."

A knock at the door made everyone jump. Troy answered it. Alex extended his hand and introduced himself and his wife. "Saw you at the funeral, but it didn't look like a good time to make your acquaintance. How is she?"

"Stubborn, as always. Come on in."

Kirsten held up a 9x13 glass-baking dish. "I brought an egg bake. I'll get it served up."

"Sounds great," Troy said. "Coffee should be ready, too."

Reggie didn't stand, but she welcomed the hugs of her friends. Sabrina stood up to help. Reggie accepted the coffee and drank some, but just moved the food around on her plate with the fork. Sabrina and Kirsten exchanged glances; they both were watching her.

"We're trying to get her to come home with us for a while," Sabrina said to them.

"I'm right here, Bri. Don't talk around me like I'm not here again."

"Hon, when did I…" Sabrina quit talking. She either remembered the time with the thorn or decided not to argue. Reggie didn't care which.

"I said I'm not going. I need to stay until everything is settled."

"Until what is settled, Reggie?" Troy asked.

"They killed him, Troy. I'm not just sitting here and taking it. I'm frying every ass I can until I get some answers." She gave up playing with the food and shoved the plate forward.

Troy knelt at her side. "Don't you think I did everything I could, Reg? It's done. They're not claiming any responsibility. It's over."

"I can't accept that and I won't."

Troy stood up, frustrated, and Alex took his place. "I know you don't want to hear this now, but Van did have a life insurance policy through work. It was part of the benefits. In a few weeks, I'll be bringing you a rather sizeable check, Reggie."

"You're right. I don't want to hear it. I don't want money, I want my husband back."

Troy yelled at her. "Well, you're not going to get him, Reggie. He's gone, dammit."

Reggie stood. "I'd like you all to leave me alone now. Thanks for breakfast, Kirsten." She went to her room and closed the door.

~*~

The four of them talked at the table for a long time. Troy and Sabrina had to get back; there was no way around it. As much as they wanted Reggie to go with them, they couldn't force her.

"We'll watch after her," Kirsten said, placing her hand on Sabrina's. "I promise we'll take good care of her. I know we haven't known them for that long, but I do love her like a sister."

"Thanks, Kirsten. That'll help a lot. I can't stand seeing her like this another day. I know she'll be in good hands with you." The two gave up the fight for tears and shared a hug.

"You a cigar man, Troy?" Alex asked as he stood up.

"I've been known to have one here and there." The men walked out back, leaving the women to gather themselves.

"He'll really be missed at the office," Alex said once they had gotten their cigars lit.

"He'll be missed, period."

"True enough. We will do anything we can. I'll keep in touch and if things get bad at all, I'll call you."

"I appreciate it." Troy let out a heavy sigh. "I wish her parents were more help."

"We have often thought about how odd that was. I had a friend like that in school. The son was referred to as the "Golden Penis" and could do no wrong. You'd think his sister hardly existed. You guys have kids?"

"We're working on it."

"That is the fun part," Alex said with a nod. "So are we."

"The money… she'll be okay?"

"She'll be okay."

"That makes me feel better anyway." Troy ground out his cigar. "I need to go talk to her and we need to head out. I'm going to have to trust the second thing in the world I love most to you."

"We'll take care of her. You have my word."

Troy knocked first then opened the bedroom door without waiting to hear a response. He was sure it would have been 'go away' anyway. As luck had it, the bedroom door didn't have a lock. He sat next to Reggie in the picture window seat. She was staring out into the yard.

"You know I love you, Reggie. You scare me when I think you're about to lose it and get all emotional on me. How is it said in those damn cat pictures you and Bri love so much? 'Get all 'Emo' on me'?" She leaned into his chest and he held her. "I'm sorry, Princess, but you have to snap out of it."

She ran her fingers through the carpet that covered the window seat. "Van built this for me. As soon as I said I've always wanted a window seat he ran right out, bought everything and made it for me."

"He loved you so much, Reg. If he weren't already gone, he'd be dead sure as hell to see you hurting like this. You gotta snap out of it, if not for yourself…for him. He wouldn't want this." He kissed her forehead and pulled her tighter to his chest. "I don't want to leave you here, but we can't make you come with us. I don't want you kickin' and screamin' about being babysat, but let Alex and Kirsten help you when you need it. Okay?"

She nodded.

"Promise you won't do a disappearing act on us."

"I'll call every day. I promise."

He knew he shouldn't have taken her at her word, but he didn't have a choice.

~*~

Reggie quit her job the following day. They begged her to just take a leave of absence. They said she could have as long as she needed, but she turned down their offer. She didn't know what she was going to do, but she couldn't go back to living life everyday like nothing had happened. Every detail, every chore, no matter how mundane, reminded her of Van.

Tuesday she drove to Minneapolis to talk with anyone that would listen to her. She was determined to camp out in front of whoever's door she needed to in order to get some answers. She should have known better than to try to take on the whole US Government, but being rational had never been her strong point. Why start now? Not when it was something this important.

After four days of being sent from department to department, she finally found herself in the office of a man who would be the end of the line for her. The office walls were covered with animal heads of every sort. Stuffed ducks, pheasants and other wild birds filled the shelves. A bearskin covered one wall. She was sickened the second she walked in. Ten minutes after being seated in the office by the secretary, a man in a suit joined her and sat behind his large desk. He introduced himself as Roy Goodyear; she refused the handshake.

"You're a civilian?" It was the first thing out of her mouth. She had been dealing with nothing but military people in every shade of uniform with too many medals. Everyone had excuses; very few had manners or time.

"This surprises you?"

"This is a military matter. I assumed I would be dealing with military personnel."

"It's a government matter, Mrs. Kimball. I assure you, you're still dealing with Uncle Sam when you're dealing with me. You won't find many faces above mine as far as the VA or military hospitals go for the entire state unless you go to the President of the United States himself. You don't see the president in a uniform now, do you?"

"Frankly, I don't give a goddamn what the president wears. What I do care about is that your organization killed my husband and no one will talk to me."

He opened up the file in front of him and flipped through a few papers. "I see the exact opposite. I have depositions from several people that you *have* talked to."

"Talked to but didn't get any answers. All I get is the same bullshit runaround."

"You were given the answers; you just didn't get the ones that you wanted." He shut the folder and placed his elbows on his desk, lacing his fingers together. "What exactly is it that you are after, Mrs. Kimball?"

"I want you people to fess up to killing Petty Officer First Class Donovan William Kimball, my husband. My kind, sweet, caring, give-you-the-shirt-off-his-back and save-your-ass-while-he's-at-it husband! He was twenty-seven years old and you people killed him!" She stood up. "Do you want his last four?"

"You're not even saying how much you want?"

She was taken aback by his comment and sat back into the chair. "Excuse me?"

"How much is this information worth to you? One million? Five? How much are you after, Mrs. Kimball?"

She finally understood and bolted out of her chair again. "I'm not asking for any money! I don't want your goddamn money! I want you to admit what you've done. I want to make sure that some other poor woman doesn't go through what has happened to me. You robbed me of the love of my life! You ruined our future…my…life." She collapsed back into the chair. Her eyes filled, but she had no tears left.

"Your husband had a reaction to the numerous medications in his system in combination with the anesthetic. Period. End of story. It happens in hospitals all around the world every day, military or not, and is no fault of those in charge. Do your research. A thirty-year-old woman died in Minneapolis last month from a reaction to plain old Tylenol. My wife's aunt died in St. Paul going in for an eyelift. She had a reaction to the anesthetic. These things happen. It's a sad fact of medicine, Mrs. Kimball. There is nowhere else for this to go. You simply need to accept it as fact."

He opened up his folder again and flipped through the papers. "Until you are married again, you may keep your military ID and your Champus insurance. The lifesaving incident was military-related and we have done our part there compensating him for it. It's not standard procedure, but we will continue to do so in his absence and send the payments to you out of respect to him. He was a good man. It's the least we can do to honor his memory. If he hadn't injured his back, he would have gone far with us. This matter, however, is officially closed, Mrs. Kimball. We've done everything we can and then some to help you. You can spend a fortune on a lawyer but you are going to get nowhere. Think what you want, but we did nothing wrong. Just accept our checks and move on."

She stood up and approached his desk. Reaching into her purse, she pulled out her military ID and whipped it at him. "You can keep your ID and stick it wherever you see fit. I don't want your damn money either. I'll get by without your guilty charity." She leaned on his desk and looked him square in the eyes. "Shove those checks up your ass. If I so much as smell one of them within ten miles of me, I'll come do it myself."

Reggie stormed out of the office and made it to the parking lot, not even remembering how she arrived there. She was unwilling to accept defeat but the matter was closed. Dishonoring Van's memory with the hate her heart felt for the organization wasn't what she wanted. Without it, they wouldn't have met. She closed her eyes and pictured him in his uniform. He was never more handsome than when he came home wearing it. He was one of the rare ones, one of the few who joined because he wanted to make a difference in the word, unlike his CO who joined so he'd have a right to boss people around with his rank. She quickly shoved the memory of Garner out of her mind, vowing never to give the military a thought ever again – least of all, him.

That night, she drove to Big Lake and spent the night on the grave of her husband after she once again found her tears and sobbed herself to sleep.

27

Reggie drove the three hours home to pack a few things then drove back to Minneapolis. She parked in long-term parking and purchased a ticket for Florida. She wanted to go see her parents. They had their excuses for not being able to make it to the funeral and she forgave them for it, but now she really needed them. Sabrina had actually called them for her, since she couldn't bring herself to do it. She had been more upset than Reggie had ever seen her before. Reggie would have given anything to see the look on her mother's face when Sabrina yelled, "Kiss my black ass!" into the phone. God, she loved her.

Reggie called her parents from a layover in Chicago. They were surprised about her sudden plans, but said they'd be there to pick her up. She had to build up the courage to call Sabrina and Troy from Georgia. For the first time, she didn't mind several layovers for a normally easy flight or even ask about the price.

"Do you know you've had Bri worried sick?" Troy shouted into the phone. "What the hell are you doing, Reggie? I almost got on a goddamn plane again!"

"I'm sorry. I had to do a few things, Troy. I couldn't let it go."

He let out a loud sigh. "Is it over, Reg?"

"It's over."

"Did you find what you wanted?"

"No, but it's over; I can promise you that. I'm sorry I worried you but please, don't ever think you need to fly to my rescue again. You two have your own lives to worry about. I'm okay."

"You're family, dammit. It's what family does."

"I love you guys. I really do."

"We love you, too. You know that. I don't know why you're going to your parents; you should be coming here."

"I need to see them, Troy. I have to go catch my flight. Tell Bri I'm sorry and I'll call her from my parent's house."

"Will do, Princess."

By the time she arrived in Florida, there wasn't much to do except fall asleep. She received hugs hello, apologies again for not being able to go to the funeral, and they exchanged superficial pleasantries. After saying their goodnights, she retired to the guest room.

This wasn't her childhood home or bed, but she slept oddly well when she stayed under her parent's roof. When Reggie woke up the following morning, her dad was tending the garden and her mother was sitting in the screened porch having coffee. It looked a lot like the screened porch she and Van had in their crooked little house in Marathon. Her parents had never come down to see it; she wasn't going to mention that.

Reggie and her mother sat quietly sipping their coffee, enjoying the sounds of the morning. Having spent many a morning on their porch alone while Van was working, Reggie welcomed the familiar bird songs. She recalled delighting in the occasional egrets that landed in her yard; they were almost as tall as she was. Silently she chuckled at the memory of the morning she found a huge iguana that had somehow made its way into the screened area. She had to call one of the 'dysfunctionals' to get it out for her. Van couldn't have been called away from the station when he was on duty. His crewmate was more than happy to come over and help her. It had been someone's pet that either escaped or was carelessly released. In any case, it had become the crewmember's new pet, which he had promptly named 'Reginald'.

Reggie looked over at her mother, admiring her features for a very long time. Even at fifty, she was still stunning and could probably pass for thirty. The few times they had shared outings at the mall on Oahu, they had always been mistaken for sisters. She had the good fortune of inheriting her mother's genes, but she didn't care. Van had always fussed about her beauty, but she never felt worthy of the praise. Now she could care less about being looked at by another man again

Reggie looked past the garden to the neighbor's house, where an elderly couple played with three children who were obviously their grandchildren. Reggie had never gotten the chance to know her grandparents. She wondered if it was a fight that kept her parents from seeing them or if it was a family tradition to distance yourself from your children. It had never been explained and she never pressed the issue. Her parents did move here to be with her brother though; maybe they were changing.

"Does Ryan come by with the kids much?" she asked her mom.

"Usually on Fridays for dinner. He doesn't always make it, but that wife of his shows up and brings them along."

For as long as he'd been married, his wife Ivy was referred to as 'that wife of his'. That was an upgrade from 'his future ex-wife'. They had been married for eight years and had been very happy. Reggie suspected her parents wouldn't have been happy if he had married the Queen of Sheba. They treated her nice enough to her face, though. Ivy believed in family bonds and always went out of her way to be sure his parents were included in the kids' lives. Reggie really liked her, although they rarely talked. They didn't have a lot to talk about. Ivy discussed PTA meetings and soccer games while Reggie could only describe the wonderful new home she completed a material list for.

"I'm looking forward to seeing the kids again."

"Exactly how long are you planning to stay, Dear?"

"I'm not sure. I just needed to get away. Is this an inconvenient time for you?"

"No. I was just curious. Aren't you going to lose your job if you take too much time away?"

"I quit my job, Mommy." As childish as it may have sounded to someone else, Reggie still called her parents Mommy and Daddy. What they lacked in physical affection for her, she had unknowingly tried to make up when she reached out to them verbally. She longed to stay the little girl who used to get goodnight hugs, healing kisses on her boo-boos, and an occasional 'I love you'.

"That wasn't very smart, Dear. What are you going to do? How will you pay your bills? I certainly hope you haven't come here looking for money."

Reggie threw her head back in frustration, refusing to do what she always did in fights; stomp away. She wasn't letting her mother get to her. "I'm not here for money. We're…I'm fine for money. I needed to be with family, that's all." Maybe it wasn't such a good idea coming here after all.

"At least you'll still be getting his benefits, right? Betty Jo over at the VFW said since he was on disability, it goes to the spouse."

"I'm not getting anything from the military, Mommy."

"Well, I'd look into it. Betty Jo said—"

"I'm not getting anything. Case closed." Her voice was louder than she intended.

Her mother was unaffected by her tone. "He did have life insurance though, right?"

"Can we not talk about money?"

"I'm worried about what you'll do."

"Why start now?" Reggie hadn't wanted to start a fight, but she couldn't keep the words from coming out.

"Don't give me that attitude of yours, Missy. We took good care of you. You and your brother went to the finest school there was. Those dance classes of yours weren't cheap either. You may not think so, but we made sacrifices for you; not to mention your father and I staying on Oahu for a year beyond what we wanted so we could be there for you."

"Right. Then you left me to fend for myself. I was barely eighteen."

"I was aware of your age. You did always seem older than you were, Dear. You were always 'Miss Independent'."

"Because I had to be."

"You seemed more than happy to marry that McMillan fellow so quick. We couldn't have stopped you if we wanted. How were we to know what he was, if you didn't? You always jumped first and asked questions later."

"Thanks for being there for me for that, too."

"And what could we have done that the doctors weren't doing?"

"I don't know, Mommy. Love me?"

"You know your father and I love you."

"It would be nice to hear it now and then." Reggie walked in the house, grabbing her purse and phone. It wasn't far to a playground. She wanted to be alone and sit on a swing.

28

Regina's parents lived in Jacksonville. It was too far away to drive to the Keys, at least on a whim. She didn't even know if anyone from Van's old crew would still be there anyway. After giving it a lot of thought, she called the cell number she last had for Derrick. It had easily been a year since they talked. She was sad that they slowly drifted apart after the move. Everyone moves on, gets a new crew or career, and makes new friends. Being back in Florida suddenly made her miss him like never before.

Instead of hearing "We are sorry. The number you have called is not in service at this time," like she expected, she got, "Derrick's bait shop. Master-baiter Derrick at your service."

She chuckled. "Derrick?"

"Reggie? Hey, Baby! My screen is broke. I don't have any caller ID. Damn, it's good to hear your voice. You calling your favorite old lover boy all the way from Minnesota?"

"I'm in Jacksonville, Derrick. I'm at my parent's house."

"Get the fuck outta town! I'm in Mayport at my sisters. Shoot me an address, I'll be there in half an hour. Tell that old man of yours tough shit. He can come along for the ride, but you're mine today."

Shit. Word hadn't spread here about Van yet.

Reggie didn't want to go back to her parent's house so she told him the name of the park she was at. He reassured her he knew the area well and would find her. Thirty-five minutes later, he pulled up and she received more than enough bear-hug to make up for what she didn't get from her parents.

"So, where's the old man? He decide to finally step aside and leave you to me? If so, your timing stinks. I was married last month. Been meaning to call you two. I've been a little, you know, busy."

She gave him another strong hug and a loud, "Congratulations." When her smiled faded, he knew something was wrong.

"Let's go somewhere and talk." He wrapped his arm around her and walked her to the car.

~*~

Derrick drove to a restaurant he knew well. It had the best jambalaya in the state, according to him. He gave the order to the waitress for two helpings and two beers. It was only ten o'clock, but they would open the bar up for a regular like him. He was at his sister's house every long break he had. His sister teased that he didn't go to see her; he wanted to go to the restaurant. Reggie didn't have an appetite, but the thought of an old Florida favorite was beginning to change her mind. Again, she strained to remember when she had eaten last.

Reggie gave him a very condensed version of the chain of events, explaining it as the VA hospital doctors had explained it to her, not wanting to put any doubt in his mind about how she felt about it.

"Why didn't you call me, Reggie?"

"I didn't call anyone. I couldn't talk about it at all. It still seems too unreal. He was too young to die, Derrick."

"Don't take this bad, Reg. You know I loved him like a brother from another mother, but I'm really not surprised."

She sat back from his embrace with a shocked expression. "But why? His pain wasn't that bad when we were here. He didn't have to take much by way of pills. I never would have dreamed his heart would have given out. How could you?"

"It wasn't the pills, Reggie. I'm surprised he went that way; I'm not surprised his life was cut short. I always thought he'd bite it helping some little old lady across the street."

She could only look at him blankly.

"He was an adrenaline junkie sure as if he were a stuntman dead set on breaking record after record. But," he paused, "he was a hero to the end, Baby. He may not have felt like it, but he was. He didn't only save the life that injured his back. You know that, right?"

"He never talked about work. I could only assume the things he did. I guessed he didn't want me worrying about him all the time."

"Didn't work, did it?"

"No," she admitted.

"You remember the morning he came home after he had been shot?"

"Like I could forget that if I wanted to."

"He took that one for me."

"For you?"

"I had left without my vest that night. I was in a mood and sick of the damn bulky thing. He noticed and gave me a good ass-chewing over it, but there was nothing he could do; we were miles out already. I knew better. I could have gotten in a lot of trouble for being out of uniform, but I was stupid and I left it behind. Anyway, that bullet was mine. He shoved me out of the way but you know what, Reg? He would have done it even if he wasn't in a vest and I was. It was who he was."

Leaning into his chest, she wrapped her arms around him, holding him tight. "These stories don't make me feel any better, Derrick. You and his friend Troy talk about someone I didn't even know. I didn't see that side of him."

"But it's who he was, Reggie."

"He's still gone and I still miss him as much as ever."

"A part of him had already died when he was thrown out. He wasn't going to be happy selling and repairing computers and he certainly wouldn't have accepted being a burden to you if he ended up in a wheelchair."

"It wouldn't have been a burden to me."

"He would have seen it differently."

"I've missed you, Derrick." Reggie made her hug even tighter.

"Missed ya more, Sweetheart. And before you start with me, I promise I've never left without my vest again."

"That's a good boy."

~*~

Reggie only managed to stay a week at her parent's house. The stress outweighed any other feelings she had. Frustration was not the best substitute for sadness, but her desire to cry at every turn had finally been suppressed. She did have a great visit with her brother and his wife and two kids. The two of them had never been overly close. He had six years on her so they didn't share any of the same interests growing up. They had the love of being family and she could have gone to him in a pinch for anything, but she wasn't going to sit and cry on his shoulder. He didn't know her well enough to look deeper when she said, "I'm fine, Ryan, really."

Reggie flew back to the Minneapolis airport, wishing she had paid the extra three hundred dollars for the ticket to fly out of Bemidji. She wasn't looking forward to the long drive. Then she thought about swinging by Van's grave on the way. It made the drive worthwhile.

Sitting on the grass with fresh red roses for him, she wished she hadn't snapped at him for the time he had bought her the single flower in Florida. Had she known he would be stolen from her so soon, there were a lot of things she wouldn't have snapped at him for doing. So he left his socks all over the bedroom…so he never could quite find the recycle bin…these things were hardly fight-worthy. Making up was so much fun, though. Maybe he did do it on purpose. He had said on more than one occasion that he loved to see her good and pissed. She smiled at the memories and did her best to curl up to the tombstone, imagining his arms around her.

She left the gravesite briefly to run to the liquor store then returned with a small bag. Sitting again with him, she drank a Leinenkugel's Berry Weiss and poured a Honey Weiss on the grass. She didn't know how she'd find the strength to go on without him. Who else would have her, anyway? Looking away from the tombstone, she saw his mother coming. "Goodbye, man of my dreams. I'll love you forever."

Reggie spent the next six months mostly in a daze. She divided her time between repainting the house, inside and out, and gardening. A couple hours each day were spent at the animal shelter with the cats and kittens, but she had to stop doing that as well. One of the newer co-workers had discovered LOLCats and started to hang pictures all over the shelter. When 'I can haz cookie now?' was placed on the jar of cat treats, she let them know she couldn't come back, although she didn't offer an excuse. Even though Van wasn't with her anymore, she couldn't bring herself to getting a cat.

Alex and Kirsten stopped by often, but things weren't the same. They were her and Van's friends, as a couple. She always felt like a 'third wheel' no matter what they did now and she eventually made better excuses for not going out. She still talked to Sabrina and Troy, but she had been searching for excuses to begin to keep them at arm's length, as well. Each time Sabrina called, Reggie made excuses for not being able to return home for a visit. Lately she avoided more calls than she accepted.

Reggie finally came to terms with the fact that she had to move. There was too much of Van in this town and in this home. Even with all the improvements they had done, it was a tough market to be selling a home. After three months of virtually no showings, Reggie talked to the bank. She needed to go; she couldn't wait for a buyer. She signed the mortgage back over to them, waving away the rights to any equity they had built up. A garage sale got rid of most of her furniture and household items. Everything left was donated to Goodwill. She drove out of town with a trunk full of clothes, a box of pictures, a few keepsakes that were gifts from Van, and the life insurance check she had gotten from Ted. It had still remained in her possession, un-cashed.

At Highway 35, she sat, deciding which way to turn. A memory of Van popped into her head.

~*~

"Do you think we'll stay here forever, Van?" she had asked one night as they lay in a hammock together, staring at the stars.

"I don't know. I like it enough, I guess, but I feel like we have one move left in us. Don't you?"

"Sometimes I feel that way, too. I don't mind the cold, but winter can sure get long."

"That's my thought exactly. I want snow, just not so darn much cold. You ever thought about Colorado?"

"I don't know what it is about it, but it always sounded wonderful to me. We should go on vacation sometime and check it out."

"Then we'll have to do that," he said as he pulled her close.

~*~

A car horn honked, snapping her out of her thoughts.
Reggie turned west.

29

Reggie drove until she couldn't keep her eyes open and rested only once at a designated rest area. There were plenty of cars coming and going; she knew she was safe enough to take a nap. She drove over the state line into Colorado after noon the following day and stopped at the first rest area she found with a service station. A map was among her purchases. She gave it a quick once-over as she ate her pumpkin seeds. They had never taken their vacation to check the area out. They figured it was years away; there would be plenty of time. When they did take their vacations, they had gone to Maui to see Sabrina and Troy.

Reggie stared blankly at the map, having no idea about one town or another. Having no desire to aim for a large city like Denver or Colorado Springs, she turned on a simple county road.

About an hour after driving past a sign that said to turn for Pike's Peak, she found herself lost. She decided she couldn't be lost if she didn't know where she was going, so she threw the map into the back seat and continued down the dirt road. Eventually she came to a paved road again and followed it into a very small, very quaint town. A few people milled around on the streets, in and out of shops that made Reggie laugh a Minnesota phrase she thought she'd never use in a million years.

"Oh, for cute!"

There was a store called 'The Little County Cottage' that was a quilting shop. Next to that was a craft shop that looked like a large version of a little girl's playhouse. She squealed when she drove by an old-fashioned malt shop then decided to pull over to get something to eat. It was as if she stepped into a fantasy land, not at all like she was lost in a town she didn't even know the name of.

Sitting in a booth, she people-watched while she ate a cheeseburger, fries and vanilla shake that the friendly waitress highly recommended. Reggie enjoyed the banter of the men and giggled softly as she strained to listen to the women gossiping. It was like one of those small towns you see on TV. If you didn't know what you were doing, at least your neighbor did.

On the placemat was a cartoon map of the town with various ads and coupons from the local businesses. It showed a lake nearby. This was too perfect. Propped behind the napkin container was a real estate flyer. Picking it up, she flipped through it with great optimism. One place in particular caught her eye instantly. It was a small two-bedroom place fifteen miles from town and listed as newly remodeled, furnished, and available for immediate possession. She paid her bill and walked over to the real estate broker's office that, as fate had it, was right across the street.

An hour later, she was beaming ear to ear as she walked through the house. It was perfect. Included in the asking price was twenty acres of property. The realtor pointed out that her closest neighbor was about a quarter of a mile away.

"If it were light out, you could see it off in the distance." She pointed out the West window. "Nice fellow. I don't see him in town a lot, though," she added as if she was expected to reveal his background as part of the service.

They walked back to their cars, Reggie deep in thought. She knew she shouldn't be so rash about a decision like this. Common sense told her to ask where she could get a hotel room and sleep on the idea for a day or two. She needed to think on it, come back in the morning, look at it again, and wander around the property. Instead, she said, "When can I sign?"

"Pardon? My, my we sure move fast. We can go back to the office now and you can sign a purchase agreement, then we have to deal with the financing."

"I'll be paying cash." Reggie reached in her purse and showed the realtor the check for two-hundred-thousand dollars.

"And you'll have a little to spare." The realtor smiled with wide eyes at the sight of the dollar figure. "I'll meet you in the bank at eight sharp, as soon as Pete gets it open. We'll get you settled in here right away."

Reggie loved that the realtor referred to someone at the bank by his first name. She adored the casualness and knew she'd grow to love the town. The realtor led them to the vehicles, but Reggie said she wanted to sit on the lanai for a while, if that was okay with her. When the realtor tilted her head, Reggie laughed and said, "Sorry, the porch." Old habits die hard.

Until that moment, Reggie didn't know that she'd ever be able to cash that check. She didn't want to accept payment for Van's death. In her mind, that wasn't something to be rewarded for. Alex talked to her on several occasions about Van going with a higher premium, wanting to know she would be taken care of if anything happened to him. It didn't matter, it still didn't seem right. The company had called her several times over the last few months. They would inquire as to why she hadn't cashed it and encourage her to do so. She started hanging up on them and eventually stopped taking the calls altogether. Thinking of the house as one last gift from him, knowing it was what he would have wanted for her, was the only way she could accept it. Ideally, it's what they would have done together, but she had finally come to accept the fact that he was gone forever. She thought long and hard before she slipped her wedding ring off her finger.

~*~

"Let me be the first to welcome you to the neighborhood. The name's Ben. Benjamin Bentley at your service," the man said with an outstretched hand.

"Hi." Reggie reluctantly returned the handshake. She was carrying her few possessions into her new home when she was startled by the voice. She was supposed to have only the one neighbor; apparently he noticed her car already and came right over out of curiosity. He looked about twenty-five. The top of Reggie's head didn't even reach his very broad shoulders.

"You are…" he asked.

"Sorry, Reggie."

"Reggie? Never met a girl named Reggie before."

"Regina. Regina Kimball. I prefer Reggie."

"Reggie it is." He flashed a smile that would have made her knees go weak, had she been interested. "Can I help you with anything?"

"I'm almost done. Thanks, though." She picked up a box and walked towards the house. She turned around. "Nice to meet…" Before she said 'you', he was right on her heels, carrying a box.

"Just tell me where to drop it." He rushed to get ahead of her to hold the door open.

"Thanks, right there is fine." She pointed by his feet. After putting the box down, he looked around the room with his hands in his back pockets.

"They sure have cleaned this place up nice. I haven't gotten over to take a peek."

"I didn't see it before the remodel, so I couldn't say." Reggie stood by the door, hoping he'd get the hint to leave.

"It's great that they left the furniture. We made it to fit the space. It wouldn't have been right trying to put it anywhere else."

"You helped make the furniture?"

"Doc and I spent a lot of weekends in my shop. He insisted on helping with it. Things moved a lot slower, but he enjoyed it."

"It is very nice. I'm glad it was left, too. I didn't move very much with me." She hadn't intended to get so chatty with him. He was friendly enough; she just didn't want company. She especially didn't want a young, handsome man in Van's house…a very handsome man. You could easily get lost in his green eyes. His wavy brown hair looked perfect, although he probably only ran his fingers through it for styling.

"I like all the woodwork stripped. I'd been telling Old Doc Banker to let me do it for him for years. They were great neighbors. Being this far out from everything, you tend to rely on each other for things."

"I'm pretty self-sufficient." She wished he'd leave and remained standing by the door, holding it open.

"I'm sure you are," he said with a grin.

"I'm sorry, but I really have a lot of work to do."

"I thought you were almost finished?"

"I meant, bringing everything in. I still have a lot to do inside and I'd like to get started."

He frowned, "But you don't want any help?"

"No, thank you." She said it as politely as she could muster. "I'd like to take my time to get things set up."

He looked over at the few boxes and three suitcases. "You have a moving truck showing up later? 'Cause I can come back if you'd like."

"I left… my home with very little." She didn't know why she didn't even want to tell him she had come from Minnesota. He was nice enough; she just didn't want a nosey neighbor coming over all the time because he was bored or missed the last owner and his playmate. Hoping he worked long hours and his job kept him away for days at a time was probably too much to ask. She picked this place for its isolation; maybe she should have waited a day before buying it. "I'll have to run to town later and get some things, too. I didn't bring much with me. I don't want to be rude, but I have work to do, Mr. Bentley."

"Call me Ben, Reggie."

"Fine. Thanks again for your help." She stayed leaning on the door.

Finally, he took the hint. "Just holler if you need anything at all."

"Thanks. I will." She had no intentions of doing so. Closing the door, she leaned against it with a heavy sigh. *Dammit.*

30

Reggie put away her clothes in little more than an hour. She stood in the walk-in closet, staring at her humble wardrobe, deciding she would need to do a little shopping to add to it. Her work uniform for far too many years consisted of jeans and work-related t-shirts. She wanted to get herself a few nice things and maybe get some more sundresses, like she used to wear on her days off in Hawaii. Colorado would bring more warm days than Minnesota had to offer. She found herself beginning to get excited for a fresh start again. A new pair of shoes would pick any girl's spirits up.

After unpacking the few knick-knacks she had spared from the box of donations and placed a few pictures of her and Van over the fireplace, she headed into town to buy kitchen items. A large local hardware store had everything she needed. She bought glasses and coffee mugs, dishes and silverware, pots and pans, and a few glass baking dishes. Of course, the manager and sales girl wanted to know everything about her, no doubt to rush to the fountain shop and tell everyone about the new girl who moved to town but oddly, she didn't mind. Reggie was pleasant, but kept her explanations simple. Moving here from Minnesota to get away from the cold was all she offered for information.

It was getting dark when she arrived back home. Tired from the day, she sat out back with a glass of wine and enjoyed the sounds of the night. After almost an hour of crickets and owls, a loud "Yahoo!" made her jump. That was followed by a splash. She found a flashlight and headed down the trail in search of the source of the sound. The realtor told her there was a pond a little way down the trail, but she hadn't taken the time to go hunt for it yet. Hearing the splash again, she knew she was close. She finally came to a clearing and found it. For the size it was, she would have called this a lake, not a pond.

The way the water shimmered in the moonlight, it had to be a fresh lake from a spring and not a stinky, stagnant pond. She suddenly found the source of the 'yahoo' she heard earlier. She should have known. It was Ben. There was a large tree off to the side with a rope swing.

"Howdy, neighbor," he said as he waved. "I see you found our little pond."

"Our pond?"

"We kinda share it. Didn't the realtor go over the property lines with you?"

"I didn't ask. They said I'd get a plot book in the mail in a couple weeks." She walked a few steps closer, looked over the size of the lake some more. "I may just be a female and all, but I would call this a lake."

"It keeps the property taxes down if we say 'pond'. Why don't you join me for a swim?"

"I don't think I packed a swimsuit," she lied.

He had swum over to her and was standing chest high in the water. "It didn't stop me from jumping in," he said as he stepped closer. The water reached well below his naval before she shouted.

"Stop! I'll take your word for it!"

He laughed. "What's the matter? Afraid you're going to like what you see?"

"No. I'm afraid the water is cold and I'll have to point and laugh."

He laughed harder. "You are a real ball-buster, aren't you?"

"You just keep your pants on and keep to your side of the proverbial fence and we'll be fine neighbors." She turned to walk away. "Good night, Mr. Bentley."

"Wait a second." She stopped, but didn't turn back around, afraid he might have stepped out of the water. "Throw me my towel. I'll walk you back."

"I can find my way back, thanks." She took another step.

He called out as she took another step. "Stop, Reggie. I'm serious. There's been a mountain lion hanging around for the past couple of nights. Let me walk you back."

"A mountain lion?"

"Throw me my towel, unless you want me to—"

"I'll get it." She found his towel, took a few steps backwards, and tossed it to him. He wrapped it around his waist and joined her on the shore.

He walked over to her and held her shoulders. "And would you please call me Ben?" She had no response to that. He dropped his hands, walked over and picked up a shotgun that was propped up against a tree. "Do you have a gun?"

"No." She had gotten rid of her gun before she left Maui and all of Van's guns after his funeral. She didn't want them. It was one more thing to remind her of him and one more way to think about how she had almost lost him.

"You should get one. I can teach you how to shoot, if you'd like." He held her elbow as he walked back towards her house.

"I know how to shoot. I'm pretty good actually. I just don't like guns." She shook her arm free.

"You should get one anyway. You never know what will pop out at you here. I had to shoot a 'coon that looked like it had rabies last week."

"Rabies?"

"I took it in. They tested it and it was negative, but it was sure actin' crazy."

"I couldn't shoot a living creature."

"Then you'll have to keep my number handy, won't you?"

She sighed heavily. "Why would you risk getting attacked just to go for a late night swim?"

"Because until you've tried it, you'll never get it." They reached her back porch. "Besides," he said as he tucked a strand of her hair behind her ear. "I lied about the mountain lion. I just wanted to walk you home. Goodnight, Reggie."

She was furious, but she wasn't going to let him know it. Not shouting obscenities at him as he walked away killed her, but she wasn't going to let him know how much he upset her. He wasn't going to win this round. It took a little more effort not to slam her door, but she caught herself in time. Still fuming, she poured herself another glass of wine. She swirled the red liquid in the glass as she tried to devise a plan. It was a toss-up whether or not to try even harder to avoid him or find a way to get even. It should have been a no-brainer which one was going to win.

~*~

The next morning Reggie drove to town to stock up better with groceries. The house had a wonderful walk-in pantry and chest freezer to fill up. She could easily avoid going to town for two weeks at a time, longer if she could do without milk, fresh fruits and veggies. Without Van to cook for, her meals had become very simple. She usually skipped breakfast and just had coffee. Lunch was mostly grazing here and there on whatever she had handy and she usually threw a salad together at dinner with some grilled chicken or made a single helping of pasta.

Other than the grocery store, she did have one other destination in mind. There was no sporting goods store in town, but the hardware store had a modest selection of guns. The manager didn't hide being leery about her at first, but she assured him that she knew how to use one and had completed a safety course. That wasn't a lie.

Before moving to Maui, Reggie had purchased a small handgun for personal reasons. She never wanted to have to use it, but she had it in her nightstand at home just the same. Troy had taken her and Bri to the range often; they were both very good. As far as shotguns went, she wasn't comfortable with anything bigger than a 20 gauge. She didn't see the need for anything bigger anyway but after looking them over, she chose a handgun. When she asked for the Smith & Wesson Model 22, the manager grinned.

"You like the classics?"

"I used to have one like it."

"I like a lady who knows her guns." He reached for it then the ammunition.

She really couldn't point out a Colt from a Glock, but she was familiar with the one gun and thought it would be best to stick with what she knew. She wasn't about to correct the manager since he thought she knew more than she actually did. Accepting the gun, she hoped he wouldn't try to talk guns with her any further.

They went outside and she shot a few rounds at a target. The manager commented on her skill as they shook hands goodbye.

That night before sunset, she lay flat in some bushes by her house and waited. It didn't take long to hear someone crunching in the path. When Ben finally approached, she fired at a tree a few feet away from him. She expected him to jump or holler in fear; he did neither. He barely flinched, but he did stop in his tracks.

"Gordon said you picked up a gun. I'm glad you took my advice; I just didn't think you use it on me."

Fuming, she stood up, refusing to let Ben see her frustration. "Is that you, Ben? I was afraid you were a mountain lion." Casually, she brushed herself off.

"You really should be careful. You could have hit me if you were any good."

"I have great aim. I already told you I couldn't shoot a living creature. Fortunately for you, you still manage to fall slightly in that category." She turned to walk towards her porch.

"Bet you dinner I have better aim."

"I don't partake in the manly ritual of a challenge, Mr. Bentley. As a matter of fact, call me a chicken and see if it matters."

"Are you chicken? And I keep telling you to call me Ben."

"I'm only chicken that I won't have enough restraint not to shoot off one of your more favorite parts if you don't start keeping your distance. I moved here to get some peace and quiet."

"And what a great place for that it is," he said, undaunted. "Come on, I'm getting hungry. Best outta six cans buys burgers at Ike's."

"Cans?"

He pulled her along. "I have them all set up."

There was a small range set up off the path a little way between their houses. Ben and the old owners must have traveled a lot between their places because the path was well worn. He had a floodlight on over the shooting range and targets. As soon as Reggie knew she was within range, she shook her hand free of his and fired off her shots. She knocked can after can off the log as Ben stood there with his mouth agape. There was one can left standing, but she dropped her gun to her side. "I only had six shots and I've already used one," then she added, "and I already ate." She turned to walk away. He let her go.

31

Three days had passed without seeing Ben. Reggie had mixed emotions about that. She was finally successful in scaring him away, but she grew lonely without him pestering her. It was an odd feeling for her. She tried to shake it off and pretend to enjoy the quiet. That was getting hard to do; things were becoming too quiet.

The lake was beautiful that day, perfect for soaking up some sun, but she was again disappointed that Ben didn't make an appearance. She took her time walking back to her house, sad not to hear so much as a peep from his home. After deciding to call it an early night, she showered, put on her favorite kitty pajamas and curled up on the couch with a new book.

A machine rumbling like a motorcycle pulled up in front of her house. She opened up the curtain and caught Ben getting off a four-wheeler. He made it to the front door and gave it a hearty bang before she was there to open it.

He smiled at her attire. "Sylvester fan?"

"I wasn't expecting company." Reggie stepped out on the porch, closing the door behind her, making it obvious she wasn't inviting him in.

"Let's go for a ride."

"I was getting ready to settle in with a book."

"Come on. The trails are more fun than a book. Grab some shoes."

"I really don't want to go, Ben. Maybe some other time."

He smiled, apparently glad that she finally called him Ben and not Mr. Bentley. "That's crazy talk. It's a perfect time. The weather couldn't be better. The sun is about to set and is gorgeous from Oak Hill. Grab some shoes and let's go."

"Really, Ben, I—" He surprised her when he scooped her up in his arms. "What are you doing?"

"You've been a hermit since you moved in. You need to get out of the house."

"Is that some kind of professional opinion?" she asked when he placed her on the seat of the machine.

"It's *my* opinion and no charge." He leaned in closer to her. "Now, where are your shoes?"

"I'll be fine," she said, stubbornly, then reached back and held on to the rack on the back of the ATV. There was no way she was going to hold on to his waist when they drove.

"Suit yourself." He climbed on, started the engine and drove off towards the forest. He didn't take the trails too fast or rough. He climbed straight to the top of the mountain that was beyond their properties. They caught the sunset just in time. Of all the things from home, she missed the sunsets the most. She did enjoy it more than she was going to let on.

"Breathtaking, isn't it?"

"Yes, I suppose."

He pointed off to the distance. "Look over there."

"Are those deer?" She slid off the four-wheeler to take a closer look.

He hurried to the ground and pulled her down. "They'll take off if they catch our scent." She lay still next to him, grinning ear to ear as she watched the doe and twin baby fawns play.

He looked over at her and smiled. "Now there, see? Doesn't hurt so much, does it?" He touched the corner of her mouth.

That made her stop smiling and she stood up. "The sun is down. Can we go back now? She walked back towards the four-wheeler when she suddenly screamed and hit the ground with her knees.

"What happened?" Ben asked as he rushed to her side. She rolled over and grasped her ankle. "Holy crap, Reg. That's a mother of a thorn. I told you to grab your shoes. Hang on, I'm going to pull it out." Her eyes remained fixed on his.

He waved his hand in front of her face. "Hello?"

"Hmmm?" is all she could say. She was having a horrible case of déjà vu. She hadn't looked at the wound; she wasn't in her usual distress from seeing anything remotely gory, but she was terribly confused. Although she was staring at Ben, his features became Van's. She stared at his hair, his lips, his Adam's apple and deep into his eyes. Finally feeling 'home', she smiled, despite the discomfort in her heel. There was a sharp pain causing her to suck in a deep breath, then in an instant the eyes before her turned green once again and the face became Ben's.

"You all right?" he asked as he tossed the branch aside.

Her eyes welled with tears, not because of the pain in her foot, but for the one that now filled her heart. A crying gasp escaped as she brought her hands to her face.

"Ah, hell." Ben leaned down and brought her to his lap. "It's okay, Darlin'." He rocked with her and stroked her hair as she allowed herself to cry freely. Let him think the thorn hurt that bad. She didn't care. The tears needed to flow. It had been a while and she wanted a good cry.

~*~

After a few minutes of comforting her, Ben stood up with her still in his arms. "I'll take you back to my place. We'll get it cleaned up." He walked over to the four-wheeler and straddled it with her still clinging to the front of him. He steered with one hand while the other held her tight. There was nothing serious about her injury. There was no rush to get back to his place. He took his time on the trails, taking the bumps and curves with great care, thoroughly enjoying the closeness of her next to him at last.

When they reached his house, he pulled up to the porch and killed the engine. She still hadn't budged or said a word. "You okay?" She nodded into his shoulder. "Notice how I'm not saying 'I told you so' about grabbing your shoes?"

"Oh, shut up." She buried her face deeper.

He carried her up the stairs and placed her on the porch swing. It was made out of the same type of wood that her furniture was, supported by two chains hanging from the roof over the deck. "I'll be back out in a second."

Again she nodded and wiped away the tears. He came out in a few minutes, carrying an ice cream pail.

"Ice cream?"

He pulled out a small bottle of tequila. "Not exactly. This here is what you might call a redneck first aid kit." He sat next to her and dug through the items in the pail. It held antiseptic cream, Band-Aids, aspirin, and a few other items. He handed her the tequila.

"Is that to sterilize wounds?"

"Nope. It's to drink. Take a swig."

"I don't like tequila."

"I don't care." He pushed the bottle to her chest. "An outburst like that was hardly over a thorn in your foot. You want to talk about it?"

"Not particularly." She removed the cap from the bottle and took a long drink, coughing as she put the cap back on.

He pulled her foot into his lap and rubbed at her heel with a pre-packaged alcohol pad. She pulled her foot back at the stinging, but he brought it back again and gently blew on it. He covered it with a large Band-Aid, then gave it a defiant kiss and grinned at her.

Reggie pulled her foot back and dropped her legs down so she was sitting normally on the swing. "Thanks for the redneck first aid."

"My pleasure." He scooted closer and stretched his arm behind her. He longed to lean in and kiss her, but he stopped himself, straightened back up and removed his arm. "I wish I could put a Band-Aid on whatever else is ailing you." He took the bottle from her, swallowing a long draw of the tequila as well.

"Would you mind taking me back? I don't want to walk all the way. My heel feels like it has a heartbeat."

"As a matter of fact, I would. I don't bite, Reggie. You don't need to be afraid of me."

"I'm not afraid of you! I just want to go home."

"To what? An empty house? You don't even have a TV. I know you're not in a hurry to watch a show."

"Please?"

"Let me make you dinner first. I still owe you that burger for the shooting."

"What if I said I was a vegetarian?"

"Are you?"

"No." She took the bottle from him and downed another swig. "Where have you been anyway?"

"You miss me?"

"Like a thorn in my foot." She crossed her arms and glared at him.

"Workin'." He stood up and led her in his house. "I'll start the fire; you can start making the salad."

They shared pleasant conversation over burgers and a Caesar salad. Ben didn't want to push things; he left the subjects up to her. She offered very little about herself. He knew she wasn't currently working, but he didn't ask how she managed to get by without a job. She made reference to previous jobs working at lumberyards, but that was as personal as she got. Having noticed a tan line from where a wedding ring used to be, Ben was curious what her story was, but he wasn't going to push it right out of the gate. He certainly wasn't going to inquire if she was hiding from a lover, which is what she seemed to be doing. It was a toss-up between that and brooding over one that left her.

Since the subject was on lumber, he explained to her about making log furniture to support himself.

"The wooden furniture, like the pieces that are at your house, are in big demand. I build smaller things like coat racks and such, too, when I'm asked. It's good money and I make my own schedule. I can take off fishing whenever I want to, well, almost anyway. I had to deliver a whole mess of furniture for a small hotel out of Colorado Springs. That's where I was the past couple days. A lot of it had to be finished getting put together on the spot." He smiled at her. "I'll be sure to let you know next time I'm going to be gone for a few days."

"I assure you, that's not necessary."

He led her back out to the front porch. "I'll be right back." After a minute, he came out with a jacket and two beers. He put the jacket over her shoulders and handed her a beer.

"I thought you were taking me home after dinner."

"The beer is dessert."

"I've already had one with dinner, not to mention the tequila."

"So have another." He sat on the porch swing and patted for her to sit next to him.

Reluctantly she dropped down.

He tapped their bottles together as if in a toast. "See that barn?" he asked as he pointed to it.

"That dilapidated building is a barn?"

"It will be when I'm done with it."

"You think you can fix that?"

"I know how to swing a hammer."

"I think the tool you are looking for the name of is bulldozer."

"It has a good foundation and frame. I can re-side and roof it. It'll be as good as new."

"What's the wood in the shell?"

"Pardon?"

"What is it? Redwood? Oak?"

"How do I know?"

She let out a heavy sigh and walked towards it. "Uh-uh," he said, stopping her. "Not barefoot again." He ran in and picked up a pair of sneakers for her.

"I'll fall for sure in those," she protested as he dropped his size thirteen shoes in front of her size seven feet.

"Want me to piggy back you?"

She stepped into the sneakers.

Ben was a few paces behind her as they walked out to the barn, grinning the whole way. He didn't think about re-doing the barn until that moment. The way she talked about the lumberyard, he knew she'd have a say on the subject. She took the bait; he only hoped she never found out it was bait. He patted his back for his quick thinking, of course, now he had to re-build his barn. Glancing down at her ass, he grinned. *Worth it.*

After studying one of the main support beams, she turned to him. "You don't know oak when you see it?"

"Oak? No. Why would they use oak on a barn? Isn't that for finish wood like a table or something?"

"Not a hundred years ago, which is how old I guess this building to be."

"One hundred next year, actually. There's a sign on the other side. That's why I'd like to restore it rather than tear it down."

She walked over to the siding, taking her time examining it. She placed her head on it, looked down the wall, and ran her hands over it. Satisfied, she turned to Ben again. "If you take these boards off right, you can re-mill them and they'll look brand new. This redwood is in awesome shape. It must be heart since I don't see any termite damage at all."

"Heart?"

"Termites aren't supposed to like redwood but like everything else, it isn't what it used to be. Things are harvested so much younger these days. Termites go at redwood now with almost as much vengeance." She was staring at the wood, but he was staring at her. When she caught him, she stopped and returned the stare. "What?"

"You know your stuff."

She leaned down to pick up a small rock then scratched at the surface of the siding. "Smell that."

"Smell it?"

"Just smell it."

He leaned in and smelled it. "Sorry. Doesn't do anything for me."

Leaning in with her eyes closed, she let out a sign. "I love the smell of redwood." Apparently she could tell Ben was staring at her. She quickly opened her eyes and stood up straight. Swallowing a few long swigs of the beer, she finished almost half of it. "You going to take me home now?"

"Will you help me with the barn?"

She laughed. "What can I do?"

"You've said more about it in five minutes than anyone has said in fifty years. Help me, Reggie. I don't know this stuff. Some contractor will rob me blind."

"I can't help you build your barn, Ben."

"Not build it, but help with the lumber. Help me count of how many yards of material I need or whatever."

"Board feet; not yards." She corrected him with a smirk.

He held back a grin. He knew what it was called. He would have called a homerun a touchdown if it would get her to help. "Do you know how to figure that stuff out?"

"Any monkey with a tape measure could figure that out."

"Well, obviously I've failed primate school."

She laughed again. "I'll come over tomorrow morning with what I need."

He held her shoulders as he planted a kiss on her cheek. "I'll owe you big time!"

She crossed her arms. "Would you kiss your contractor like that?"

"Maybe, if he had your ass." When she spun around to walk away, he took hold of her arm. "I was teasing. I'll keep my distance. I don't want an enemy out of my only neighbor. I may need to borrow a cup of sugar someday."

She held up the beer. "For the great desserts you make?"

"Precisely."

"Will you take me home now?"

"Sure thing. I'll get your chariot."

32

Reggie sat at the kitchen table sipping her coffee, getting excited to go over to Ben's and actually feel useful again. She jumped when there was knocking at the kitchen door. It could only be Ben. She didn't understand why he came over so early when he knew she was going over there.

"Good morning, Gorgeous," he said when she finally pulled the door open and leaned on the frame. He stood with his arms behind his back. "Sorry. Did I wake you?" Her hair was not brushed; she tried smoothing it down with her hands, a little embarrassed at her appearance.

"Not really. I'm up."

"I should hope so. It's almost eight. Half the day is wasted."

"Half the day? What are you… some kind of five a.m. freak? I said I'd be over this morning, Ben. I didn't promise you it would be at the butt-crack of dawn."

He laughed. "I like to get my days stared early. Besides, I had an errand to run. I wanted to make sure you didn't come over already and miss me."

"Would you like some coffee?" It surprised even her that she asked.

"Sure, if you have some on." She had walked towards the coffee pot, an unspoken invitation to follow, but he hesitated.

"One thing, though."

"What's that? I don't have cream, but I do have the powdered stuff."

"I drink it black, thanks. It's just...I don't know how my friend here takes his."

She turned around ready to be upset that he brought company as well when she saw what he was holding in his hand. "A kitty!" She rushed to it, plucking it from his hands.

"My sister's cat had a litter. This little guy looked like the one on your pajamas so I asked if I could have him. She was excited to get rid of it, since he was the last one not spoken for."

"He's adorable." Reggie snuggled nose to nose with him for a while, but suddenly became sad and gave him back.

"What's the matter?"

"Nothing. He's very cute, Ben. You'll have fun with him."

"He's not mine. He's yours."

"Mine?"

"I got him for *you*."

"For me?"

He passed the kitten back to her. "For you. I don't want a cat. I thought you'd like the company. You're home alone so much."

"Are you allergic?"

"No. Are you?"

"No." Reggie closed her eyes and again brought the kitten close to her face. She didn't realize a tear had escaped until Ben's hand brushed it away.

"Are you all right?"

"I'm fine." Without hesitation, she leaned in to give Ben a kiss on the cheek. "Thanks. That was very sweet of you. I've wanted a cat for a long time. I haven't thought about actually doing it since I moved."

He was grinning, apparently surprised by the kiss. "I have everything you need in my truck. I'll be right back." He hurried down her porch steps.

She poured two cups of coffee and went outside to the deck, sat on one of the wooden chairs, and placed his coffee on the table between them. She put the kitten down so it could explore its new home. It wandered off, eager to investigate its new surroundings and the potted ficus tree.

Ben came up the steps with a litter pan, a plastic container of litter, and a canvas grocery bag with kitten food, a pooper-scooper and a couple of toys.

"I want to pay you for that stuff."

He sat down and picked up his coffee. "Nope. My sister made care packages for all the kittens. She wanted to be sure they were given to good homes and started off on the right foot. He's had his first shots and, as much as it goes against my feelings on the matter, he has an appointment to be neutered at exactly six months. That was a stipulation. Kinda like getting one from the shelter."

"I would have done it anyway. He'll be better off." She grinned and sipped her coffee. "If she's such a stickler for that, how is it her cat got pregnant?"

"It adopted them, not the other way around, and she was already pregnant. My sister has a soft heart and my brother-in-law can't tell her no. It helps that he's a large animal vet. The neuter will be on them. He's doin' it."

"No, I'll pay for it."

"That's not an option. Just accept it."

She wanted to argue, but knew it was pointless. "Thank you."

"You're welcome." He held up his coffee in a mock cheers.

"Does the little man have a name yet?"

"Sort of," he said with a chuckle.

"Sort of? How do you 'sort of' name a cat?"

"My niece calls him Derf."

"Derf?"

"It's Fred backwards. She's a leftie and they used to try to get her to write right-handed. Everything came out perfectly backwards. Now she does it for fun."

Reggie smiled. "I can live with Derf."

"I'll let her know." After taking the last gulp of coffee, he stood back up, leaving the empty cup behind. "I've probably worn out my welcome. I should get going." He looked over at the kitten that was now half-way up the ficus. "Better you than me. Later neighbor." He gave her a playful salute. Her eyes gazed over at the gesture, but he didn't see it.

She stood and called to him. "Ben!"

Midway down the stairs, he turned back around. "What is it?"

After a hesitation she said, "Thanks again for the kitty."

"You're welcome, again. See you in an hour or so?"

"See you in an hour."

33

With Ben's help working the tape measure, Reggie had the whole barn measured in a little over an hour. They went into his house and she began to work some figures on a yellow legal pad. He stared at her sketches in amazement. She could draw a 3-D picture more accurately than he could draw a stick man.

"What are you thinking for animals, Ben? Should I count in for a stall or two or maybe a small pen of sorts?"

"I don't know. What do you think?"

"It would be perfect for a couple of horses. It looks like you have old fence posts up for a pasture from what I could see."

"There was a section of pasture fenced off that held some cows years ago. I removed all the barbed wire a couple years back."

"So a pen for some cows then?"

"I don't think I need to go through the hassle. My sister has more than enough to keep my freezer full."

She put her pencil down and stared up at him. "Why do you want to fix a barn if you're not even planning on getting any animals, Ben?"

"I didn't say I wasn't planning on it. Eventually, I would. I wanted to do it one step at a time. I told you already; the barn is almost a hundred years old. I'd like to see it restored." She did some more figures then slammed her pencil down on her pad. "What is it?"

"You little sneak!" She stood up so fast, she sent the chair flying backward.

"What?"

"Nice act, Mr. Woodworker. 'Gee, Lady. I don't know what heart redwood is'. You lied to me!"

"I didn't lie to you, Reggie."

"Bullshit. 'I don't know how many *yards* I'll need?'"

"Okay, I lied about that one."

She huffed towards the door but he stood in front of her and stopped her, gently grabbing her shoulders. "Damn, you sure are pretty when you're pissed."

Her shoulders dropped and she stared up at him blankly. "What did you just say?" she said at almost a whisper.

"No offense, Reggie. Look, I wasn't lying to you, not totally, anyway. I don't know how to do what you're doing. I do want to fix up the barn and I was thinking how much fun it would be if me and the pretty neighbor lady could go horseback riding sometime, only first I need a place to keep some horses, then of course…get some horses." She stared up at him, not making a sound. "Come here." He led her to his shop out back.

He opened the door and hit the light. The room held a couple different styles of chairs that were put together, one partially stained. He had blueprints of a few different styles of couches pinned up to a corkboard that stretched almost an entire wall. There was a pile of six- to eight-inch round logs with the ends shaved down, not quite to a point. "This is my workshop. I only ever deal in—"

"Pine," she said, cutting him off. She walked over and looked at a few pieces of wood. She picked up a piece, again closing her eyes, and held it to her nose.

"I really need you. Help me, Reggie. Please."

She put down the log and picked up a skinny branch from the floor that was still covered in bark. It had obviously been scrap in the bundle he received; it wasn't for his furniture. She swung it around a few times like you would a sword then she spun around and moved it right up his inner thigh, stopping short of hitting him where it would count most. "Don't ever lie to me again, Ben."

He held his hands up as if she were holding a gun to him. "I promise. Not even a small fib. It's going to be really hard to resist though 'cause you are really pretty when you're pissed."

She moved the stick up the couple inches it needed to make its target and he hit the ground with a groan. "Stop calling me pretty or the deal is off."

"I surrender." He half-laughed, half-winced. In either case, he was on the floor holding his crotch in pain, but smiling.

"I'll be back tomorrow with a list for you."

"No dinner date?"

"Nope. I'll be having dinner with my cat." She closed the shop door and walked away.

~*~

At eight o'clock that night, Ben showed up at her kitchen door. He knocked for several moments, doing Bob Marley's *Knocking on Heaven's Door,* before she gave in. She opened it a crack to look. He was holding a bouquet of wild flowers. "Sorry I fibbed a little about the way to measure wood." She accepted the flowers, but didn't say anything. "Are you sorry for wrenching my nuts?"

"Not particularly."

He ran his fingers through his hair with a smirk. When he looked up, she had the same look on her face as she had earlier when he had first said she was pretty when she was pissed. "What is it, Reggie?"

"Huh? Nothing." She gently shook her head as if trying to clear her mind. Ben was about to ask to come in when Derf came running out of the house. "Derf, no!" Reggie pushed past Ben to chase after him. He followed them down the steps, but he had lost sight of the cat.

"Dammit!" she cried. "He'll get lost!"

"He'll be fine. Cats are good about knowing where home is."

"But it only just became his home. He'll run away." Her bottom lip quivered. She'd only had the kitten for a few hours, but he sensed she was horribly attached to him already.

"I'll start lookin'. You run and grab some flashlights." She ran back up the stairs and into the kitchen to get them. Ben continued to walk around the house making a "pssstt pssst" sound, trying to get the kitten to respond to him. Reggie came running back out.

"Do you see him?"

"Not yet, but I'm sure his eyes will show up sure enough when a flashlight hits them." She handed him one and he turned it on. The second flashlight she brought didn't work so she stayed at his side.

She called his name and said, "Kitty, kitty" in a high voice. Within a few seconds there was a meow. She called him again. "Derf. Kitty, kitty." There was another meow, but they still couldn't see him. Ben moved the flashlight back and forth, but there were no eyes shining back at them. The meow was louder this time. They thought it was coming from the crawl space under the porch and squatted down to look. Reggie shook her flashlight again and it finally flickered on. She continued to search the crawl space while Ben stood up. He thought the meow come from above this time. He let out a chuckle and reached up.

~*~

When Reggie heard his laugh, she turned around and stood up. Ben was reaching up to grab Derf, who was up on the railing of the porch. Facing Ben, she hadn't seen the kitty. While Ben's arm came up, she wrapped her hands over her head and dropped to the ground hollering, "No!"

Ben dropped his flashlight and fell to his knees. "Reggie? What is it?" She sat motionless until he pulled her to him. "What happened?" She finally began to relax in his arms then pulled herself out of them just as fast. "Um, nothing. Sorry. Did you see him?" She tried to stand up, but he pulled her back down.

"You thought I was going to hit you."

"That's silly. I know you wouldn't hit me, not that I haven't given you plenty of reason to." She forced a laugh.

"You were ducking a blow. Who hit you, Reggie?"

"I told you, Van. Nobody hit me."

"The name is Ben, Doll-face. Who's Van?"

"What? I did not say Van."

"Yes, you did. Was he who hit you?"

"Nobody hit me, *Beeennn*."

"Are you here hiding from someone who was beating you?"

"Don't be silly."

"You're always alone in your house; like you're afraid to be seen. Is that what this is, Reggie?"

"A bee buzzed my ear. I hate bees." She stood up.

"You little fibber."

The kitty meowed and Reggie looked up. "Derf!" She ran up the stairs, picked him off the railing and held him close. "Thanks for helping me look for him." She ran into the house and closed the door without another word.

Ben stood, wondering what the hell happened. She was ducking a blow; there was no mistaking that. She didn't want to talk about it and he wasn't going to push her, but there was no way he wasn't going to keep an even better eye on her now.

34

The next morning, Reggie showed up with a material list like she promised. Ben was sure not to mention anything about what happened the night before. He vowed not to push so hard and to try to be a great friend. He'd never forgive himself if she withdrew herself even further because he pried too much.

He was no fool. If she had a husband who abused her, she'd be dumb enough to forgive the bastard and eventually go crawling back. Setting himself up only to have his heart broken wasn't on his agenda. "Suck it up and find a woman, Bentley," he had chastised himself last night. "You can try going farther than a quarter of a mile away to your neighbor's house."

He could tell she was shy at first, waiting for him to ask about last night. When he didn't, she loosened up. The enthusiasm and knowledge she had impressed him. They talked about making a minor change to the inside for a tack room, since he had decided on a couple of horses, so she recalculated the measurements.

"You know," he said, "I was thinking about that fence I tore down."

"You wishing you didn't now?"

"No. I hate barbed wire. I was thinking though about rebuilding it in wood."

"That will cost a small fortune."

"I don't know. I have a connection, obviously." He motioned towards his shop. "All the posts are there. It wouldn't take much work to put up a fence."

"What are you thinking?"

"What are *you* thinking?"

"Since you're going through the trouble of remodeling a hundred year old round-roof barn, and you're insisting on a wood fence…if money were no object, I'd say to make an X-fence."

"An X-fence?"

"You know." She held her arms crossed, making an 'X'. She looked up at him. "You bull-shitting me again?"

He put his hands to his crotch. "Would I dare?"

"I'm still not sorry," she said, putting the pencil to the paper. Her hand froze again. He had just sat across the table from her and noticed her stop drawing, mid line. He put his hand on hers.

"What's the matter, Reg?" He placed his hand on hers. She looked up at him, blankly staring into his eyes. "Reggie?"

"No. I am."

"Am what?'

"Sorry about the nut shot."

He laughed it off. "Ah hell, I had it coming. But, you know, if you wanted to massage them a little for me…"

She laughed and continued to draw. "Thanks, but no thanks. I'm not that sorry." She quickly finished the drawing, adding a header and a bottom support to the 'X' then turned the paper to face him.

"Now that, I like. You want to go measure it up with me?"

"We'll have to do the distance between each pole. My guess is with barbed wire, they weren't too picky for distance between them. We'll have to map the whole thing out."

"I have a 'fridge full of beer."

"Then I accept."

It took them through two o'clock measuring the distance between each fence post. Reggie sketched out the layout, carefully making notes of the different distances. They weren't too far off from all being eight feet apart, but just enough that each board would require its own measurement and cuts.

"You ever thought about doing this again, Reggie? 'Cause you sure know your stuff," Ben asked as they were on the last few posts.

"I don't know. It's practically all I've ever done. It would be nice to do something else, I just don't know what."

"I never would have placed you in a lumberyard. You're too…" he caught himself before he said 'pretty' again.

"What do you think I would be, Mr. Bentley?"

Crap. He was in trouble again. When was he going to learn to keep his mouth shut? "Stop taking offense at everything I say, Reggie. You don't see a lot of women in the lumber field. I didn't mean anything by it."

"Why don't you say it?"

"Say what?"

"Stripper."

"Come on, Reg."

"You'd have been right." She placed the tape measure on his four-wheeler and walked away.

Ben waited until she walked out to the lake at sunset later that evening before he went over to talk to her. If he had learned anything, it was that she needed a few hours on 'simmer' before she was done being angry.

"It's good money," he said to her back as she stood there staring out at the water.

She never even turned around. "Don't make excuses for me."

"I'm not making excuses for you. It's good money. I know first-hand."

"Let me guess. You always had a pocketful of ones and were a sucker for anything over a B-cup." She finally turned around and glared at him.

He whipped his shirt off and flexed his pecks. "They're not B's, Sweetheart." Holding her hips, he rolled his stomach up and down almost touching hers, but not quite. He rocked himself back and forth slowly towards the ground, stopping when he was eye level with her stomach then slowly came up until they were touching noses. "All male review, Doll-face. Three years in a row straight outta high school. Paid for college. You?"

Ben thought she was going to faint. She dropped down on the grass and he joined her.

"We do what we gotta do, Reggie. Why do you have to take it as an insult? If you were good at what you did and you made money, so what?"

She leaned into his shoulder. "I'm sorry. I just got tired of being ogled all the time. I know it sounds like I'm a hypocrite because that's what goes with the job, but I hated it – every minute of it. I guess that why I'm so sensitive about it."

"Let me lick you up and down."

Her head whipped around. "What?"

"Jodeci *Let Me Lick You Up and Down*. Drove the girls crazy."

She snorted a laugh then covered her mouth. "Jodeci?"

"Know it?" He grinned, knowing full well she had to.

"*Come and Talk to Me* was mine."

It was his turn to laugh. It was funny they liked the same band for their performances.

"It was almost the best day of my life the day I walked out of there for the last time."

"What *was* the best day of your life?" he asked as he stroked her cheek.

"It doesn't matter," she replied, looking away.

He gently held onto her face and turned it to face him. "I'm sorry. I'll try to keep the sexist pig comments down. Okay? Just give me a chance to be your friend, Reg. Quit running away from me." He leaned in and gave her a quick gentle kiss on the cheek.

She smiled at the kiss, but changed the subject. "You went to college?"

"Now I should be offended. Am I all bod and no brains because I work with wood instead of wearing a suit and going to an office all day?"

"Of course not. I'm surprised, I guess, to go through all that and not use it."

"I don't do office. I went to college for myself. I had to pay my own way, too. It was more for the challenge of it. You know, 'it isn't worth doing if it isn't hard on you'… some kind of mumbo jumbo like that."

"That which doesn't kill us only makes us stronger."

"Yeah, like that." He helped her to her feet and they walked back to the fence to finish up the last few posts. There was just enough light to finish the job. When they finished, Ben convinced her to go to town for a burger with him.

~*~

Reggie didn't remember when she had so many laughs over a meal. Her sides and cheeks hurt by the time they were done.

Ben dropped her off at her house right after dinner, not attempting to extend their evening together in any way, walk her to the door, or kiss her goodnight.

"The roofers are showing up tomorrow for a quote. So are the guys who will rip off the old siding to get it milled."

"You move fast."

"Again, I have connections. Pop over whenever you want and play supervisor."

"I may do that. Thanks for the burger."

"You're welcome. Goodnight, Reggie."

~*~

Reggie went over the next day, bright and early, to be sure the contractors Ben hired were up to the challenge of the restoration. He had told her that when he started looking into it, everyone tried to talk him into ripping the old roof off and putting up a more modern, simple pitch, but he stayed firm that he wanted it to remain the way it was. He did agree to tin instead of asphalt shingles, which Reggie was okay with, not that it was her decision, of course.

She assigned herself to the job of removing the nails from the old siding as the contractors dropped them to the ground. They had scaffolding up the entire side of the barn. Ben helped her with the process and carried the boards away as she was done, stacking them in the truck that would haul them to the mill.

~*~

Ben was surprised at how much he cared what Reggie thought about every aspect of the project. He realized that he shouldn't be; she was the reason he was doing it. He loved working beside her, becoming distracted more than once then hitting his hand with the hammer.

"You'd better watch yourself, Bentley. You'll need those hands later to make furniture and pay for all of this."

"I'm gonna need my hands for something better than that later, if I have my way," he said, under his breath.

"What was that?"

"Don't you worry. I have this project covered. I've been planning it for a while," he lied. He had to go to the bank and take out a small construction loan against his house. He looked over at her as she bent down to pick up another board. *Yup. Still worth it.*

The next few weeks went pretty much the same way. Reggie was helping where she could, correcting the contractors when they wanted to stray from her plans, and having a few beers with Ben when the day was over. He worked late nights after she had gone. He still had his furniture to put out, but he didn't want to leave her alone with the wandering eyes of the contractors. He had, on more than one occasion, reprimanded a worker or two with a look that alone said it all.

Ben surprised her one Saturday night after everyone left. He brought her over to his back porch, leading her with her eyes covered by his hands. "Ta da," he said as he removed his hands.

"A porch swing!" She squealed as she sat down on it. It was made the same way, with the round pine logs, as all his other pieces. It was free-standing, not attached by chains to the roof like the one at the front of his house. "It's lovely, Ben. When in the world did you find time to do this?"

"It didn't take that long. When I can't sleep, I go out to the shop. I received an order for one so I made two." He sat down next to her. "You really like it?"

"I really do. You're really good. I should have you make me one when things slow down."

"This one *is* for you."

"No! Really?"

"Really." She threw her arms around his neck. He accepted the hug and held her tight. "It doesn't even come close to paying you for all the work you're doing for me, Reggie. I really appreciate it."

"It's no big deal, Ben." She released him from the hug and ran her fingers across the back of it.

"Yes, it is." He held her chin in his hands and kissed her.

35

Ben pulled up to Reggie's cabin on the four-wheeler at one o'clock on Sunday afternoon. As usual, she headed him off at the pass. She came out the front door and closed it behind her as he was coming up the stairs.

"You hiding an old lover in the basement or somethin'?"
"No," she said, crossing her arms." It's a mess."
"You've seen my place, Reg. I hardly care."
"Well, I do. What's up anyway?"
"It's a gorgeous day."
"You always think it's a gorgeous day."
"I was working on the barn this morning. I was hoping you'd show up."
"I picked up a book I started before we began working on the barn and I couldn't put it down." She lied. It scared her that she was getting attached to Ben. It was difficult for her to stop the kiss last night, but she did. She was grateful he let her leave when she claimed to be worn out from the long day.

Ben had taken everything she dished out, but he was still wonderful to her anyway. He deserved better. She wasn't over Van by a long shot and was far from ready to move on. It wasn't fair to Ben to continue to let him believe this was turning into something. It was especially hard on her that certain things he did reminded her of Van. It wasn't fair to Van's memory and it wouldn't be fair to Ben to be compared to him.

Needing to put a little distance between herself and Ben; she decided she couldn't go over there today. She should have known it wouldn't stick.

He reached for her hand and gave it a tug. "Let's go."

As he tried pulled her forward a few steps, she planted her feet firmly. "I don't want to go anywhere, Ben. Why do you always insist I need to go somewhere?"

He moved in close to her and leaned down, so he was eye to eye with her. "Because life is too short to waste a beautiful day." He walked to her door and picked up her sneakers that were outside. Except over the winters, she still had her Hawaii habit and kicked her shoes of at the door. He dropped them at her feet.

"I see you're giving me no a choice again," she protested as she pulled them on.

"Nope." A few seconds after he started up the four-wheeler, she joined him. Glancing down at her shoes, he said, "I hope that's not a good pair." He usually didn't blast away full throttle. This time though, Reggie had to grab a hold of his waist to stay on.

They rode a few miles in silence. He drove fast on the straight-aways, but it didn't bother her; in fact, she liked it. He maneuvered the trails in the forest like a pro. She felt safe with him even though she knew they should have been wearing helmets. They went so deep into the forest she thought she'd never find her way back if she found herself alone or needing help. Sounds of other ATVs could be heard off in the distance. When they reached the top of a hill, she could see at least a dozen machines below.

"Are they friends of yours?" she asked with a hint of fear. Suddenly she felt like they were the lone biker coming across a gang of Hell's Angels.

"I recognize most of the machines," he said before gunning it down the hill. Ben stopped at the bottom next to a camouflage green, very large machine that proudly advertised 'Arctic Cat', and killed his engine. "When are you going to get a real machine, Carlson?"

"Kiss my ass, Bentley. I'll take this bad boy over your Polaris any day." He smiled at Reggie. "You're far too good lookin' to be with this bum."

She blushed and dropped her head to his back.

"Brian, this is my neighbor, Reggie."

"Nice to meet you, Reggie," he said, taking off his glove and leaning over to shake her hand." You buy Doc's old place?"

She shyly nodded and answered with an "Uh-huh". It had been a long time since she had been around the friendly banter of men.

"I'm about ten miles as the crow flies." He pointed to the West. "When you get your own machine, don't let this weenie talk you into a Polaris. You come see me. I'll set you up right."

"He's an Arctic Cat dealer. What do you expect him to say?" Ben turned around to look at Reggie. Only now did she realize that her arms were still around him. She let go.

"You hittin' it or are you chicken?" Brian said to Ben, putting his glove back on.

"I know you didn't just call me that." Ben started his machine back up.

Reggie placed her arms around him again. "Chicken to what?" she asked as they drove away behind his friend.

"You trust me?" She put her head to his back again and sat still for a minute, then shook it 'yes'. "Hold on, don't be afraid, and I'm sorry. Here's why I asked about the shoes. You're gonna get muddy, Darlin."

The group gathered together again after a mile of winding trails and at least two miles on a dirt county road. Reggie had counted fifteen people in their "caravan". There were two other women behind men, but everyone else was on their own four-wheeler and there was one dirt bike. They stopped at a huge pit. Half of it was dirt and small hills; the other half of it was completely mud. Ben stopped at the top of the small incline and they watched the other riders.

Everyone rode full bore around the course, but were mindful of each other. It was dusty, but the day wasn't windy so it wasn't that bad. You could avoid many of the dust clouds with a little effort.

"We're going in there?" Reggie asked.

"Unless you really don't want to, Reg."

She reached her arms around him and held tight. "Go for it!" He placed his hand protectively over hers for a moment, then drove into the pit.

He took it easy on her at first, driving around the hills, but then surprised her when he began to climb one of the bigger ones. He didn't stop at all when he reached the top; he simply leaned back a little and rode back down. A small scream escaped her, but it was one of fun. From the hill, he ran full-throttle over to a huge mud puddle and ran right through the middle of it. For a few seconds, Reggie thought the engine was going to die. It began to slow down and spurt. She suddenly felt like they were floating on water rather than driving through it. After another second, she discovered that was the case. It wasn't a mud hole; it was a small pond. The front tires finally hit bottom, but they still weren't moving forward.

Ben slid off the machine. "Scoot forward." He had his hand still on the throttle. Reggie had never even noticed it was a small lever on the handlebar, not the whole handle like on a motorcycle. "Don't let up on the throttle. Water will be sucked in and kill the engine." She moved her hand to it and kept it held down. Ben ran to the back of the machine, taking him thigh-deep in the water and mud. He gave a few pushes before the tires finally gripped, allowing Reggie to drive forward. She could only go slowly, but they were soon out of the worst of it and Ben climbed on behind her. He put his hand on hers and gave it full throttle. She squealed as mud went flying and they drove out.

He let go of the throttle once they were completely out. She turned around, laughing. "You are insane, Mr. Bentley."

"I could have told you that." He reached up to her face to wipe away a spot of mud with this thumb, but then left his hand there for a minute. He held her gaze then cleared his throat and put his hand down. "You want to drive for a while?"

Her eyes had been glazed over at his stare; she finally snapped out of it as well. "You going to stay on with me?"

He gently brushed another chunk of mud from her other cheek. "I'm not letting you go." He held onto her face and slowly brought his lips to hers.

Time froze as Reggie's eyes closed. Her heart raced while they kissed. It was just a gentle peck, but she had gone weak. She had tried everything in her power to push Ben away. She didn't think she'd ever want anyone again. As hard as she tried to fight it, she really liked him, and as horrible as she had been to him, he seemed to really like her, too. They stared into each other's eyes then Ben went in for another kiss, parting her lips with his tongue. She returned the kiss and reached her hand behind his neck.

A horn blaring snapped them out of the kiss. Another ATV was coming out of the mud hole, right at them. Ben punched the throttle and moved them out of the way. When they were clear of the other rider he said, "All yours, Reggie. Have at her."

36

They spent the afternoon in and out of the mud, up and down the hills. Reggie couldn't believe how much fun she was having or how much abuse the machines could take. Ben drove over to the pair of couples and introduced her to everyone. They were all head to toe with mud. Reggie laughed at the sight of them before she realized she had to look the same way. They opened the front to one of the machines; she laughed when it revealed that it was a cooler full of beer. They offered her one and she accepted with a smile. Nothing sounded better. The second one went down just as good. She caught herself always looking Ben's way as he talked to his friends. When he turned to her each time and smiled, she smiled back then quickly turned her head away, back to the girls. *Am I flirting?*

One of the women brought over a cooler filled with sandwiches and chips. Ben and Reggie sat together as they ate.

"I feel bad not contributing anything to the meal," Reggie said. She was assured repeatedly not to fret about it.

"Cindy always bring too much," Ben said, trying to make her feel better. "Poor Eric will be taking what's left to work all week. We're doing him a favor."

After a couple more hours of riding and conversation, the sun was going down. It would be dark in about a half an hour.

They had at least that far to go to get back home. Ben walked over to where she was sitting with the girls. "We'd better get going if we're gonna get home by dark."

"Still haven't fixed that busted headlight?" Brian laughed. "Could have set you up with a deal if you'd gotten an Arctic."

"Give it a rest, you Arctic snob."

Reggie accepted Ben's hand and he helped her up. After exchanging pleasantries and goodbyes with everyone, they climbed on his four-wheeler and headed home. It became cold fast. Reggie shivered and held Ben tight for warmth. She was cold, but she was also glad for the excuse. She couldn't let things go further with him than the kiss that caught her off guard, but she enjoyed holding him. Breathing in deep, she had almost forgotten how good a man smells, even above mud, dirt, and gas fumes. Tucking her head closer to him, she shivered harder. He removed his hand from the handlebar and rubbed her arms. "Damn, you're really cold."

"I'm okay. I didn't expect to get so wet, but it was fun. I'll be fine."

He stopped the machine and climbed off with the motor running. "Hang on a sec." Walking around to the back, he opened up a small cubbyhole. She didn't know it even had one. "Ah ha," he said as he pulled out a gray sweatshirt with COLORADO across the chest in red letters. "It's in need of a washing, but you'll be warmer." She accepted it with a, "Thanks."

It was dark when they pulled up to his house. "Aren't you going to take me home?"

"I don't know if you realize how muddy you are. There's a shower right off my mudroom. I'd hate to have you tromp mud all through your house." She was still shivering. He rubbed her arms up and down trying to warm her up. "I've turned you into a Popsicle. You take a long hot shower; I'll hose off outside then start a fire. Okay?" She nodded in agreement. "I can find something for you to put on to run you home when you're cleaned up." He walked her into the house and pointed to the spare bathroom.

She undressed and piled her muddy clothes in an empty basket in front of the washer and dryer. This spare bathroom was also his laundry room. After climbing into the steaming hot water, she stood there for a few minutes trying to warm up. After several minutes and attempts with his body wash, she decided she had finally removed all the mud from her body. She shampooed her hair twice with his bottle of combination shampoo and conditioner. Now pruney, she finally exited the shower and dried her hair off as best as she could with a towel since she couldn't find a hair dryer in any of the drawers or cabinets. There was no robe or shirts so she wrapped the biggest towel she could find around herself and walked out into the living room.

Ben had been kneeling at the fireplace but stood at the sight of her. He rushed over and led her to the fire as if she needed assistance.

"I thought you drowned in there," he said with a chuckle. Again he ran his hands up and down her arms trying to warm her up. "Better?"

"Much." She knelt down on the soft furry rug in front of the fireplace, tucking her legs under herself. She ran her fingers through the long hair of the rug. "What is this?"

"I dunno. Alpaca I think. Got it in Mexico off some kid with big brown eyes, begging for a sale."

"Softie. I like it. It looks nice here in front of the fireplace."

"Yes, it does." Ben said, but she could tell by his gaze, he wasn't referring to the rug.

He had cleaned up as well and was in a pair of sweat shorts. "You cleaned up good for just using the hose."

"I hosed off then jumped in the other shower. I'll clean the wheeler tomorrow." He knelt down next to her. "Did you really have fun today?"

"I really did, Ben. I know I was a pain in the ass…thanks for making me go. I really liked your friends."

"They really liked you, too. They want you to come along next weekend."

"You do that all the time?"

"Every chance we can. It's great. You ought to get your own machine, but then…"

"But then what?"

"But then you wouldn't be holding on to me." He leaned in and kissed her. Reaching for her chin, he held her in a longer kiss. Her eyes closed and her heart raced. He stopped the kiss, leaned back and stared into her eyes. She surprised herself when she leaned forward and kissed him. He wrapped both arms around her and pulled her close. He kissed her again, using his tongue this time and she let out a small moan in her throat. They kissed fervently for several minutes before he stopped. He looked down and picked up the corner of towel that was tucked in above her breasts and pulled it out. When it dropped, she sat, unable to move.

"My God, you're perfect." He kissed down her neck. She reached for him, wrapping her arms under his and around his back. He lay her backwards and gently rested his body on hers. Again they kissed; again she lost herself in it. She didn't remember him removing his shorts, but he was suddenly on her and she adjusted herself to welcome him inside.

When he entered her, she let out a slight cry of pleasure that was muffled by the strong kiss. She held his back tight and pulled him closer. They moved as one on the soft rug in the glow of the fire. Reggie didn't think she'd ever experience this kind of loving again and melted at his gentle caresses and soft kisses to her breasts.

~*~

Ben slowly moved with her, wanting to take his time pleasing her. When he knew she was beginning to climax, it brought his. The two tightened their grips, pulling each other closer and had to part their lips that were in an intense kiss. They buried their heads deep into each other necks.

Several minutes passed before Ben could move again. He finally rolled to his side, still holding her tight. He kissed her forehead. "Damn, Reggie. I'd say that was worth the wait."

~*~

Reggie was quiet and stroked his back. She couldn't think about anything, but where she was and how she felt, or it was going to drive her insane. She fought her feelings for too long. She gave herself to Ben and dammit, it felt good. A gentle moan escaped her and she kissed his chest. "Yes. Yes it was."

After a few minutes, Ben stood up and helped her to her feet. They walked to the bedroom and made love again. This time, things moved slower as they spent more time exploring each other's bodies. He was also perfect in her eyes. Although she thought he was a little skinny when they first met, he was actually more than nicely built. His stomach was a "perfect six-pack", and his arms had more than enough muscle. She had seen them in action and had tried hard not to pay attention to them when he worked in a tank top on the barn, but she couldn't resist running her hands over them now.

"I'm a pig for not thinking of asking earlier, Reggie, but are you…you know…protected?"

"You're in the clear, Mr. Bentley," she said with a kiss.

"No chance of 'whoops'?"

"No." She rested her head on his shoulder and her arm draped over his chest. Holding him, she drifted off to sleep. She hadn't been so content falling asleep in almost a year.

~*~

As they lay there, Ben held her possessively. He finally had her where he wanted her, but he still felt like he had to protect her from someone. He hoped she was really here to stay and wouldn't be running back to someone else soon. Vowing silently to himself, he promised he would do what he had to do to keep her.

They had shifted positions through the course of the night. He woke up with her back to him, but he was still holding her tight. Not being able to refrain, he woke her with gentle kisses and again they made love. He drove her home with her dressed in a pair of his pajamas. They shared reluctant kisses goodbye as Ben cursed under his breath repeatedly about having to make another delivery today. "See you around six?" he asked with hopeful eyes.

"I'll come over."

"I'll bring something home to eat. Unless you want to go out."

"No. I'd like to stay in. I can cook something, Ben."

He pulled her close. "I don't want to waste any unnecessary time."

She giggled and shoved him away. "Go already so you can hurry up and get back."

He gave her one last kiss and drove away.

~*~

Reggie stood at the front door watching until she could no longer see him. When he was out of sight, she ran in the house and snatched the phone out of its cradle. She didn't care about the time zone difference. A very groggy friend answered her phone with a grunt.

"Bri. I met someone."

37

Ben and Reggie spent their days and nights together over the next six weeks. They were always at Ben's; she slept over almost every night. She still hadn't invited him into her house and he never pushed the issue or even brought it up. Derf usually shared the bed with them as well. She brought him over more often than not. She didn't want him to be alone so much. Ben's home became his second home.

When the crew working on the barn would go home, Reggie joined him while he made his furniture. One of the first futons Ben had made was out in the shop. It received a healthy workout several nights when they couldn't make it to the house.

The barn was finally completed and they roamed around inside admiring the work. Ben had ordered a round bail of straw to complete the look. After breaking it apart and having a straw fight, they made love in the barn to break it in properly.

They lay in each other's arms almost purring with contentment. Ben leaned down and gave her a kiss and a tight squeeze. "Let's go dancing."

"Dancing?"

"There's a little bar right outta town. There's a DJ tonight. Come on, it'll be fun. We haven't done anything for ourselves since we started this project."

"I don't want to go dancing, Ben. Besides," she said with a giggle, "we have so treated ourselves and you wore me out."

"Baloney. Let's go." He stood up.

She sat up and let out a sigh. "You really gonna make me do this?"

"Yup. We'll swing by your place and you can get some dancing shoes on." He pulled up his jeans and reached his hand down for hers.

She frowned. "I don't suppose sneakers will do."

"I'll wait in the car," he said, thinking her apprehension was that he would want to go in the house.

Reggie finally gave in.

She ran in to her house and to his surprise, was back out in less than ten minutes. She still had jeans on but added a modest black v-neck top and heels to match. He smiled. "You clean up nice."

"You're really going to make me do this?"

"Yup."

After about twenty minutes, they arrived at the bar. It had the appearance of a nice quiet place that should have country music playing from a jukebox, but when they walked in, there was a current dance hit playing. Ben walked up to the bar and ordered a couple of beers while Reggie watched people dance on the crowded floor. There was a DJ in the corner and a disco ball overhead with colored lights flashing to the drumbeats of the music. They found an empty high table and a couple of barstools and sat down.

They had to talk loud to hear each other over the music as they scrutinized some of the moves of the people dancing. Metallica's 'Enter Sandman' came on and almost everyone left the floor. "You wanna dance?" Ben asked.

"To this? No. The DJ isn't working the crowd very well. He cleared the floor. This isn't very danceable at all."

"Some people are liking it." He pointed to a few goth-looking couples who were doing a horrible head-banging imitation to the beat.

She scoffed and took another drink. When that song was over, they hear a few notes and "It's Electric". Ben's eyes lit up. "I know you know this one, Reggie. Don't even try to tell me you don't."

He pulled her off the chair. "I don't want to, Ben."

Leaning down, he stared hard into her eyes. "Tough shit."

They walked onto the dance floor. Halfheartedly, she got in step with the crowd and followed along with the line dance *Electric Slide*. After a few times of doing the same moves she began to kick just a little higher, add a little more bounce to her step, and added a spin where others only stepped. Ben grinned and mimicked her moves. Reggie smiled and stepped it up another notch.

He went from beside her to the front and began to do the steps facing her. "Let's see it. Do the other version with me, Sweetheart." She kicked her moves up yet another notch. They moved together facing each other and occasionally she leaned into him and he spun her back out. It was a routine he knew; apparently she knew the same one.

~*~

Reggie didn't stop to think about it; she moved with the music and loved every minute of it. She particularly enjoyed watching Ben. He was a wonderful dancer.

When the song neared the end, he stepped back and put his arms out to her. She took the move for what it was and ran into his arms. Raising her over his head, he spun her around in a perfect lift that she had only trusted a few other men enough to do. He brought her slowly down and kissed her when their faces met. Continuing the routine, he lowered her until her feet hit the floor and he finished with a dip and another kiss. Their kiss was interrupted by the applause of the crowd. They hadn't realized people had stopped dancing to watch them. Reggie suddenly became embarrassed. Ben pulled her close in a hug. "Damn, Girl."

She wanted to leave the dance floor, but he held her there. The DJ read the cue from the crowd and played Prince's *Erotic City*. Reggie shook her head 'no' but Ben said, "Oh yes." She began to dance with him, but she insisted they scale down the sexy moves a little and was glad to see other couples joining them on the floor, not just watching. They grinded to the music in perfect sync with each other and took turns taking a few steps back and doing a little something special of their own. When the song was over Ben led her back towards the table. Bobby Brown's *Every Little Step I Take* played and Reggie stopped Ben in his tracks.

"You're not going to make me dance to Bobby, are you?"

"You bet your sweet ass I am," she said as she went back out and started a quick stepping of her feet. He joined her and within a minute, began to mimic her moves. They danced as if they had worked months on a choreographed routine. The DJ tapped Ben on the shoulder and motioned if it was okay if he danced with Reggie. Ben looked at her for permission. She was hesitant for only a moment, but she accepted. The DJ went into what Reggie knew as street moves and she accompanied along well.

~*~

Ben didn't mind standing aside and watching at all.

"Quite a gal you have there, Bentley," someone said from behind. He spun around to find a friend from the lumberyard in town.

"Hey, Hink," Ben said, turning around and shaking his hand. He returned his attention to Reggie.

"Where did you find that?"

He chuckled. "Next door."

"No shit?"

"She'd whip your ass breaking down a set of blueprints, too."

"You're shittin' me."

"I shit you not."

"Well, I'll give you a holler when we're looking to hire. Hell, for that pretty thing working in my office, I'd 'off' McQueen myself."

The song was coming to an end and the DJ had to run back up. Ben wanted to get back out on the floor. "Eat your heart out, Hink."

The DJ was gracious enough to play a slow song. Ben and Reggie were grateful; they didn't want to do anymore fancy stepping. They rocked in each other's arms swaying to Barry White's *Can't Get Enough of Your Love, Babe*. Halfway through, Ben insisted on a little jitterbugging and Reggie couldn't resist. It was mellow compared to what they had done so far, even though they still had a few extra turns and of course, a big dip finale.

They finally sat back down at the table, breathing a little heavy.

"I'd forgotten what a workout that can be," she said, after a sip of beer.

"I have a better idea for a workout." He leaned in and gave her a long kiss. "I've had enough dancing for one night."

"Let's go."

38

Reggie didn't think she'd ever have fun dancing again, let alone enjoy it so much with Ben. He was a heck of a partner. She would have enjoyed dancing longer if she didn't want him so incredibly bad and if the place wasn't so packed. Watching his moves had her wanting to take him right there on the dance floor. She could barely wait until they were back at his place to make love again. They continually pawed each other on the drive home.

"It's moments like this that make me feel glad to be alive," Ben said as he gently stroked her cheek with the back of his index finger. They had just finished making love by the fireplace.

"Why is that?" she asked as she turned to him and kissed his finger.

"A few years ago, I could have died."

"What?" She leaned to her side and propped her head up on her hand with her elbow nestled in the soft rug. "Were you in an accident or something?" She stroked his bare chest with her free hand. She leaned in and gave it a kiss. "No scars."

He gave her forehead a kiss. "Nope, no scars. I got away without a scratch, actually."

"Then what?"

"I had a part-time job on a boat a few years ago."

"Doing what?"

"Just fishing. No big deal. I wanted to get out of town for a bit for no particular reason. We went to Florida one summer to try to land some big game. You know, Marlin, Dolphin."

"Dolphin? You caught Dolphins?"

He laughed. "Not that kind of Dolphin-Dolphin. You know, Dolphin. It's called Mahi Mahi in Hawaii."

"Okay, you're off the hook there. I do remember seeing that in Florida." She had never mentioned Hawaii. Why did he know the reference? *It's just the name of the fish, Reg. Chill.*

"You lived in Florida?"

"For a bit."

He touched the tip of her nose. "There's so much we need to learn about each other. Anyway," he continued, "the boat started to take on water and we were sinking. We had to put out an emergency call to the Coast Guard. It had gotten bad fast."

"Really? She gave full attention to his tale. "Did you have to bail out into a life boat?"

"We weren't going to do that right away. We had to try to at least save the boat first." He stood up to add some drama to the story with actions since he had such a captive audience. He didn't even bother to slow down and put on his boxers. "We had a huge old bastard of a water pump. Sucker had to weigh three hundred pounds." He held his arms out wide to demonstrate.

She sat up.

"I was below deck sucking up water, but it was coming in too fast. I didn't even know when the Coast Guard had boarded us, but suddenly everyone was hollering at me to get out."

She stood up and dressed in a frenzy. He continued with his tale.

"I made my way over to the hatch and looked up. The pump was kind of hangin' there. I was ready to kiss my ass goodbye thinking it was falling on me but…what're you doing?"

"I have to go." Reggie ran for the door.

"Wait a second," he said as caught up to her and stood between her and the door. "What's the matter?"

"I gotta go!" she shouted, shaking free of his hold.

"Why? I'm sorry if I got carried away. I just—"

"Now!" she hollered as she opened the door and ran out. She held her sobs midway to her house then fell on her knees on the path and screamed a horrible cry. Dropping flat to the ground, she wrapped her arms around her legs and cried until a coyote's howl scared her several moments later. Once in her house, she hurried through packing a bag, and left.

~*~

Ben lay awake, worried about what had happened. He longed to go to her but thought she needed some time. Why was she so freaked out about his accident? Did she know someone who had died on a boat? That was too much of coincidence. He decided to go over first thing in the morning.

He was knocking on her door at six a.m. He wanted to go over earlier, but it was as early as he dared to show up. Normally she wasn't up early and he knew that, but she was probably still upset and he was sure she tossed and turned all night like he had. He knocked gently at first. "Reggie? You up yet?" Then it became a louder banging. "Come on. Open up. I know you're in there. We need to talk." He was surprised when he checked the door and it was unlocked. After calling out her name a few times, he grew worried when nothing but silence answered him. "Reg?"

He walked into the living room and stood there, still expecting to see her take the corner at any second and didn't want to scare her. "Reg?" He took a few steps in and looked around. She always claimed she didn't want him to come in because the place was a disaster, but it was immaculate. Not a thing was out of place. She had a few tasteful country knick-knacks, not a mess of useless collections of tacky cutesy items; no doilies, no frills, just clean and homey.

Some photos of her were on the fireplace. He walked over to get a better look at them. Reaching for a large one of her smiling in someone's arms, he picked it up to examine it better. He loved the look of her smile. In his opinion, she didn't do it enough. He gently stroked the glass of the frame, wishing it really was her he was touching. Where was she anyway? His eyes finally went to the man whose arms she was in. "Holy Shit!" He dropped the frame. The glass shattered.

Ben ran out to the garage and discovered her car was gone. "Shit! Oh, shit!" He nervously ran his hands through his hair before running back to the house. After opening the door, he paused mid-stride, realizing he knew so little about her. Who could he call or where would she go? He sat on her couch and stayed there for a long time with his head in his hands, never before feeling so useless.

The kitten came over and rubbed up against his leg. Ben smiled and picked him up. "Hey, Derf. Where'd your mom go, Little Guy?" The cat purred as Ben gave it a quick pat before putting him down. It ran away in the direction of the kitchen so Ben followed him. Derf walked over to a feeder that easily held two weeks or more of food. Next to it was a water bowl that held a smaller version of a blue bottle that looked like ones for a water cooler. It was easily a gallon. Although he didn't think she'd leave the kitten alone, she wouldn't have to come back anytime soon to feed it. *Dammit.*

Finding a dustpan and broom in the closet, he swept up the glass. Carefully removing the pieces left in the frame, he was glad to see he hadn't scratched the picture. He stared at it for a while longer, struggling to understand why she would still have this man's picture up if they were no longer together. After all the time they spent together, he had considered them a couple and he was feeling more than a little wounded. Maybe the man left her for another woman, but she was still hung up on him? That would explain why she was so cold to him early on. She had probably been pining away, hoping he'd come for her, even if he had abused her. That was probably it. Maybe when she realized who Ben was last night, she was now worried that hero and the one rescued had become friends and kept in touch. She was worried he'd find out she had been promiscuous in their separation and wouldn't come back. No, that hardly made sense either.

He wandered over to a bookcase and pulled out a photo album. His anger seethed as he flipped through the pictures. "Don't they make a cute couple," he said under his breath as he looked at the many pictures of them cheek to cheek, taken with one of them holding the camera. There were a lot of pictures with them and a bi-racial couple; they looked like they were taken in Hawaii. There were a few of the man in the picture in his uniform, holding up an award. *Probably the one for saving my life*, he thought to himself and sighed. Ben remembered now that he had gotten the man's name after he had climbed out of the hatch that day. Ben had reached down, offering the man his hand. He had been lying flat on his back on the deck of the boat, catching his breath.

"Holy crap, I can't believe you held that thing by yourself," Ben had said. "What are you? Part ox?"

He helped Van to his feet and the two men shook hands. "Petty Officer Kimball at your service and I'm just doin' my job. Now let's get the hell off this boat before she sinks."

Kimball. How didn't he catch it...but why *would* his mind go there?

As he flipped through the pages, two pieces of paper fell out.

The first one he opened was a marriage certificate. "Oh, perfect. He wants a divorce and she's fighting it." He opened up the next one and uttered yet another, "Oh, shit." It was a death certificate. Lying on her couch, holding the album to his chest, he wondered what cruel act of fate brought him and Reggie together. He didn't really view it as cruel; he really liked her. In fact, he was falling in love with her. He couldn't let her go. What was the big deal? Her husband had saved his life and he's gone now. Why should that matter?

He fell asleep on the couch clinging to the album, exhausted from not sleeping the night before and straining his brain thinking about where she could have gone.

39

Reggie's phone rang and Ben jumped to his feet, suddenly awake. He had no idea how long he had been asleep. Looking around the room, desperately hoping to see Reggie, he called out again. She was still nowhere to be found. He ran over and answered the phone. "Reggie?"

"Who's this?" a female voice asked.

"Uh, her neighbor. Who's this?"

"Her friend, Sabrina. Is she around?"

"Actually, no."

"Where is she?"

"I don't exactly know."

"Pardon? Then what are you doing in her house? Wait a second. Are you Ben?"

"She tell you about me?"

"Um, yeah."

He could sense a smile in her voice. "How much?"

"We've been best friends forever."

"What'd she say?"

"I'm not at liberty to share. Do you know when she's coming back?"

"Do you have a minute?"

"I'm all ears, Babe."

Sabrina was silent as he explained what happened. When he was done he asked, "Are you still there?"

She finally answered. "Holy shit. You have to be shitting me! That was you? How in the hell was that you?"

"Look…I don't know. I don't have the answers to why things happened the way they did. But they did and here we are. We have to find her. Do you know where she'd go?"

"That's easy. She'll come here."

"Where's here?"

"Maui No Ka Oi, Babe. Maui No Ka Oi."

"Hawaii?"

After exchanging phone numbers with Sabrina, he rode back to his house. He found the flag up on his mailbox up and a letter inside.

Ben,
I have to go away for a while. Please look after Derf for me. Bring him here if you can, I don't want him to get lonely.
   Thanks,
   R

He crumpled up the note with a muffled, "Dammit!" Maybe she was going to Maui after all. He didn't know what to do while he waited for the call from her friend.

Ben did the only thing he could manage that didn't require any brain activity: Fishing. He was actually happy to not have caught anything. After he put all the fishing gear away, he called Sabrina. A man answered, surprising him. When Ben explained who he was, Troy introduced himself.

"Sorry, Buddy. We haven't heard a peep from her yet. Bri is worried sick. She's lying down."

"Seems I bring disaster everywhere I turn, huh?"

"Van was my best friend for as long as I knew him. Don't ask me to come to your pity party."

"I'm sorry."

"He did what he did and it's done. It wasn't just his job, it's who he was. Uniform or not, he'd do it again in a heartbeat."

"How'd he die? Was it another rescue?"

"Nope. Yours."

"Mine? How so? That was five years ago. The death certificate said he died about a year ago."

"He died in a surgery. We thought the VA docs didn't know what the hell they were doing, but there is no evidence to show neglect or malpractice. I did a lot of investigating and I hate to say it, but where the medical profession is concerned, shit does just happen. It was one surgery too many or maybe too many pain pills...his system never recovered."

Ben cursed under his breath.

"It's a part of the job. He knew what he was doing."

"He knew he was going to die saving a loser like me?"

"If you charmed that hell cat, you can't be all that bad."

"I gather she hasn't taken to many men."

"Including you? Two." Troy paused. "You coming or what?"

"We don't even know that she's going there."

"She'll be here. I'll get you a place to stay and I'll pick you up. The rest is up to you."

"I really do love her, you know."

"Heaven help you." Troy chuckled. "Holler when you have your flight info."

At seven o'clock the next night, Ben's flight landed. Troy was there to greet him at baggage claim. "Ben?" he asked as he extended his hand to him.

"Yup. The 'I'm lost' look give it away?"

"Nope. It was your dreamy eyes."

The men laughed. "She here?"

"Got here around six this morning."

Ben removed his bag from the luggage carousel. "She say anything?"

"She's not talking much at all. She doesn't know I've come to get you. I know it's gonna bite me in the ass later."

"Can I ask you something?" Ben asked as they walked towards the parking lot.

"Fire away."

"Why are you helping me? Her old man was your best friend."

"Yes, he was, but he's gone. All I have left of him is Reggie. The only person I love more on this planet than that girl is my wife." Troy stopped walking. "Reggie shut down when she lost him. I was afraid we were going to lose her, too. You were the first sign of life we've seen in her in ages. I don't want to see her slip away again." He opened up his truck door. "Fix it."

After Troy paid the parking fee and they were on their way, small talk replaced the seriousness of the situation. "This sure is one heck of a home you have here," Ben said.

"Can't beat it. The cost of living is a bitch, though. If I hadn't bought when I did, I've never be able to move here now and buy so much as a bare piece of property, let alone beach front."

"That bad?"

"You'll see. My humble hollow-tile home was just appraised at a million-two."

"No shit? How many acres?"

Troy chucked. "Acres? I'd say less than a quarter of one."

"What?"

"You pay for paradise, my friend."

After a not so unpleasant silence, Ben asked, "What if I can't?"

"Can't what?"

"Snap her out of it."

"Then I'll have to kill you and hide your body with the others."

"I'm serious."

Troy lowered his sunglasses. "So am I." When he faced the road again, he grinned. "You'll get her to come around."

"I don't know." Ben ran his fingers through his hair. "Hell of a coincidence, don'tcha think?"

"What? That she fell in love with the man who ultimately lead to her husband's death?"

"That's a nice way of putting it."

"It is what it is." Troy shrugged noncommittally. "If it wasn't you, it would have been somebody else."

"But it wasn't somebody else. It was me and I love her. I love the wife of the guy who saved my life and died because of it. How can she return the love of the man that killed the love of her life?"

"Look, Ben. Don't get me wrong. I loved the guy, but he had this 'hero' thing about him."

"Hero thing?"

"He was like the firefighter that you knew would die rushing in a burning building to get that one last person as everyone else screamed, 'No, don't go!'" He let out a loud breath. "If I felt otherwise…would I be here with you right now?"

"Thanks," Ben said as their eyes met.

"You can thank me by taking that fireball back with you. Sabrina is four months pregnant and going to be a bear about not being able to go out drinking with Reg."

"She knows you're getting me, right?"

"Yeah. She's on your side, too. I couldn't lie to her if I wanted to." He made a left turn at a sign that read 'Maalaea'. "This is us."

"How do you learn to pronounce the names of the towns?"

"It'll come to you. Just don't say anything you're not sure of and FYI, Mahalo means 'Thank you' not 'trash'."

"Huh?"

"They have it on all the trash cans. I've stopped more fights between the locals and the squids with that."

"Squids?"

"Navy boys. They're in Lahaina often when there's a ship in town. Not a place you want to be unless you're lookin' for a fight."

"I'll keep that in mind."

40

Sabrina greeted them in the driveway when they pulled up. If Troy didn't tell him she was pregnant, he never would have known. "Aloha," she said as she gave him a tight hug and placed an orchid lei around his neck.

He said thanks and gave it a sniff. "There's no smell."

"Pikake is my favorite, but I didn't want to overwhelm you." She looped her arm around his. "Come inside. She's at the beach watching the sunset. I said I'd be along in a minute. We can wait for her though."

"I'd like to go to her now."

"I kind of thought you would." She walked him through the house and pointed to a room where he could put his bag.

"I'm staying here?"

"I wouldn't have it any other way. No worries. If she flips out, tough. She has her own room."

After Ben put his bag on the bed, Sabrina walked him to the sliding glass door and opened it up. She pointed down towards the boat harbor. "She's probably sitting out on the break."

"Thanks." He gave her a kiss on the cheek then ran towards the harbor.

Troy joined his wife at the door. "Think he can pull it off?"

"I hope so. If I have to cry with her one more time, this kid will be getting a Long Island iced tea very soon."

"Gorgeous spot you have here."

Reggie's head whipped around at the sound of Ben's voice. She returned her gaze to the spot where the sun had set only moments ago. Shades of purple, red, and orange painted the sky in its aftermath.

"Why'd you come here, Ben?"

"I think that's pretty obvious." He sat next to her.

"Who's watching Derf?"

"My sister is making sure he gets plenty of attention." He reached for her hand. "Damn, you make me fight for this. I love you, Reggie."

"I can't see you anymore."

"Like hell you can't. I can't let you just throw away what we have."

"Yes, you can." She wiped a tear from her cheek. "You don't know anything about this. You have to listen to me and leave. Please. Just leave."

"I don't know what? That I'm the reason your husband is dead?" Her head turned again to face him. He removed her sunglasses and stared into her eyes. "I know everything, Reggie."

"Since when?"

"Not until yesterday, in case you're thinking this craziness was some kind of hidden agenda on my behalf. I went to your place looking for you. I recognized him from the picture above the fireplace. A guy doesn't forget the face of someone that does something like that for him, you know. At least I understand why you never let me come in. Must have been something good if, after what we had, you can't even put his pictures away."

"Then you understand why I can't be with you."

"No, I don't. This doesn't have anything to do with us."

"It has everything to do with us." Reggie stood. "If he wasn't gone, there would be no us. If there was no you, there would still be a him!" She bit her lip and looked away from him.

Slowly he came to his feet and placed his hands on her shoulders. "I can't change what is done. I especially can't change how I feel about you. I don't know why fate has things so twisted up for us, but you can't fight it, Reg. It's too much coincidence to ignore. We must be meant to be together. You can't mourn him forever."

She broke free of his hold with another tear rolling down her cheek. She defiantly brushed it away. "Watch me." Reggie turned her back to him and headed towards the house.

~*~

"I figured you'd find your way here," Troy said as he sat next to Ben at the bar off the harbor, Buzz's Warf. "Didn't go well?"

"The understatement of the year."

"Well, you should be me right now." Troy sighed.

"How so?"

"She flipped when she found your bag in the spare room."

Ben spun in his chair. "She take off?"

"No. Bri wouldn't let her, but I think I'll wait a while before I go back."

~*~

The two men stumbled in shortly after midnight. Troy said goodnight and tiptoed down the hall to his bedroom. He was glad everyone was asleep.

"You have a new best friend now, Troy?" Reggie asked with her arms crossed. He could finally see her standing in front of her bedroom with the door wide open.

"No, Reg, but he really is a great guy."

"Some friend you are."

"Look, this has to stop. I miss Van, too, Reg, but he's gone. I've moved on and so should you."

She stepped closer to him and stood on her tippy toes, wanting to be more face to face. "Don't you dare tell me what to do!"

"I'm not telling you what to do, but I am saying you need to move on. Ben's a nice guy and he loves you. Van's dead, Reg, and he ain't comin' back."

She slapped his face.

Troy didn't flinch from the blow. "Hit me again."

"What?" she hissed. Reggie had been glaring at him, fire in her eyes. Her fists were clenched at her sides as the anger caused her to quake

"Hit me again. If that's what it takes to make you feel better, then by all means, hit me again."

Reggie's features softened. She fell into his chest and he wrapped his arms around her. "I'm so sorry." She cried softly into his chest as he rocked her.

"Let's get you to bed." He danced in small steps into her room while still holding her tight. By the time they reached the bed, he had her softly giggling.

She climbed in bed and he pulled the sheet up to her chin. "You want me to close the window?"

"No, the breeze feels good."

"Good night then, Princess." He leaned down and gave her a kiss on the forehead; she grasped his hand as he tried to leave.

"I'm really sorry I hit you, Troy."

"I could take you." He sat down on the bed and brushed a strand of hair from her face, tucking it behind her ear.

"I love you, you know."

"Yes, I know. It's my burden."

"You really like him?"

"I do, Reg. Drives me crazy though."

"How so?"

"Don't take this wrong or go freaky on me again, but he has a few of Van's quirks and it kind of trips me out."

"The hair thing?"

Troy laughed. "That's one of them." He reached for her hand. "Reg?"

"Hmmm?"

"You know Van would have never wanted to live out his years in a wheelchair."

"I know."

"It's not Ben's fault that he's the one that lived."

"I know."

"Knowing the outcome, Van would do it again in a heartbeat."

"Even if it meant leaving me?" Tears filled her eyes.

"You know he worshiped the quicksand you walked on, but yes, Princess, I'm sorry. He was a hero first and a husband second." Troy leaned down and held her tight. "Let him go, Reg."

~*~

Despite all the beer the previous night, Ben was up early. The sight of the ocean was far too inviting. He walked across the street to go for a swim. When he came back, Troy was in the kitchen making coffee. "How was the water?" he asked when Ben walked in.

"Felt great but your damn beach is loaded with these," he said as he held up a Kiawe branch. "Pulled it outta my foot. I'll be wearing sneakers next time."

Troy shot a glance down the hall, snatched the branch from Ben's hand and swiftly buried it in the trash. "Don't say anything to Reggie about that."

"She has a thing for thorns?" He stood dumbfounded and confused.

"Their first meeting was here. She got a mother of one in her foot and…what?" He paused at the expression on Ben's face.

"You have to be shittin' me."

"What?"

"She stepped on one when we were out four-wheeling at my place."

"She lose it?"

"I'd say. Bawled like a baby for almost half an…wait a second. Shit." He slumped down on the stool at the counter. "Those tears weren't for the thorn; she was remembering when it happened here." He put his head in his hands. "I can't do this, Buddy."

"Yes, you can."

"No, I can't. I'm competing with a goddamn ghost."

"She'll snap out of it."

Ben signed heavily. "They both still sleeping?"

"Reggie is. Sabrina is busy puking."

"Got morning sickness bad?"

"Just started. I've never seen anyone so happy to throw up before."

"You been trying for a while?"

"And enjoying every minute of it." Troy smiled as he held up his coffee as if in a toast. "You ready for a cup? Kona macadamia nut."

"Hit me."

41

Ben was on his second cup when Reggie came into the kitchen. Her hair was a mess and she didn't have a stitch of makeup on, yet she was still the most beautiful thing he had ever seen. She stopped in her tracks as if she had forgotten that he was there then claimed a stool, keeping an empty one between them.

"Good morning," Ben dared.

"Good morning. Did you save me any coffee?" she asked Troy.

"Of course." He reached for a cup.

"Should I go check on Bri?"

"She's fine. She'll be out in a minute."

"Want me to start breakfast?"

"I'm taking care of it." He pulled out the electric pan to get bacon going. "I have to do this outside. The smell of bacon cooking makes Bri want to yak."

"Since when?"

"Last week."

After he walked outside, Ben turned to Reggie. "How'd you sleep?"

"I always sleep like a rock when I'm home."

"You never said Hawaii was home."

"Well, add that to the list of things you don't know about me."

He slid off the stool and stepped towards the screen door.

"Ben!"

"What, Reg?" He stood in front of her. Too close. He could smell her body-wash and it was driving him crazy.

"I'm sorry. I don't mean to be so mean. I just don't know why you're here."

"I told you why."

"But here? How did you manage to swindle yourself into the lives of the two people I love most in the world, in less than twenty-four hours?"

He brought his head close to hers, dropping it close to her shoulder, but didn't rest it there. He wanted to kiss her so bad it was killing him. After running his face up the length of her neck, he stopped at her ear and whispered, "Maybe you're the one we all love most, too," before leaning back and staring into her eyes.

"Good morning," Sabrina said when entered the kitchen. "Anyone else vomit their body weight this morning?" Her eyes went back and forth between the two of them. "Am I interrupting something?"

"Not at all. Good morning, Beautiful." Ben kissed her on the cheek. "You are positively glowing this morning anyway, if I do say so myself. I think I'll go play supervisor for breakfast." He walked outside.

~*~

The two girls shared a stare. They were both thinking the same thing. Van had always called Sabrina 'Beautiful'.

"Well, you are. That doesn't mean anything." Reggie spun around and sipped her coffee.

They ate outside. Troy and Sabrina tried to keep the conversation going, but it was hard to do with two pouty stiffs.

"How about we hit Front Street today?" Troy suggested.

"What's Front Street?" Ben asked.

"The main road in Lahaina. It's about a half hour from here. A lot of art galleries and shops with tourist crap, but a cool town. It used to be the state capital and an old whaling town."

"Hey, isn't that where you said I should avoid?"

"No Navy ships in town. You're in luck."

"I'll pass." Reggie stood and picked up a few plates.

"Like hell," Troy barked at her.

"Excuse me?"

"I think a glass bottom boat tour is called for and you're going to schmooze Keoni for us."

She spun around in a huff and walked the plates to the kitchen.

~*~

"Who or what is a Keoni?" Ben asked Troy in a whisper.

"An old friend of hers. He owns a string of glass bottom boats. He's not so fond of me. We've had to board him a few times late at night."

"Why?"

"He's not licensed for 'booze cruises' and every now and then we need to remind him."

"I guess you're not the most popular fellow with the commercial boaters."

"You catch on fast."

Reggie came back for more dishes and glared at Troy as she picked up the fruit bowl.

"It's a no-brainer there, ugly." Ben laughed. Reggie dropped the glass bowl of fruit upon hearing that. It shattered.

"Oh, shit." She scrambled to pick up the pieces of papaya, mango, and other locally-grown fruits then screamed as she cut her finger on a piece of glass.

"Regina!" Sabrina rushed over when she saw the blood freely gushing.

Ben grabbed a cloth napkin and reached for her hand. He held the napkin on the cut and applied pressure to it. Troy reached for his coffee and shook his head.

Reggie froze for a second then swayed forward.

"Reg?"

"It's your turn to catch her, Ben." Troy took another sip.

Reggie looked to Troy, but her eyes were beginning to glaze over.

"What's happening?" Ben brought his free hand quickly to her back.

"She doesn't do the sight of blood well," Sabrina answered.

"Even hers?"

"Especially hers."

Ben didn't wait for her to faint; he scooped her up and walked to the house with Sabrina close at his heels. Troy picked up the pieces of glass, still shaking his head.

"Reggie?" Ben settled her on the couch. He lifted up the napkin to look at the cut, then applied more pressure.

"Hmmm," was all Reggie replied.

"Is she really okay?" Ben asked Sabrina.

"She'll be all right. It just takes a minute to pass."

"Good Lord. All this over some blood? How does she take that time…" Ben stopped talking. "Uh… never mind. That's somewhere I really don't need to go.".

Sabrina tugged at his shirt and motioned for him to step back outside. "She'll be fine. Come here."

Once they were outside, Sabrina explained. "She doesn't."

"Doesn't what?"

"She doesn't have that time of the month. She can't have kids." He could tell Sabrina suddenly felt guilty for saying anything. "I'm sorry. It's really not my place to say."

"That's okay. I guess that's a conversation we haven't had yet. We sort of did. I assumed she was on the pill. Why doesn't she?"

"It was an accident, years ago. Broke her insides up pretty bad. It's part of the reason she's always had such an attitude towards men. She feels she has nothing to offer and they are better off without her, so she puts this wall up. You know?" She looked to him for understanding. "I only just told her I was pregnant. I was calling that day to tell her when you answered her phone. I honestly didn't know how she would take the news."

"That's crazy. There's so much more to her than giving someone a kid."

"I know that and you know that, but try to tell her that."

"But she married Van."

"And he fought hard for that, believe me."

"You said that's part of the reason she pushes men away so bad. What's the other part?"

"That is definitely not my place to say."

"You can't leave me hanging, Sabrina."

"Look, you two seem to have gotten past that. Don't go digging anything up. Things are hard enough right now anyway. Just deal with what's at hand, okay?"

He nodded. "I should go back in and check on her."

She held him by the sleeve. "Don't let her know I told you or she'll kill me. Let her do it on her own time."

"I promise."

"On second thought, let me go in and check on her. She'll be pissed that you saw her almost faint, too."

"Is there anything I can do that won't piss her off?"

"Sorry. Nothing comes to mind."

Ben went to help Troy clean up the broken glass. "So how do you get away with it?"

"Get away with what?"

"Talking to her like that. Tellin' her what to do."

"Easy. I don't want in her pants."

"Come again?"

"I'm no threat to her. We're just friends. I take her shit and she takes mine."

"But you got her to listen to you."

"We're not out the door yet, my friend."

"You going to tell me what it is?"

"What what is?"

"Whatever it is Sabrina won't tell me about why she's such a ball-buster."

Troy threw the glass into the garbage can. "Nope. It's not my place either." When Ben let out a heavy sigh, Troy continued. "You have bigger problems anyway."

"How so?"

"Bite off one thing at a time, would you? Don't worry about her past. I mean her past that goes far beyond Van. Worry about right now." Troy sat back down. "What does she see when she looks at you?"

"Someone who is alive because her husband is dead."

"Bingo, and she feels guilty."

"I'm the one that feels guilty. How do you figure she feels guilty?"

"Because she loves you."

"She can't stand the sight of me."

"Are you new at this?" Troy laughed. "I know Reggie. You guys had something going before you found this small detail out. You'll get through it."

"Killing her husband is hardly a small detail."

"If you're going to wallow in that yourself, there's no way you're going to pull her out of it." Ben and Troy locked eyes. "Pull your head out of your ass. I can't do it for you, friend."

"You guys ready to go?" Sabrina hollered from the house.

"Be right there." Troy turned back to Ben. "Come on, Romeo. It's sightseeing time."

42

They loaded up in Sabrina's quad-cab Toyota Tacoma. Ben had noticed immediately that the island's population was truck happy. Hers wasn't too decked out as far as off-roading went, but she did have oversized tires on it and a little bit of an added lift. Troy helped his wife in then made a comment about how she'll have problems climbing into it in her later months as she slid over the bench seat in back.

"Gonna have to get you a car, Baby."

"Don't bet your white crackery ass on it." She leaned forward, wrapping her arms around his neck and giving his cheek a kiss. "You get the car, Babe." She sat back down behind Ben.

Ben couldn't hold back his laugh. He could see why Reggie loved them the way she did. They were great together.

Reggie opened up her purse and pulled out a small bottle. She downed it before they even pulled out of the garage.

Sabrina realized what it was and grabbed it from her hand. "An airplane bottle of tequila?"

"The cart was unattended on the plane."

"You're not drinking in the car while I'm driving, Reggie. Whiskey Tango Foxtrot?" Troy said, angrily. Ben looked over at Troy. "Sorry. Military talk. WTF? What the—"

"Got it."

"I'm done, Dad. It was just redneck first aid for my cut," she said, holding up her finger and looking at Ben.

Troy didn't say anything. Sabrina offered him the empty bottle. He tossed it in the trashcan at the end of the driveway as they drove out.

"Heaven help us," he said under his breath as he headed for Lahaina.

The girls talked in the back about the pregnancy, Reggie's house, and Derf. The guys talked about Troy's job, Ben's woodworking and some island legends. Troy had honked his horn going through a small tunnel on the way and that sparked a conversation the rest of the way about the island gods and some of the superstitions. The volcano goddess Pele's dog was said to chase you if you didn't honk as you drove through. He also had to explain about the ugly chain link style fencing that ran along the cliffs.

"Used to cost the county a fortune in car repairs from falling rocks. Now they figured they're covered. It's ugly as sin, but I guess it does the trick."

~*~

Troy looked into the rearview mirror at Reggie. She was sulking in the back seat with her arms crossed pulling off a pretty good pout. It no longer had an effect on him. "Anything in particular you want to do since you're home, Reg?"

"Not do, eat. Is Safeway still in the Cannery Mall?"

"Yes."

"Can we swing by on the way home so I can get some taco and ahi poké?"

"Of course, Princess."

Reggie finally smiled.

~*~

Reggie knew she was being pouty, but she never could stay that way with Troy. She kept looking at Ben while they drove. It was hard not to get lost in his profile or to not think about how good he felt when they were together. She longed to be sitting with him, to share her home with him, but she couldn't.

"What's poké?" Ben asked as he turned around and faced Reggie.

"Raw fish or octopus with oils and seasonings," Sabrina explained when Reggie didn't answer him.

"Raw?"

"It's really good. We'll have to get you to try some."

"It'll be good for a laugh, if nothing else, to see the look on your face." Troy chuckled.

"Is this all part of the island hazing ritual?"

"Something like that." Sabrina patted his shoulders. She scooted forward and rubbed her hands down his arms, playfully. "Oh, Honey. Feels like you have some competition here." She turned to Reggie. "Have you felt this boy's arms?"

Reggie gave her a 'knock it off' glare.

"How tall are you, Ben? Six-three?"

"Six-four."

Again she turned to Reggie. "Small change, Regina?"

Troy belted out a loud laugh he couldn't control and Reggie said, "Bri! Quit it!" before she laughed as well.

"Is this an inside joke?" Ben asked.

"Sorry, Buddy. The women in this family are what we call 'kolohé'."

"And that is?"

"In Hawaiian it means rascal," Troy explained. "It's better than saying—"

"Watch your mouth, Baby," Sabrina said, cutting him off.

"I was going to say pupulé, sugar, not bitch." They all laughed.

Ben looked over his shoulder and smiled at Reggie. "Pupulé is crazy," she said with a soft smile back.

"I'm going to need a Hawaiian dictionary if I'm going to keep up."

~*~

Reggie glanced up at him and couldn't help a grin, but turned her head away and focused her attention on the water. "I wish it were whale season."

"So you two will have to come back," Bri said, placing her hand on Reggie's leg. She unbuckled herself and slid over, wrapping her arm around her friend. "I love ya, Girl." Reggie returned the embrace and fought the desire to cry. She was so confused she didn't even know if they were happy or sad tears fighting to come out at the moment.

"I love you more, Bri."

Once in Lahaina, Troy parked at the banyan tree. It was a good place to begin exploring all the shops and attractions with Ben so he could play a proper tourist, but Reggie wasn't happy. She could only think of where she and Van had their first kiss along the street right there. For Ben's sake, she was going to try hard not to wallow, but she was beginning to feel like it was going to be impossible. Memories of Van were everywhere she turned. Needing a minute, she wandered towards the marina.

Her stomach was suddenly feeling queasy. "Self-inflicted ulcer no doubt", she mumbled as she rubbed it. "Bri? You craving ice cream yet?"

"I don't need to be pregnant to be wanting ice cream, Hon. Let's go."

They went to the little ice cream shop in the Pioneer Inn and had huge waffle cones. Reggie wasn't sure if she wanted the ice cream to soothe her stomach or to prove she could get past the memory of having ice cream there with Van.

Ben looked wide-eyed at the potion he was given, then at Reggie. She smiled and tip-toed up, whispering in his ear. "Don't worry, Ben. If your crackery ass can't finish it, I can."

Reggie really did want to try to help him have a good time. He probably paid through the teeth for his tickets, as she had, getting a last minute flight. She both loved to look at him and found it hard to do so, but there was no reason for her to forget her manners. Despite her time away, she was finding out how easily island hospitality came back to you.

~*~

Ben laughed at her comment. He longed for her to pause in a kiss as she put her feet flat to the ground but she didn't and he didn't push it. He hated that, after the intimacy they shared, he was back at the 'I'm longing for you to kiss me' stage, but he wanted to give her the space she needed.

As they approached the row of various activity boats, Reggie turned to Ben. "The name is appropriate for a glass-bottom boat, don't you think?"

"I suppose I'd say yes if I knew what that word meant. I'm not even going to try to say it."

"Nielé means nosey," she explained.

"Then yes, it is a perfect name for a glass-bottom boat. I just hope I'm not getting quizzed later." He watched her walk towards the boat while waiting off to the side with Troy and Sabrina.

Ben was surprised at how his emotions toyed with him while he watched her being greeted by the man Troy pointed out as Keoni. For some reason, Ben expected an old 'salt' of a sailor, but he was a very young, handsome local boy. He picked Reggie off her feet and she wrapped her legs around his waist. He spun her around in circles in a tight hug.

Troy must have sensed the tension. "They're just good friends. They never dated. It's a little overly island-style greeting."

"A little?"

"Easy there, Cowboy," he said, patting Ben on the back.

Reggie received hugs from two other crewmembers then talked with Keoni again. He was shaking his head in a 'yes' then she pointed over and his face dropped. He said something to Reggie and she playfully cuddled up to his chest. He laughed and kissed the top of her head then waved everyone over.

"I see why you needed her," Ben said to Troy.

"I knew being Mr. Popularity was never going to be a part of my job."

Reggie introduced everyone and they climbed onboard. Troy and Keoni shook hands, but exchanged a stern look; each was giving an unspoken 'I'm keeping an eye on you'. The girls went top deck so Reggie could get some sun while the guys settled into the benches, allowing Ben to see the reefs and all the tropical fish once the boat was on its way.

Ben turned to Troy. "What's the whole song and dance with Reggie? Why not just buy a couple of tickets?"

"Because one, they're over-priced for the tourists. And B, nobody pays for things around here when you know the owners and three," he leaned in and whispered, "don't let her fool you. Reggie loves getting away with it."

Ben sat back surprised. "I really took her for a 'hating using the advantage of her body' thing."

"Maybe to a point; like attention from guys when she…" Troy paused.

"I know she danced."

"Okay, good. So you two aren't just bed buddies. You do know a thing or two about each other."

"She wouldn't let me in her house," Ben admitted.

"She had pictures of Van up?"

"Yeah, I saw them when I was looking for her the other day. With what I thought we had…" he didn't want to finish his thoughts.

"Give it time." Troy stood up. "Mai Tai?"

"I thought you busted them for that?"

"They can serve on their license for their trips. They're actually free with the ticket. They aren't allowed to sell booze and try to make an extra buck or weasel in on other businesses. They're not licensed for night cruises… kind of like busting a pilot for flying without setting a flight plan."

"And selling booze while flying."

"Right."

"I'll take two."

Troy laughed. "Anyway, back to the subject, Reggie has a lot of friends here. She knows a lot of business owners and everyone likes to give it away to her. Don't go flying punches when you see her hugging half the town. I won't have your back."

"Fair enough. You really going to drink the dude's booze when you didn't buy a ticket?"

"Okole Maluna, my friend." Before Ben had a chance to ask, Troy said, "Bottom's up."

43

After they arrived back at the pier, the four meandered in and out of art galleries, had a great late lunch at the Hard Rock Café, and walked into a few bars for a drink when they were thirsty.

"I wish this place was like Key West, Reg," Sabrina said. "It was so much fun walking bar to bar with drinks in hand. Of course, it would be more fun for me if I could actually drink."

"But you're my good little mama, aren't you?" Troy said with a hug.

"Bite me, White Boy."

"Anytime, Baby." They shared another long kiss. Reggie and Ben looked away, trying not to get embarrassed over it.

Reggie did hug a few people in the various shops. She knew quite a few of the local artists. Ben was amazed at the price tags set for some of the work.

"You sure know a lot of people, Reggie," Ben said, trying to tone down the hint of jealousy.

"It's just like your town, Ben."

"Our town," he corrected.

"Everyone knows everyone," she continued. "I did a lot of material orders for these places. These buildings are all restored. Where I worked was the biggest outlet for the finer hardwoods and marbles."

"You measure up counters and stuff, too?"

"Yes."

"'Cause I've been wanting to re-do my kitchen."

"Nice try." She ducked into an ABC store for a snack. She came out with a bag of something shredded and orange.

"What's that?"

"Li hing mui. It's a seasoned plum. Try it." She held a piece up to his mouth and he took a bite. He made a face and spit it into a trashcan. Everyone laughed.

"That's disgusting."

"It's an acquired taste."

"You are pure evil, Reggie," Troy said as she walked ahead of them.

"If the foo shits…" Reggie waved her hand as she walked ahead. Sabrina ran to catch up with her.

~*~

Troy and Ben stayed behind a few paces.

"Foo shits? More Hawaiian?" Ben asked.

"Shoe fits. There's no 'F' in the Hawaiian alphabet". Ben turned around. "Where you going?" Troy asked.

"Back in that store to look for a friggen Hawaiian dictionary."

They drove to Kaanapali and wandered through the various hotels playing tourist. Reggie wanted to show Ben the tropical penguins at the Sheraton and the exotic birds that filled the lobbies of all the hotels. They stole a quick dip in one of the pools to cool off after Troy carefully looked around for security guards and wait staff that weren't occupied slinging drinks and food to the guests.

Ben understood now why Troy said to wear a pair of swim trunks rather than shorts. Afterwards they walked down the beach, watching the tourists on the various water toys. Troy even swam out to help a young girl who had gotten frightened as she had gone out too far on her boogie board.

"He's never off duty." Sabrina laughed as she hooked Ben by the arm.

They went home after dark after a simple meal of pupu's over a last round of drinks. No one was terribly hungry after their big, late lunch.

"Pu-pu's…hardly an appealing word for appetizers if you ask me." Ben shook his head.

They swung by to get Reggie her pokè on the way back. Ben declined a taste of it.

When they pulled up back home, Reggie went out into the backyard instead of going in with everyone else. She stood in the middle of the yard with her eyes closed. Ben watched her from the window.

"Reggie said she missed the smells of home," Bri explained. "Why don't you put on some music." She pointed to the stereo and large rack of CDs. "The speakers go out into the yard."

He looked through them and pulled one out. "No way." He held up the *Dirty Dancing* soundtrack.

"Oh, she knows it," Sabrina said with a grin.

Ben put it on and walked outside. Sabrina turned the yard lights on as the music played. Ben walked over to Reggie in true Patrick Swayze fashion, waiting for Jennifer Grey to walk over to him. To his surprise, Reggie smiled and claimed her place at his chest. He pulled her close and they began to dance after the gentle rocking of her head. They flawlessly completed the routine as Troy and Sabrina stood at the sliding glass door watching them. At the point where Patrick would have gone off in a solo routine on his knees, Ben stayed, holding Reggie tight. He leaned down and kissed her.

When their lips parted, Reggie wiped away a tear. "I'm sorry, Ben. I just can't." She ran off towards the beach.

~*~

"Damn her!" Sabrina cried as she turned into Troy.

44

Sabrina went to bed and Troy joined Ben outside.

"Those are some fancy feet you have there, my friend."

"Whatever," Ben replied, again running his fingers through his hair.

"She always tried to get Van to dance; he just didn't like it."

"So is that in my favor or against it?"

"Don't go trying to figure out a woman's mind. It'll make you batty."

"Pupulè," Ben said with a straight face.

Troy laughed. "You do catch on quick."

Ben turned to him. "Will you please tell me what happened to her?"

"Don't ask me that. It ain't my place and it really has nothing to do with what's going on. Trust me on that."

"She wigged out one night when I was reaching up for her cat. She hit the deck. I know somebody hit her," Ben said, firmly. "Was it Van? Is she carrying some kind of sick 'I'm not good enough for anyone 'cause the one I really loved abused me' trip? 'Cause I can't compete with that, Man."

"It wasn't Van that hit her so get that outta your head before I plug you myself."

"Who then?"

Troy let out a long breath. "Don't you think, if I knew who it was, that I'd have killed the bastard long ago?"

"You knew about it though."

"Yes, I knew about it, not until years after the fact. Look, I've told you; I didn't even tell Van about it. That's Reggie's business. If she wants to leave it buried, leave it buried."

"It has something to do with her not being able to have kids, doesn't it?" The look on Troy's face told him he was right. "Tell me, Troy. I want to be able to help her."

"You can't help her by digging up bad memories."

"I'm not going to dig anything up; I just want to know what I'm dealing with."

Troy stared at the ground for a long time. "Buy me a shot and a beer," he finally said, looking up at Ben.

The two men left the house and walked to the bar at the harbor. Two shots and a beer later, Troy finally stopped fidgeting with the label on his bottle. "Van wasn't her first husband."

"He wasn't?"

Troy shook his head 'no'. "The first one didn't last long. She got married right after she graduated." He paused and took a swig of beer. Ben patiently waited for the story to continue. "Her parents split the islands almost the second they handed her the diploma. She had two month's rent paid for as a graduation gift and not much money of her own in the bank. Working part-time at a clothing store in the mall doesn't do much for your wallet around here. Anyway, she fell in love with a rich California boy with a big fancy house and car, making her all kinds of promises. They married after a month of dating and she got pregnant right away." He downed the rest of his beer and looked around as if he was afraid of being overheard. Ben signaled the bartender for another round.

Troy finally continued. "What she didn't know was that he had a taste for the finest drugs money could buy. He was a dealer. She found out and left him, but he came her after, vowing to beat the kid out of her if he couldn't have it." The two men locked in a stare. "He succeeded."

"Jesus."

"What he did to her also fixed it so that she could never have another." Troy paused for a moment, as if he wanted to let that sink in. "It had to have been bad. I imagine that's why she can't take the sight of blood. I've seen some bad shit, but I can't even imagine…"

Ben's elbows went to the bar and he sunk his head in his hands in frustration. "And where is this prick now?"

"No one knows. He fled the island and hasn't been heard from again. She received divorce papers in the hospital. We didn't meet her until a few years later. Trust me; I did what I could to try to find him."

"Van never knew about this?"

"Nope. He knew she'd been married for a few months after high school, but that's it. I promised her I'd never tell him and I didn't. They were good for each other. She really did okay."

"Where are her parents?"

"In Florida with her brother. Nice enough people, but some parents just pick a favorite kid sometimes. She was left here to fend for herself. She's a tough nut and they figured she'd be okay, I guess. They didn't even go to Van's funeral. They were off in Paris or something."

"Greece." The two men spun around in the direction of the voice. "If you're going to talk about me when I'm not around at least get the facts straight. It was Greece." Reggie turned and ran out of the restaurant.

"Ah, shit." Troy jumped off the bar stool.

"No." Ben grabbed his arm. "Let me." He ran out the door after her. "Reggie, would you stop, please?"

She slowed to a walk, but kept going. "I didn't ask you to come here. I didn't ask for you to go digging up my past."

Ben stopped her. "Stop running away from me, Reggie. Bad things happen to good people every day. Why are you punishing yourself for something you had no control over?"

"I'm not punishing myself."

"The hell you're not. You run away from everyone who loves you."

"Everyone who says they love me hurts me!"

"I'm not going to hurt you. I'd never hit you; you know that. I don't care if we can't have kids. I want you, Reg."

"Can you promise not to die, Ben?" she said with tear filled eyes.

"No one can promise that."

"I just want to be left alone." She shook herself free and went back towards the house.

45

The next morning, Reggie joined Troy on the lawn for coffee. "Where's your friend?" she asked as she sat down.

He didn't look at her; he drank his coffee and said, "He split."

"What?"

"Whatever you said to him last night worked. He left."

"When?"

"I don't know. He must have called a cab. I didn't take him. The room was empty this morning and his bag is gone. Seriously…do you even care? You've been nothing but a bitch to him since he showed up."

She was taken aback. He'd raised his voice at her and even given her the 'what for' a time or two, but he had never talked to her quite like that. "He deserves to have a family with someone who can give him one."

"Cut the crap, Reg." He stood up and tossed what was left of his coffee into the grass. "Stop playing that card."

"How about the 'every time I look at him I'll see Van' card, then? Van's dead because he's alive. How am I supposed to live with that?"

"That's right. Van's dead. You know he'd do exactly the same thing again in a heartbeat, too. I don't think you miss him near as much as it pisses you off that he was willing to lose his life to save someone else and not just stay home to play house with you. It's what he did, Reg! You know damn well he hadn't been happy since he left the Guard. He sure as hell didn't want to live in a wheelchair and be taken care of the rest of his life. He's dead, Reggie. He's gone and it seems to me he saved a mighty fine replacement of himself for you." He shouted, "Dammit!" as he picked his cup up and threw it at the wooden fence. It shattered on impact. He walked off towards the beach as Sabrina came flying out the door.

"What is all the shouting about?"

Reggie dropped to her knees in tears. Sabrina hurried to her side.

After another draining tear session and Reggie's take on the conversation, Sabrina finally spoke. "He's right, you know."

"About what?"

"All of it. I love you, Regina, but all of it. You can't keep punishing yourself."

"I'm not! Why does everyone keep saying that?"

"You are, Hon. You didn't ask to be abandoned by your parents. You didn't ask to be beaten. You certainly didn't ask for your husband to die. You can't keep punishing yourself by continually pushing everyone away."

Reggie dropped her head onto Bri's shoulder. "You're lunatic husband said Van gave me Ben."

"In a way, he's right."

"Not you, too." Reggie sighed.

"I've heard of some strange coincidences, Hon, but this takes the cake. What made you go to that dinky town of all places? You had no ties there. How did you happen to buy a place right next to the very guy your husband saved? Call it fate or call it the Lord works in mysterious ways. Call it whatever the hell you want, but for crying out loud, stop fighting it. He loves you."

"Well, I'm sure I fixed that."

"I doubt it," Bri said with a hug. After a long silence she asked, "Do me a favor?"

"Anything."

"Have a Long Island and breathe it on me. You're stressing my pregnant black ass out."

~*~

The girls were sitting on the lounge chairs when Troy walked back into the yard after lunch. Reggie had a Long Island iced tea and a small battery-operated fan, blowing the scent towards Sabrina, who chuckled with glee at her attempt. Reggie stood when she Troy got closer. He closed the distance to her in a few paces and picked her up off the ground with a bear-hug.

"I'm sorry," he said with his head buried in her neck.

"No, I am. You were right about everything. I have been a horrible bitch." He held her face and kissed her cheek. "Will you do one more thing for me?"

"What's that?"

"Take me to the airport tomorrow."

"You sure you're ready to go?"

"I'm sure."

"You want me to go with you?"

"Thanks, but no. I have to stand on my own feet sometime. Besides, you need to take care of prego over there."

"I've already done my part." That brought him a smack on the arm from her that he welcomed with a smile.

46

Reggie walked up her porch stairs, noticing right away that Ben had brought the swing over for her. She only took enough time at home to empty the contents of her suitcase in the laundry room and open a few windows to air the place out. There was a nice cool breeze coming in and she welcomed it. Maui was so hot when she left. She was looking forward to coming home and having to put on sweatpants. She walked over to Ben's house, enjoying the smell of the air and the trees in the place she knew she truly wanted to call 'home' from now on.

She heard hammering so she walked towards the barn. Ben was working on the fence. He looked over just briefly before he finished driving a nail he was working on. "I didn't expect to see you so soon." He reached in his pouch and brought out another nail.

"I wanted to come home. That fence really isn't a one-man job."

He scoffed, probably at her use of the word 'home'. "I'll manage. Did you come for Derf or are you here just long enough to pack up?" He sank another nail, she thought with a little more force than the wood required.

"Did you even listen to me? I said I wanted to come home."

"Yeah, I heard you." He threw his hammer in the toolbox and whipped off the pouch of nails. "Loud and clear. I'll go get your cat."

"Ben…"

He stormed towards the house without turning back. In a couple minutes, he came back out. She was waiting on the porch for him. He gave her the kitten and a bag of food, jumped off the porch and walked towards the barn.

"Can't we talk?"

"Nothing to talk about, Reggie."

"I think there is."

"Wrong!" He swung around and bounded up the six stairs in two long strides. He stood face to face with her. "Wrong! I get it. I'm out of your life. I'm not playing second fiddle to a ghost anymore. I won't have you thinking about him every time you see me. I'm sorry I'm not the one that's dead, Reggie, but I can't fix that."

"But…"

He cut her off when he leaned in even closer to her face. "Go. Home." He bound off the porch again and returned to the barn.

She walked back, snuggling with the kitten and refusing to cry. After the long trip and the emotional roller coaster she had been on lately, she simply didn't have the strength for it. Immediately after entering her house, she flopped on the couch with her arm over her eyes. Derf leapt off the couch and ran for the kitchen, happy to be home. Reggie was asleep in seconds. Jetlag and too much thinking had finally gotten the best of her.

~*~

The kitten knew no boundaries. Despite Reggie's diligence with a water spray bottle, which she was taught to use as rule enforcement with the naughty kitty, he was still always up on the counters. He made his way up the chair, across the counter and on the stove. He was happily leaning down and licking bacon splatter from the knob when he slipped and caught himself, but not before turning the knob on and starting the gas appliance.

The windows were still open to air out the house and the breeze was coming in as strong as before. It only took a few passes of the curtains for them to catch fire.

~*~

Ben saw the glow as he was heading back to his house. "Shit!" He dialed 9-1-1 on his cell phone and ran for the four-wheeler. He jumped off it when he reached her house, before it even came to a complete stop. He had been calling her name as he drove over, but she was nowhere to be found. There were flames coming out of every window as he stood on the porch calling her name again. He reached for the doorknob, but it burned his hand and he pulled it back. He could hear the sirens, but they were still too far away. He was worried she was in there. The fire wouldn't wait for help.

After kicking in the door, he immediately spotted her lying on the couch. "Reggie!" He rushed in as creaking came from above. A beam in flames fell down between where he was standing and the couch. Holding his arm up, trying to shield his face from the flames, he jumped over the beam. He made it to the couch and picked up her limp body then jumped back and ran outside to fresh air. "Reggie!" he shouted as he shook her, but she didn't budge. He put his head to her chest, but he couldn't hear anything over the pounding of his heart. After putting his cheek close to her lips hoping to feel air coming from her nose, he worried when there was none. He began CPR and got a few breaths into her. She finally gasped for air. He dropped his head in relief and turned her on her side. She coughed loudly several times, trying to take in more fresh air. When an ambulance and fire truck screeched to a halt, he immediately picked her up and ran to them.

He shouted, "She needs oxygen!"

They opened the back of the ambulance. He stepped up and put her on the gurney then moved out of the way while they went to work on her. "How long was she in there?" one of them asked.

"I don't know. She left my place twenty minutes ago."

"Do you know how the fire started?"

"How the hell would I know that?" It hadn't even occurred to him. Did she start it? Had he been so bad that she…? That was crazy. She didn't even like him; she wasn't about to commit suicide over him. He wanted to hold her, but instead he had been so horrible to her. No doubt if she woke up, his would be the last face she'd want to see. He climbed out of the ambulance.

One of the EMT's jumped down from the back and closed the doors. "She's in bad shape but stable. We're going to take her in. You should ride along." He pointed to Ben's arm. It was red and blistered. He didn't even realize he'd been burned.

"I'll drive in later."

"You responsible for her?"

"Huh? Uh…I suppose." He didn't know why he said that. "I'll be in shortly." He gave them her name and they drove off. He walked over to the firemen who were concerned only about keeping the fire from spreading to the trees. "Nothing to do now but save the foundation." Old firemen's joke; Ben didn't laugh.

"Ah shit."

"What?" the chief asked.

"She had a cat in there."

The chief looked at the house. "Not anymore." He looked down at Ben's arm. "You really ought to have that looked at."

Ben looked down at it again. "I'll go in a bit. I want to spend a few minutes to see if the cat was able to escape." After half an hour of searching and finding no sign of the kitten, Ben drove into the hospital. He didn't realize how bad he looked until the nurse at the ER desk jumped to attention at the sight of him.

"I'm fine," he assured her. "How's my neighbor doing?"

"She's a lot better. You the hero of the hour?"

"Hero? No, I just got her out."

"That, Honey-bun, is a hero," she said with a flirty wink. "Let's get you in back and get that arm looked at."

"Can I see Reggie? Uh… Regina first please?"

"She's sleeping, but I suppose you can peek in on her. Just for a second though."

The nurse led him to the room where Reggie was then left him alone while she went into the next room to get it set up to take care of his burns. He reached for Reggie's hand with both of his and gently stroked it. She shook her head and whispered, "Ben" but it didn't matter. Through the oxygen mask and the soft moan, all his mind heard was "Van". He let go of her hand and walked into the next room.

When his burns were treated and wrapped, he went back into her room and sat in a chair in the corner. He kicked his feet out in front of himself and fell asleep.

~*~

Early the next morning, Reggie opened her eyes slowly and looked around. She was suddenly scared, having no memories of being brought into the hospital. She sat up and called out, "Troy!"

Ben hurried to her side. "Hey."

She had fear in her eyes. "Why am I here? What happened?"

"There was a fire, Reg."

"A fire? My house!" She kicked her legs over the side of the bed trying to get out. He grabbed them, put them back on the bed and gently pushed her shoulders back.

"Don't try to get up yet. You've had smoke inhalation bad."

"How did I get here?"

"An ambulance brought you."

"The last thing I remember is falling asleep on the couch. It caught fire? How?"

"They're looking into it."

Reggie's eyes fell to his bandaged arm. "How did I get out, Ben?"

"I saw the flames from my place, Reg."

"You carried me out while the house was in flames?"

"It's not as bad as it sounds." He walked away and looked out the window.

"That's not true," the fire chief said as he entered the room. "Sorry for the intrusion. I know it's early, but I heard voices. We discovered what caused the fire. I wanted to let you know as soon as possible."

Ben turned around to face him. Reggie sat up.

"There was a dial turned on for the stove. My educated guess is it caught the curtains on fire."

"How would the stove get turned on?"

"Did you start anything before you laid down? Water for tea or anything?"

"No."

"Are you sure?"

"I'm positive. I went straight to the couch after I walked in."

"Your boyfriend here mentioned a cat."

"I'm not her boyfriend."

"My apologies. It's not often you see a neighbor go into something burning that bad." Reggie's eyes went wide. The fire was worse than Ben was letting on. He was obviously defensive about being called her boyfriend. She wasn't going to make a fuss about it. The way he felt about her, she was surprised he saved her at all.

"It's not common, but it's a possibility. It could have been the cat. The switch was broken. You didn't need to push the left front one in to turn it on, did you?"

She shook her head no. It didn't bother her and she never even thought about getting it fixed. "Wait a second." Something the fire chief said finally hit her. "You said cat. Did Derf make it out?" she looked at Ben with a pleading in her eyes.

"I couldn't find him."

She dropped back in the bed and turned her head to the wall. She refused to cry again. She was sick of crying. It was just a silly kitten.

"I'm sorry," the chief said. "I wanted to let you know the cause. I hope you feel better soon." The chief left the room.

"I'm going to go see when they're going to let you out." Ben left the room as well.

47

Ben came back at noon with a shopping bag. She was sitting up in bed, awake, but hadn't touched her lunch. She was playing with the Jell-O when he walked in; she didn't hear him. "Food suck?"

She jumped at his words. "I'm not hungry."

"You need to eat something."

"I said I'm not hungry." She pushed the plate away and slumped back on the bed.

"They're letting me take you outta here. You must be a real gem of a patient."

"Kiss my ass."

"Yup. That's pretty much what they said." He dropped the bag at her feet. "Put these on."

"What are they?"

"Why don't you look and find out?"

She huffed and sat up. "Sweats?"

"You needed something to wear out of here. I wasn't about to guess your size and buy you jeans and tops. We can stop somewhere on the way home."

"Home?"

"My house. For now anyway."

"That's not necessary, Ben. I can go to a motel."

"You have no driver's license, no credit card, and no cash. You're stuck with me, Doll-face. Now get dressed." He left the room and closed the door.

They drove in silence on their way to his place. When he reached her driveway, he stopped and glanced at her.

"Is there anything to see?" she asked.

"Nope."

"Then no." She waited for another few moments before speaking again. "Do Troy and Sabrina know?"

"Yep."

"Are they coming?"

"Nope."

"Is that all you can say? Yep…Nope."

"Nope."

"You're infuriating. You know that?"

"Yep."

She crossed her arms and stared out the window. "Why isn't Troy coming?"

"You're unbelievable."

"What?"

"All this time, I thought you've been burning a torch for your old man and here you're in love with your best friend's husband."

"I am not in love with Troy!"

"Like hell." He stopped in front of his house and slid out of the truck.

Reggie huffed after him and slammed her door. "I'm not in love with him! They're my best friends. We've been through a lot. They have always been there for me."

"His is just the first name you scream when you wake up?"

"That's a long story," she said, storming off and heading to the lake. She sat at the edge and threw pebbles in the water. His shadow fell over her.

"Seems to me we have a world of time."

She wrapped her arms around her legs and pulled herself in a tight ball. "Every story you drag out of me or my friends makes me out to be some kind of victim and I don't like it."

"So quit being a victim." He walked away. After a half an hour, she walked into the house. He had some chips and sandwiches on the table. He pointed to it. "Sit and eat some lunch."

"I told you earlier, I'm not hungry."

"I don't give a goddamn. I'm not having you passing out on me. Sit and eat something."

"Are you planning on being this incorrigible the whole time?"

"That's entirely up to you, Doll-face."

"I swear if you don't stop calling me that, I'll kill you in your sleep!"

"I sleep with my gun." He left the room.

Reggie sat at the table and nibbled at her sandwich. She was hungrier than she pretended to be and finished an entire one before she knew it. After checking his refrigerator, she found some milk and drank a large glass. The whole milk tasted great. She only bought herself skim milk but was happy to indulge here. When she was done, she carried the glass to the sink to rinse it. It slipped in her hand and broke when it dropped. When she went to pick up the pieces, she again sliced her fingers.

~*~

Ben came running at the sound of glass breaking. When he reached her, she was staring at the blood dripping from her finger. "Not again." He removed a hand towel from the drawer and reached for her hand. It surprised him when she said, "No," and pulled her hand back.

"Don't go crazy on me. Let me get some pressure on it and stop the bleeding."

"It's not so bad," she said, watching it drip. "It's such a funny thing…blood."

"Reg?"

She stared as it dripped a drop every few seconds. Ben tried again to grab her hand and again she pulled it away. "You never think about it, but it's always there. You have no idea how bad you need it until you lose it."

"Reggie, stop. It's still flowing really bad. Let me put pressure on it."

"No!" She gave it a slight squeeze, causing it to drip a little faster. "All these years, the mere sight of it…this," she said as she made it drip again. "So I'm losing a little blood. Big deal. It's not like it's a baby…or a husband…or a…," She choked up. "A…a stupid cat!" Clutching her hand at her stomach, she fell to her knees.

Ben dropped next to her, wrestled her hand away and applied pressure to her finger. She clutched at his shirt with her free hand and buried her face in it, crying loudly. He stroked her hair until she was cried out then picked her up and took her to the couch.

"I'm going to get a Band-Aid. I'll be back in a second."

~*~

When he came back, she had already fallen asleep. He figured she was exhausted from all the drama and crying. He put the bandage on and since she was asleep, he gave it a kiss. Discovering he was more tired than he realized, Ben went to his room and dropped on his bed, falling asleep within a few minutes. Hours later, he awoke to Reggie gently shaking him.

"Ben, get up," she whispered.

"What is it?" He sat up and held her shoulders. "What's wrong?"

"Get your gun."

"What? Why?" He dropped to his knees and grabbed his shotgun from under the bed.

"There's an animal scratching at the door."

"Why are you whispering?"

"Well, I don't want to scare it away!" she said, as loud as she could and still be whispering. "What if it has rabies? Why else would it be scratching to come in?"

She turned to go back out the door. He poked at her side and made a grunting sound. She screamed and jumped on his bed. "Very funny! Go see what it is." The loud whisper made him laugh. Being woken out of a sound sleep, they had forgotten to be rude to each other. He smiled at her standing on the bed.

"This isn't funny. Go see what it is." Her hands were on her hips but he could see she was fighting a grin as well.

"Yes, Dear." He went out the back door and approached the front door slowly. Ben laughed then opened the door and called to her. "Come here."

She slowly came out of the bedroom. "What did you find?"

He was standing in the doorway with his hands behind his back. When she was closer to him, he held out his hands. In them was her kitten.

"Derf!" She ran and took the cat from him, rubbed his nose to hers then laughed as she swung him around.

"I guess he knew his way here. It was kind of his second home."

"Do you still have any food for him?"

"No. I sent it all with you, but I can open up a can of tuna. He's probably starved."

The two of them sat on the kitchen floor and watched the kitten wolf down the tuna. They looked up and smiled at each other, then Ben's face relaxed. He stood and leaned against the counter.

"Sabrina is supposed to stay in bed. That's why they're not coming."

"She's having problems?"

"The doctor ordered bed rest for a few days. They expect her and the baby to be fine. It's not that they didn't care, Reg. Troy asked me to look after you."

"I'm sorry he put the burden of me on you," she said, losing her happy moment as well. "It was probably too much on her with me being there. I shouldn't have gone home."

"It had nothing to do with you. Is everything that happens on this planet your fault, 'cause I have a nasty bunion starting and I'd love to be able to blame you for it."

"What did I ever see in you, anyway?"

"Not much of anything but a ghost apparently." He pushed himself off the counter and walked away.

48

Over the next few days, they hardly spoke. They remained civil when they shared the same space, but that was as little as possible. Even though Ben insisted she take the bedroom, Reggie slept on the couch.

"I don't want to be in the way anymore, Ben," she said that night after he hit the lights and said goodnight.

"I'm an asshole, but I'm not going to throw you out on your ass, Reggie. You can stay as long as you need to."

"I'll start looking for an apartment tomorrow."

"What're you going to do for money?"

"I have enough to rent a place. The insurance shouldn't take too much longer. I'll be okay for a while. In any case, I'm really not your problem. It hasn't been fair to you."

"Whatever," he said as he shut his bedroom door.

The next morning, Ben woke up early and was surprised to see the couch empty. It wasn't made up yet either. He looked around, but couldn't find Reggie outside. He finally found her the bathroom, throwing up. He waited for a moment and knocked gently on the door. "You okay in there?"

"No. Please go away."

When the door finally opened, he walked over to her. "Holy crap. You look horrible."

"What every woman wants to hear. Thanks."

"Go get something on. I'll take you in to the doctor."

"I don't need a doctor, Ben."

"Have you looked in a mirror?"

"Ahhhh." She spun around, grabbing her bag of clothes before she went back into the bathroom.

~*~

They had been to town shopping a few times so she could get some clothes and such. It would have been more exciting to rebuild her life and wardrobe if she had somewhere to put them. She wanted, more than anything, to climb in bed with Ben at night and share what they had before. She missed the closeness, the familiarity of his body, his smell. She blew it and now he hated her. She could have left a few days ago, but she was hoping that by being together, maybe something would happen and he would fall for her again. Trying to be been civil and helpful, she had made the meals and helped with the fence, but he was always distant, never saying much. He refused interviews regarding her rescue, completely shrugging it off. He couldn't have cared less about her. She needed to get away from him before it ate her up.

~*~

While Ben pulled the truck up to his front door, his anger just about destroyed him. He longed to bring her to his chest when she stepped out of the bathroom. She obviously didn't feel well and he wanted to comfort her, to make her feel better. What did he do? Tell her she looked like hell. *You are a number one first class asshole, Bentley. If she wants to go, then let her go. You can't keep doing this to yourself. She doesn't love you, you schmuck. I'd even go as far as to say she hates your guts.* He opened his door and stopped talking to himself. He hurried over to open her door and help her. She returned a courteous smile. No more, no less.

He dropped her off at the doctor's office and said to call when she was done. "I have errands I can do. I'll only be a few minutes away."

"Thanks." She closed his door and he drove off.

~*~

"Pregnant? I can't be pregnant. Doctor Griffen...I can't get pregnant."

"I beg to differ. You can and have. You do know how this happens, correct?" he said with a grin.

"I know how it happens! It just can't happen to me."

"Can and has...unless you, of course, abstain from sex and this is an immaculate conception."

"You don't understand. I had an...accident when I was eighteen. They told me I couldn't get pregnant. I've never been able to get pregnant."

"Apparently you've healed."

"I hardly get anything for a period. I usually barely even spot." She stopped for a moment and remembered things getting heavier a few months ago. She refused to get excited about it and wrote it off more as a nuisance than anything. When it stopped again, she didn't even think twice about it.

"There are exceptions to every rule, especially where nature is concerned."

"I can't..." She stopped arguing. Her thoughts went to Ben. What would he do now? He'd hate her more than ever.

"Is this not welcome news? I would think you'd be excited after all these years, if you've said you've tried and now you've finally succeeded."

"My husband is no longer around."

"I see." He said it in a way that meant he really didn't understand the situation. She wasn't about to explain it. "Since you're not sure of the date of your last period, I can only guess at this point by the size of things. My guess is that you are eight weeks along. I wouldn't recommend terminating the pregnancy this late in the game. I can make a call and see—"

"No!" she shouted. "No. I'm not terminating the pregnancy. I'm eight weeks along?" That would put her conceiving practically the first time she and Ben made love.

"You've never had any tenderness in your breasts? No other signs of discomfort?"

"There have been a lot of strange things going on. I haven't slowed down enough to realize…" she thought about her stomach being queasy on Maui. She wished she hadn't had so much to drink that day.

"Kimball," he said, reading her name again. "You're the girl who lost her house to a fire, aren't you?"

"Yes."

"Are you getting by?"

"Yes." She slid off the table. "I'll be fine. Doctor?" She hesitated. "I really had no idea. I kind of drank a lot a few days back. Is the baby going to be okay?" She was really worried since Sabrina always made it a point not to drink if she even thought there was a possibility she could be pregnant.

"You'll be okay, just lay off the booze from here on out. Okay?"

She nodded.

He ripped a piece of paper off a notepad. "This is a prescription for prenatal vitamins. Fill it as soon as you can. I'd like to see you next month for a follow up."

"Thank you."

Ben was sitting in the waiting room when she walked out. She hid the paper with the prescription in her pants pocket. She hadn't even bothered to purchase a new purse.

He stood up and walked to her. "What did he say?"

"Nothing. Just a passing bug. I told you I didn't need to come in. Why are you back so quick, anyway? I thought you had errands to do."

"I found you an apartment. I thought you'd want to see it and move out right away."

"Oh." She placed a hand on her stomach. "I guess so. Thanks."

"You're not going to toss your cookies again, are you?"

Now that she knew she was pregnant, her pants were incredibly uncomfortable and tight. She also wanted to fill the prescription right away.

"No. I'm better already. Can we stop at a store please? I'd like to get a few things."

"Sure. How about after you look at the apartment. It's not furnished. You'll need a few things anyway."

"Okay."

She lacked enthusiasm for the apartment, but it would do. It was a lot bigger than her one bedroom on Oahu and less than half the rent. "When can I move in?"

"We can move you in tonight. The manager said they would prorate the rent. Light and electric are on; you'll just have to get it put in your name. That shouldn't be a problem since you'd have a history with them with your house." She stared in the bedroom and her thoughts drifted off as he talked. She pictured a baby crib in the corner and her eyes filled with tears. Her hand rubbed her stomach. Two months. *Will I be able to feel the baby kick soon? That's when...*

"You feeling okay, Reg? You're zoning out on me."

She wiped at her eyes. "It needs a good dusting in here, but it'll be fine. Thanks for finding it, Ben. It'll be nice to have me out of your hair."

"Yeah, I suppose. Let's see about at least getting you a bed, table and a few chairs for starters."

"I don't have enough yet for things like that. I'll get by with—"

"You can pay me back. You can't sleep on the floor, for cryin' out loud, Reggie. Quit being so damn hard-headed."

She wanted to cry, to hit him, to say she loved him and that she was carrying his baby, but she couldn't. She wouldn't. Not ever – to any of it. She'd stay here with the bare necessities and move as soon as she received the insurance money for the house. It was ruled as an accident and the case was closed. They couldn't drag it out forever.

49

Two months later, Reggie was leaving the grocery store with her small canvas bag of fruits, veggies, and fresh piece of chicken to broil for dinner. She enjoyed shopping day by day as she needed things. The daily walk to the store was enjoyable as well as great exercise. The doctor said things were progressing completely normal. She was given a clean bill of health again today and had no restrictions set on her. Upon closer inspection with an ultrasound, the doctor found her uterus to be perfectly normal and another surprise as well. She was still beaming from the news.

She always walked very early or very late and had never run into Ben. They hadn't spoken since she moved out. The apartment didn't allow pets, but Ben agreed to take care of Derf for her. She missed her cat almost as much as she missed Ben. Initially, she thought maybe she could visit him, but she had started to show almost immediately so she had been avoiding Ben completely. She was glad he hadn't called wondering why she hadn't come to visit the cat. He truly must not have wanted to see her either. Baby-doll tops were back in fashion and she was able to conceal her stomach well, but they wouldn't last forever.

She suspected that the people at work knew, but no one said a word. She lucked out on getting a part-time/temporary job in the library. That was the one place she didn't think she'd run in to Ben, and she had been right. She just needed something to fill her days until she could move on and this was perfect. No stress, no lifting, and virtually no men. When the job was done, she could walk away without feeling like she abandoned them. She was only needed for another month at the most. She would have her insurance check by then and leave town.

Reggie was off today and a sundress sounded more comfortable than maternity pants. She took her time strolling home. A horn honked as she passed the park. Hoping it would be a co-worker was too much to ask for. It was Ben. *Shit.* She dropped her bag to the front of her stomach and smiled. If she was nice to him, he'd go away. *Right?*

Climbing out of his truck, he walked over to her. He didn't look like he was particularly happy to see her. "Hi, Reg."

"Hi, Ben. You look nice." He was in a t-shirt and jeans. *You couldn't come up with something else?*

"Uh, thanks?" He looked at her and his head tilted a little. "You're looking pretty radiant yourself."

"Pfft... this old dress?"

"You have a whole new wardrobe, Reggie. You can't get away with that line. I can't put my finger on it but you look...different."

"It's been a while, Ben."

"Yeah it has. I thought you'd want to come visit Derf."

"I haven't been able to. I do miss him horribly."

"Your car broken down?"

"No, I like to walk to the market. It's really a nice stroll."

"I'll walk with you. It would be nice to catch up." He reached for her bag.

"Really, Ben. I've got it." She held on to it tight.

~*~

"You are one stubborn broad," he said as he let go. She had let go at the same time and the bag hit the ground. "I'll get it." Ben bent down, stuffed everything back in the bag and went to stand. His face was eye level with her belly. He hesitated for a second before standing up. Her eyes were watery; he didn't understand. A breeze brought the dress tight to her stomach. There was no mistaking what he thought he saw when he was crouched down.

"You're pregnant?" he said, louder than he intended. "How are you pregnant?"

"I think you know how, Ben." Her lip quivered and she turned to walk away.

"Oh no, you don't, Miss Cold-as-ice. I see. You just didn't want anything to do with me. Who's the…" She bit her bottom lip. He knew her expressions better than he knew his own. He looked at the size of her stomach and stepped closer. He put his hand on it. "It's mine, isn't it?"

"No." She swallowed hard and tried to avoid his eyes.

"You're lying, Reggie." He pulled her towards his truck. "Get in."

"No." She pulled herself free of his hold. He bent down, picked her up and put her in the truck. "Stay put!" he threatened with a pointed finger. She listened.

He walked around and climbed in, looking over at her briefly before closing his door. "How long have you known?"

"Since the day you drove me in to the doctor."

"Dammit! That was over two months ago. How far along are you?"

"Four months."

"Four months? How could you not tell me, Reggie? Why?"

"Because you hate me!" she screamed.

Yup. That's what she thought all right. He did a great job of that. "I don't hate you, Reg." He spoke in a much softer tone than he had been using with her up to that point.

"Right," she mumbled.

He started the truck and drove back to his house. He parked the truck by the porch and walked around to help her down. "Visit Derf first, then we need to talk."

Ben enjoyed watching the excitement from both of them. It was obvious the kitten remembered her. When Derf finally got his fill of loving several minutes later, he picked up a toy mouse and ran away. Ben held her hand as they sat on the couch together.

"How is it you're pregnant? I thought you couldn't get pregnant, Reggie."

"I didn't think I could. I was always told I'd never be able to get pregnant. I've hardly ever…you know…that time of the month, since I was eighteen. When I did kind of start again a little, they said there was still no way I'd ever get pregnant. I swear I didn't think I could get pregnant, Ben. I'm sorry."

"Sorry? You think I'm upset?"

"Aren't you?" Her lips trembled as she spoke.

He threw his head back on the couch and let out a grunt in frustration. "I'm not upset, Reggie, not about this. I'm only upset you didn't tell me two months ago."

"What about your 'no chance of a whoops' comment that first time?"

"I was just trying to sound responsible. I wanted you from the second I laid eyes on you. I wouldn't have cared if you got pregnant that night."

"I think I did," she said, softly.

"Have you told Troy and Sabrina?"

"No. I couldn't."

"They call me asking about you. Bri's really been on me about dragging you back over here."

"I haven't told them, Ben. Honest."

"I believe you. I don't think they could hold that from me if they knew." He held her hand. "Why wouldn't you tell me, Baby." *Baby.* All his emotions for her were flooding back. He longed to pull her close, to let her know he was there, that he wasn't going to let her go ever again. He wanted to keep the promise he had made months ago on the four-wheeler. *I'm not letting you go.*

"You couldn't stand to be in the same room with me, Ben. Why would I think you wanted a child with me?"

"I couldn't stand to be in the same room with you because I can't be near you and not want to rip your clothes off and have my way with you." He stood up. "You're so gorgeous and perfect and goddamn cute when your pissed." He went back to her side. "I want you, Reggie. I want you so bad I can't stand it."

"What are you talking about? You hate me. You hate me for everything I've said. You hate that I couldn't get over my husband dying. You never said it, but I know you hated that I could never let you in my house. I couldn't, Ben. It wasn't that I was hung up on him then. To me it was Van's house. I hated getting insurance money for him dying. I wanted you to come in, I really did. I just couldn't." She dropped her chin to her chest. "You think I'm in love with one of my best friends. You—"

He stopped her combination talking and crying with a hard kiss then leaned back and stared into her eyes. "I love you, Reggie. I've been in love with you since the day we met. I don't hate you."

"You were so mad at me the day I came home… the day of the fire. I didn't know why you even bothered to save my life when you hated me so much. You cared less about being called a hero. I thought you were sorry you saved my life."

"I didn't like being called a hero, is all. I'm not that caliber. Van and Troy are that caliber; I'm nobody. I wanted to save the woman I loved and if I couldn't save you, I wanted to die trying." He held her face in his hands. "I don't hate you, Reggie." He leaned in and gave her a softer, slower kiss. His mouth covered hers and she welcomed his tongue greedily. A moan escaped her throat and she relaxed backwards into the corner of the couch. He eased himself closer to her, mindful of her stomach.

They kissed like they were trying to make up for all the lost days at one time. It seemed like an eternity before they quit. Ben stopped only briefly, looking into her face and kissed her again. He put his hand to her breast then leaned back.

"Wow." She looked up at him dreamily, not wanting the kiss to be over. "Think the kid will share these with me?" She nodded and pulled his face back to hers. They shared another long kiss. This time, he ran his hands across her stomach over and over. He suddenly jumped back. "What was that?"

"A soccer match." She put his hand back. He smiled up at her in amazement.

He hadn't caught what she meant, except the fact that the baby was active. He dropped his face into her neck. "I've missed you so much, Reggie. Come back to me. Please. I swear I'll make you happy. Don't leave town and don't rebuild your place. I want you here with me. We'll add on. You can draw it up any way you want."

Reggie turned his head so she could kiss him once again.

"I'm not letting you go again," he said. They kissed more ravenously, greedily savoring each other until Ben thought he was going to burst. She reached to the front of his jeans and undid the zipper.

He broke the kiss and looked up at her, confused. "Can we?"

She shyly nodded 'yes'.

He slid off the couch and carried her to his bed. He removed his shirt and jeans then removed her underwear and slipped her sundress over her head. He leaned down and looked at her naked bulging stomach. "I can't believe how stunning you are pregnant," he said as he rubbed her belly. He leaned in and gave it a kiss then rested his head on it for a moment. He picked his head up and looked at her.

"Do you know if it's a boy or a girl?"

"I didn't want to know. Do you?"

"No." He kissed her belly again.

He scooted himself up and passionately kissed her some more before positioning himself carefully on top of her. With all the gentleness he could muster, he entered her. They melted in ecstasy instantly, neither believing they were finally together again. They made love with more passion than they ever dreamed possible.

"Marry me, Reggie," Ben said with his arms protectively around her when they had finished. "I'm not taking no for an answer."

"Will you make me another swing for a wedding present?"

He laughed and pulled her close. "One that will fit three, Darlin'."

"You'd better make it four."

His head shot up. "Twins?"

ABOUT THE AUTHOR

June, who prefers to go by Bug, was born in Philadelphia but moved to Maui, Hawaii when she was four. She met her "Prince Charming" on Kauai and is currently living "Happily Ever After" on a hobby farm in a small town in Southern Minnesota.

She enjoys riding her Paint horse, Ringo, around the small ghost town they are playfully reestablishing with the neighbors, making gifts for her friend's children with her embroidery machine, and playing in Photoshop. Her son and daughter are her greatest accomplishments. She takes pride in embarrassing them every chance she gets.

OTHER BOOKS BY JUNE KRAMIN

Through The Mirror and Into Snow (written as Ann T. Bugg)
Into the Forest and Down the Tower (written as Ann T. Bugg)

UPCOMING RELEASES BY JUNE KRAMIN

I'll Try to Behave Myself (Fall 2012)
Money Didn't Buy Her Love (Spring 2013)

Off To Camp and Discovering Art
(written as Ann T. Bugg) (Fall 2012)
Down the River and Awakening The Rose
(written as Ann T. Bugg) (Spring 2013)

Made in the USA
Charleston, SC
09 October 2012